# WHISKEY
# HEART

# WHISKEY HEART

_a novel by_

## Rachel L. Coyne

American Fiction Series

© 2009 by Rachel L. Coyne
First Edition
Library of Congress Control Number: 2008934506
ISBN: 978-0-89823-246-2
American Fiction Series
Cover design and interior book by Lindsay Stokes
Cover photograph by Alexandra Neumann
Author photograph by Gerald Carlson

The publication of *Whiskey Heart* is made possible by the generous support of the McKnight Foundation and other contributors to New Rivers Press.

For academic permission please contact Frederick T. Courtright at 570-839-7477 or permdude@eclipse.net. For all other permissions, contact The Copyright Clearance Center at 978-750-8400 or info@copyright.com.

New Rivers Press is a nonprofit literary press associated with Minnesota State University Moorhead.

Wayne Gudmundson, Director
Alan Davis, Senior Editor
Donna Carlson, Managing Editor
Allen Sheets, Art Director
Thom Tammaro, Poetry Editor
Kevin Carollo, MVP Poetry Coordinator
Liz Severn, MVP Fiction Coordinator
Frances Zimmerman, Business Manager
    Publishing Interns: Samantha Jones, Andrew Olson,
        Mary Huyck Mulka
    Editorial Interns: Michael Beeman, Mary Huyck Mulka,
        Nathan Logan, Kayla Lundgren, Tarver Mathison,
        Amber Olds, Jessica Riepe, Alyssa Schafer, Andrea Vasquez
    Design Interns: Alex Ehlen, Andrew Kerr, Erin Malkowski,
        Megan McCleary, Lindsay Stokes

Printed in the United States of America.

New Rivers Press
c/o MSUM
1104 7th Avenue South
Moorhead, MN 56563
www.newriverspress.com

For Jessica Munson

*And what profit has he who has labored for the wind?*

Ecclesiastes 5:16

# 1

When my mother was eight, her house burned down in the dead of night with her little brother in it. So on nights when my father did not come home, she was always torn between her fear of leaving us alone and her need to search my father out. Sometimes she never could decide. Those nights she'd go sleepless. Wrapped in one of her gray sweaters, she'd stand at the end of the driveway, where she could see both the house and the road in from town. She'd stand there until morning, with her arms folded around her.

Most nights, however, around closing time or at the end of her patience, whichever came first, she would wake us all: me, my older sister Abra and my older brother Mason, and Pearl and Taylor, the two youngest, wrap us in blankets and pile our half-sleeping bodies into the back of our Chevy. We dozed while she drove from bar to bar, house to house, looking for him.

Those nights often passed like dreams for me, as if I were floating, yet somehow also wedged between my siblings' elbows; awake, then asleep, then awake, listening to the tired old engine starting, then restarting. Often, the next day in school, when my first-grade teacher would shake me awake, I could not remember those late-night journeys. And I could never explain my exhaustion.

Momma spent hours searching for Daddy, maybe most of the hours of her life and mine too, I guess. It required a certain patience, or I don't know what to call it, perhaps an anger, that only my mother had. By morning our backs would ache from sleeping sitting up, but she always found him. She had a talent for seeking him out, as if it was the work Momma was meant for. She was called to it, as some people are to religion or writing.

As a child, I thought this was proof that my father and mother belonged only to each other. That was love, and only that, because in my mind they were perfect complements. Their love had all the logic of geometry. It was ordained by math. She was always seeking, and he, well, he was always hiding.

My father was not a bad man, just a drinker; a man who never knew enough from enough. But he left home each morning for work, his thermos in hand.

Her persistence carried them both to unbelievable lengths. When he realized that she was capable of checking every bar for five towns around, he took to drinking in the next county. In a few months, she forced him even farther afield. For a while, he was driving two hours for beer on tap and a chance to pass out in a booth.

After that, he switched to drinking at friends' houses. She would call their wives. Then he started going home early with women he met at the bars. Momma would wake his friends, pounding on their doors until they surrendered the woman's name, or address, or whatever they knew—attitude, hair color, dress size. So my father had to give it up, the womanizing I mean. In the end, he drank alone down by Comfort Lake, then on our front porch or, in the winters, in his chair in front of the television, where we were not supposed to disturb him.

The first time I ever laid eyes on my cousin Tea, my father was still in his philandering stage. He'd taken up with one particular woman, whose flowered dress with its low neckline I can remember clearly, but whose face escapes my recollection.

That night, I think Momma had been forewarned. Usually, we drove aimlessly with the radio turned on, playing softly for her, but not so loud as to keep us awake. But that night she kept her foot on the gas and didn't look away from the white line of the road until we'd driven past three towns and wound up on the outskirts of Stillwater.

We found my father sitting in front of the woman's house, smoking a cigarette. I remember that it was a big, square house with a broad porch and red Chinese lanterns strung all around. My father didn't budge when he saw the car, just flicked his cigarette out into the night.

Gold light and soft music were coming out of the screen door. My father kept one eye on that door and one eye on Momma as she killed the engine and climbed slowly out of the car. Right as she got to the porch steps the woman came to the door with her mouth open, as if she were just about to say something to my father. She had a dish in her hand and a towel. But when she saw Momma, she gave out a yelp like a lapdog and dropped the dish.

Momma climbed the steps. In a voice that was soft and low but clear and dangerous enough for me to hear in the car, she said to Daddy, "If a dog's got something that's hers, she don't need to do nothing but piss on it." She straightened her back and shook out her red hair. "You want me to go that far,

Abe? Do I need to piss on you to keep you home?"

The woman rocked back a little and put her hand protectively on Daddy's shoulder. "Talk like that in front of your kids?" she demanded, poking her chin out at us.

Momma's dangerous eyes flicked from Daddy to the woman. "Are you going to fuck my husband in front of my kids?"

The woman gasped again. She drew her hand back from Daddy like he was all of a sudden superhot, and nearly ran back into the house, slamming the door behind her. Then from behind the door we heard this weird howling that shook even Abra awake. Another dish shattered. Then another. Strange and wolflike, that woman was crying for my father. The noise made me afraid.

Momma turned toward us and headed back for the car. She paused on the steps long enough to say to Daddy, "Looks to me, Abe, like you won't find much peace here tonight."

"Don't think I will," he said calmly and collected his coat and followed Momma to the car. When he stood, he swayed like the Chinese lanterns in the summer air. It took only moments for the rocking motion of the car to lull him to sleep.

Momma navigated the country roads alone. All around us, the ripe corn rose up like great walls. Don Williams sang "Amanda, light of my life" on the radio. I must have dozed off like Daddy, because when the car stopped I jerked awake with a start to find Momma was twisted around looking at us. She was crying a little, but when she saw that I was awake she smiled and said, "Ain't this song just the saddest you ever heard, Kat?" And then she turned away from me.

I thought she was reaching to restart the car. Instead, she opened her door and climbed out. She ran her palm across my window as she walked by. I turned in my seat to watch her go. Through the back window I saw her walk down the road. Then suddenly she veered off and plunged into the corn.

My breath stopped. For me, it was an act so like jumping off a bridge or a tall building. The corn swallowed her instantly and entirely. And suddenly, it was night and I was utterly alone without my mother. The feeling of that sank right down through me and buried me beneath the Chevy's bald tires.

When I finally moved, it was with a suddenness that surprised even me and startled Abra awake. I lunged for the door and in the same moment, her longer, stronger arms circled around me. Her nails lifted my skin. Perhaps she felt the same panic as me, but was more desperate. I threw a punch that I would see for the rest of my life in a small jagged scar over Abra's left eyebrow. She shrieked like an old bothered crow and I ran. I dove into the corn after my mother, Abra's shrieks ringing out behind me.

Picturing my father, suddenly angrily awake, towering, drunk, behind me, I ran on and on blindly, calling out for my mother.

But she was gone, though in what sense I am still not sure. I froze. The sudden terror of my situation glued me to the spot. Every year children got lost in the corn and search parties had to go out looking for them. The corn was double my size, and thick. I could see only a few feet in either direction, and it was cold and night. I felt as if I had passed to the other side, though perhaps at that moment I was only a few feet away from the road.

Perhaps, had things worked out differently, I would have calmed down and turned back to find my family sleeping in the car, but something rustled in the corn just out of my sight. Then several crows, perched on the corn tops, took flight, screaming like my sister. Their wings touched my cheeks. I imagined their beaks tearing at my hair.

Fear can be a door that you open and close behind you. It can be a small blank room that swallows memory and all sense of self. I lost myself in terror and didn't return until near dawn, when I found myself in my own backyard, my feet bare and torn, my mouth gritty, and my teeth stained with rich black dirt.

The moment I emerged from the corn was the first time I saw my cousin Tea. She was sitting on our front porch, thin and pale, where her mother had left her, with her whole life—clothes, sketchbooks, paints—in four cardboard boxes tied up with twine.

I don't know why, but without needing to say anything, we put our arms around each other and held on as tight as two people can. She held me like a baby, and I knew at that moment that I had dropped clean off the earth. That was the last moment of my life. The earth in Tea opened up and she buried my body beside her heart.

# 2

**B**est of all, when I drive, I like that noise of tires on the highway, I like that clean noise. The noise of movement, I guess. When I drive the world parts before me like liquid. Like complete halves with nothing touching, nothing meeting. The road itself is between them. All of life should be like that.

There had been a man in my life once. A man who was so long gone now that his name hardly ever touched my lips anymore. He never understood about driving. I don't miss him, but there hasn't been anyone since. When he left, I took to the road again with a sigh of relief. I got a job in another city and then another and another, each separated in my memory only by the sound of the pavement under my tires.

When he left, he told me I was a good woman. But he knew I was someone else's woman. Maybe I belonged to the highway or the car or Tea. Or maybe even to Momma.

Maybe I was Momma's woman. Never would have thought it, but here I was, driving home. Home. Never thought I'd come back here. Never thought I was the kind of woman who would come and go and come again. Like Momma, who never could decide whether to stay or leave, love or let be.

I always believed I was the type of person who could go and just stay gone. People who love you deserve that much—to have a certainty about you. Like me and my cousin Tea. We never lingered. Not in this life anyway. Tea died at the age of twenty-nine, must have been five years ago now. And me, I've driven a thousand miles for every year lived at home.

But that clean noise of the highway can only carry you just so far. My car stalled just before dusk on a dirt road, miles into the Minnesota corn. It was still hot, so I got out of the car and shut the door. The slamming of the car door jarred me. I suddenly looked down at myself, amused to see that I was wearing pink flip-flops, an old pair of jeans, and a T-shirt but no bra.

I frowned, shaded my eyes, and squinted down the road. There was no denying it. I was home. I might not know how or why, but this was definitely the land, the very acre of my birth. Momma's house, my brother's house, and Daddy's grave all lay just across this field. Even the corn was familiar. Across the ditch from me, it grew tall, clutching at the ground with its hard, red roots.

I had never noticed corn much until Tea came to live with us. On this stretch of the prairie, it was as pervasive as the air you breathed. It wasn't just a part of the landscape here. It was the landscape and the land and the roots beneath it. My first August with Tea, she brought me out to the edge of a field and pulled up a plant by its stalk. "You see that?" she said excitedly, pointing at the blood-red root. "Our hearts are that color."

Dusk was unfurling its wings around me, all purple and black. I started walking, threading the thin strip of gravel between the road and the deep ditch. As I walked, the wind rose briefly and pushed through the growing dark in the corn. The earth sighed and I felt its still hot breath, smelled the humid funk of fields and the sun-soaked corn itself.

I walked on and thought about the roots I had tried to lay elsewhere. I thought maybe I could plant them so deep and so red that I'd never come back here again. I wondered how a woman could drive more than a thousand miles from New Orleans to Comfort Lake, Minnesota, and not remember a single mile of it.

≈

My grandmother's house was a flat, low structure. Behind it, separated by a pitted dirt yard, was my brother Mason's house. He lived there with his wife, Constance, and too many children. Farther on still was the barn and half a dozen sheds. Mason farmed Grandma's land for her and raised horses. There was a collection of cars in the driveway and so I stopped there, rather than walking on to my mother's house. I found Grandma in the yard picking bugs from her beans, dropping them into a mason jar that reeked of kerosene. She worked bent over double, using her left hand to strip the beans of any wildlife. Her right hand, molded into a useless lump by the fire, she cradled to her chest. Years before, she had lifted my mother from her smoking bed, wrapped her in a blanket, and run with her through their burning house, leaving another child and most of her sanity behind.

One of Mason's children, a boy of maybe two, clung to her legs while she worked, but she paid him no mind. Grandma straightened slowly when she saw me. The sun was behind her, but she shaded her eyes when she looked at me.

"Kat," she said, as if I'd never been away. "You cut your hair, girl. Your daddy won't like it."

"Is Momma here?" I asked, pointing off across the yard. "Is that her car?" There were two pickups and a Chevette down by the barn.

Grandma turned slowly in the direction I was pointing and nodded. "Naomi's here," she said. "They're all here. But in the corn. The stock got out and they're in after them." I turned to look at the corn. It grew all around the house and yard, right up to the porch in back. When I turned back to my grandmother, she was gathering up the little boy in her arms. She had surprising strength in her and tucked the boy's head tenderly beneath her chin and turned towards her own house. I watched her climb the steps, wondering what I should do next.

"Don't you wander into the corn, girl," Grandma called over her shoulder. "Your daddy'll have a fit. They'll be back soon enough."

"Daddy's gone," I said gently. But she didn't hear me.

The door had hardly closed behind her when the corn parted violently. I spun around at the noise and Mason's horses emerged, pressed close in a great pack, with all of Mason's children clinging to their bare backs. With skinny arms they hugged the horses' necks as their bare heels beat sweaty flanks.

Mason's only daughter was in the lead, bent low over her horse, her hair streaming out behind her. The boys hollered and whooped when they saw me. They swarmed and circled. For a moment I was swallowed whole. Then overwhelmed. Then in the same instant they were gone, rushing headlong toward the barn, assaulting the objects that lay in their path.

Momma followed more sedately behind, pulling a clumsy calf along behind her with a length of rope. She stopped short when she saw me, and I felt a jolt of nervousness shoot through my stomach.

"Hello, Momma," I said softly.

Momma looked at my flip-flops, my torn jeans, and my loose breasts under my T-shirt. "What happened?" she asked.

I shrugged and looked away, my eyes stinging ominously.

Momma let the calf loose and came forward. I thought she might shake me, so I stepped quickly back. "Kat, what happened?" she repeated sharply. "Why are you home?" She looked at me hard. "Why are you crying?"

"I'm not crying," I said almost angrily. I crossed my arms across my chest, feeling very bare and exposed.

Momma's face became even more intense. Then she sighed. "Of course you're not," she said, all the anger melting out of her. She glanced away, absently gathering up the young cow's rope again.

Mason's daughter arrived then, half jogging up from the barn where the horses were now jostling in the fenced yard. I hadn't seen her in years, but she looked about thirteen now and had long, golden hair that rustled in a windy way when she moved. Like all of Mason's children, she was slim and straight and resembled the horses he raised.

"You remember Jordan?" Momma asked.

I nodded.

Jordan looked me over in a frank, appraising way. "I like your flip-flops," she observed. "I'll take her down," she said to Momma, reaching for the rope.

We watched Jordan depart in silence. The calf wanted to linger, but Jordan would have none of it. She pulled hard with her strong young arms, then whacked the calf solidly on its side. In minutes they were making steady progress, with the calf nuzzling at Jordan's side.

"What about that man of yours?" Momma asked, when Jordan was out of earshot. "Where's he?"

"Bob," I said. "He's gone."

"You have a fight?" she asked.

"No," I said uncomfortably, looking down at my feet. "That's not why I'm here. He's been gone for a long time. Gone gone. The kind of gone that doesn't come back."

I felt an instant surge of regret. Momma stiffened and her mouth flattened into a plain, tight line. "I've gotta go back into the corn, before it gets too dark," she said. "There's another cow out there still. You go on home. I'll be there in a little while." Then abruptly she turned and headed back toward the corn.

I stared after her, blinking my stinging eyes. I knew I should never have come home, but wanted to follow Momma all the same. I watched until her back disappeared completely into the rustling, swaying corn and felt myself shudder. I looked up at the sky. The moon was out now, clear and big, though there was still plenty of light.

The yard got darker, but I didn't quite know what else to do so I stood and stared into the corn. I thought about Momma, about my grandmother's burned hands, ridiculous, passionate red roots, and my own heavy heart. My mind added them together and by some secret law of memory's arithmetic, I found myself thinking about Tea again.

She had told me once about prairie fires, about how a single controlled spark could grow into one long horizon of fire that was beautiful and terrifying to behold. Tea had never seen it, but her great-grandmother had. Back then they would burn the prairie so that new life could grow through the root-bound sod. There hadn't been a true fire on this stretch of the prairie in years. But the corn remembered it. In its blazing red roots, Tea had said, the corn remembered.

I looked back into the corn and shuddered again, feeling uneasy, strange and tired in my own skin. I thought about my stalled car and longed for that steadying noise of the highway under my tires. I didn't want to be here. I didn't want to be home, the only place where you could be burned and born on the same hot breath of August. Damn you, Tea.

# 3

I walked the rest of the way home to Momma's house. When I got there, I found Abra standing at the end of the long dirt driveway, waiting with her arms crossed. Of all of us, Abra was the only one who looked anything like Momma. She had Momma's height and the well-defined bones of her face. Abra wore her hair long, but braided and pinned close to her head, plain and severe. Tonight she had her hair covered, hidden beneath an ugly brown square of cloth.

Abra didn't smile when she saw me, and for a moment I thought she was going to pretend I didn't exist. She looked down the road and then back at me again, glancing at my clothes, my flip-flops, my face. She shook her head and looked down at her hands. Abra had large hands, and the bones of her wrists stood out like knots on a tree. Finally, she gave herself a little shake and said abruptly, "I'm just leaving."

I don't know what I was expecting, coming home, but it wasn't this. I took a minute and watched my sister closely. Abra hadn't changed much. If anything, she seemed taller, the bones of her face broader. Almost as if she'd become a harsh exaggeration of herself. She'd lost weight. Not much, but just enough to make her seem less womanly than before. Though Abra was only five years older than me, she seemed closer in age to Momma than to me.

At last, I asked flatly, "Are you going to the restaurant to work?"

She shook her head. "Not tonight. No."

I stared at her for a moment, expecting her to say more. When she didn't, I kept talking, wrapping my arms around my loose chest. "You got a ride coming for you?" I asked, ignoring the hard set of her mouth.

"Yes," she answered impatiently. At thirty-two, Abra didn't drive. I knew it. It was still the same. She lived here with Momma and they drove to work together.

We were quiet for a long awkward moment. Then she nodded off down the road and said, "They're coming now. So you can go on up to the house."

Following the direction of Abra's gaze, I saw nothing but the growing dark. "You're sure?" I asked, feeling the strange desire to linger, if only because I was not wanted.

"They're coming," she said again firmly.

I stared hard down the road. Still nothing. Then, a long way off, two yellow headlights appeared in the dusk.

Abra wore a heavy woven handbag on her shoulder. It was brown and ugly like the kerchief on her head. She zipped it closed with a hard yank and resettled the bag on her arm, scowling at me. As the car got closer, Abra's lips grew straighter and flatter. I stared curiously at the approaching car. There were three people inside.

Abra stepped in front of me, blocking my view, and said firmly, "You go on to the house now. Momma'll be home soon."

I had now been dismissed twice, so I went. Still, I took my time leaving, feeling a little curious about my sister and the friends she didn't want me to see. I walked slowly up the driveway, looking back over my shoulder.

Maybe it was the other way around. Abra might not want them to see me.

The car stopped. It was a dark blue Chevy, the bulky kind of car that the sheriff used to drive. The man driving leaned across the passenger seat and opened the door for my sister. The car light made his face all hard angles and shadows. I guessed instantly that he was a church man, a deacon maybe. There was something both clean and oily about the way his hair was newly combed. I could see the traces of the comb running through it, like a newly planted field.

Two women sat in the back, their heads bowed as if they were praying. Like Abra they wore scarves tied neatly around their hair. As I walked up the dirt drive, I sensed I was being watched, so I paused and looked around at them. The women gazed openly at me. The man stared straight ahead, his face set. The expression he wore made me wonder briefly if I knew him, but he turned to speak to Abra as she was getting into the car and I lost his face. There was a brief murmur of voices, male, then female. The car door slammed and they were gone.

I kept walking up the drive, accompanied only by the odd sound of my flip-flops. Alone, I felt tired. When I reached the house, I found that Abra had left the porch light on but locked the door. My key no longer fit. With a sigh, I curled up in a ball on the front porch and slept.

≈

When I woke, the dark had come in earnest. Slightly bluish light emerged through the screen door. The solid wood door behind it was ajar. Someone was home. I was stiff, but it was a familiar stiffness. Tea was a painter. I had been her model, sitting in aching quiet for hours while she worked.

From inside the house came the noise of blows hitting home, followed occasionally by a scraping noise that I couldn't quite place. Then something hit the ground with a dull thud. I rose, stumbling into the house, hugging myself as I walked, pulling everything in tight, to avoid accidents with the shadows and half-lights. I found my mother standing in the dimly lit kitchen wearing her bathrobe.

She was defrosting the refrigerator. On the kitchen table, the contents of the freezer were thawing slowly in the hot night air. I glanced at the clock on the wall. It was framed by two hands praying and it read two o'clock.

Momma wielded a hammer and chisel against the stubborn ice in the freezer. Her blows were solid, ringing hollow and heavy across the kitchen. Beyond Momma, at the kitchen window, was a slight pulsing, like a heartbeat of light that caught my eye. The window was covered with dusty, ghostly life. It had become a completely eerie, gray patchwork of moth bodies and wings.

I looked back to find Momma watching me. The tools she held were familiar. On the floor beside her, Tea's old tool chest was open. I felt my heart contract a little at the sight of the familiar, battered box.

Its contents were strewn on the floor. Red was the color my cousin had been fondest of. Flakes of it were everywhere, chipping off the tools and crumpled tubes of paint.

There was still some life in the dried pigments, though. Where the flakes mixed with the melting ice, a slick red pool was growing. The stain seeped across the floor to my mother's pale bare feet. Following my gaze, Momma seemed to notice the paint for the first time. She blinked at it and sighed.

"The door won't close," Momma said finally, responding to my unasked question. "I came down for a glass of ice water and now the door won't close."

I stepped across the room, over the bloody puddle of watery paint and melted ice, and took the hammer and chisel from Momma. She settled into a kitchen chair while I started to work, sipping ice water as she watched me.

I swung hard. Chips of ice fell on my bare feet. I must have been feverish, because each drop of unexpected cool was like heaven. "When did you change the locks?" I asked.

Momma stared out the window at the moths. "After Tea died, I couldn't find her keys. Lord knows what she did with them or who she gave them to."

I took a few more swings. "Why didn't you wake me?" I asked.

Momma shrugged. "You know that expression, let sleeping dogs lie."

I missed the chisel. The hammer hit the aluminum of the freezer door with a loud, discordant thump. I shook my head in disgust, looking at the dent. Momma said nothing. The silence that spread out between us was cold and white like ice. It settled down like a sheet being laid out on a bed.

I went back to work. For a quarter of an hour, the only sound in the kitchen was the noise of hammer connecting with the chisel and the ice cubes rattling in Momma's glass. Finally Momma rose, found the mop, and began working on the puddles of melted ice and paint on the floor.

"I tried to wake you," she said eventually. "You wouldn't budge. How long did you drive?"

I shook my head because I didn't remember. I tried the freezer door. It closed easily now.

Momma and I began refilling the freezer, arranging hamburger, chicken, thick farm sausages, and to my great surprise a few frozen dinners. There were five of us kids. Momma had always made our dinners "from scratch." I had always thought the expression appropriate, since family dinners at our house were always about as pleasant as an open wound.

The arranging took almost an hour. Momma stretched it out, opening containers, sniffing meat, rattling things to judge the staying power of certain leftovers. We just were getting to the stage where squeezing and pushing were necessary to fit everything in, when Momma asked, "Are you going to go out and look at the grave then?"

I handed Momma a package of hamburger and didn't answer.

"We couldn't bury her at St. Stephen's because of the suicide. She's out at the Lutheran cemetery—"

"Tea didn't kill herself, Momma,"I interrupted.

"It wasn't me who said she did. It was the police. The coroner," Momma said blandly, not looking at me. "So we buried her at the Lutheran cemetery. Are you going to go see her?" she asked again.

I shook my head. "No point to it. Tea's gone. It's not like it would matter to her or anything."

"It might matter to you," Momma suggested. "Graves aren't for the dead. It might make you feel better to go out there and bring some flowers."

"Feel better about what?" I asked defensively.

Momma sighed and looked away. "You could have come home for the funeral, Kat. It would have meant a lot to have you here."

"Like I said, Momma. It's not like Tea would've cared."

"I cared," Momma said so fiercely that I started in surprise.

Momma sighed and shook her head. "It would have meant a lot to me if you'd come home," she said more quietly. "Not just for Tea, but your father, too. You could've come home when he died."

"That was years ago, Momma," I said softly. I swallowed hard and looked away. Suddenly my chest felt tight in a way that I didn't like. Momma was too close. The room was too close. I backed away from the freezer, bumping into the table.

I sat there and took a long drink of Momma's ice water. I poked at the pile of leftovers and premade meatloafs on the table. Among Momma's Tupperware I found a dozen mysterious containers of foggy plastic with red lids. They were about the size of a pill box. I rattled one. Nothing moved inside.

I looked back at Momma.

"Those are all Tea's," Momma responded before I had asked the question.

"What's in them?" I asked.

"Don't know."

Momma took the little container from me and wedged it between the paper-wrapped packages of meat. "As long as you're home, I wish you'd take care of Tea's things. Everything in the attic. I wish you'd clean it out. It's unsafe with everything . . . with God knows what all crammed up there. It's a fire hazard."

I almost smiled. I didn't know what Momma had inscribed on Tea's gravestone, but "fire hazard" was probably a more fitting epitaph. My half-smile faded when I saw Momma watching me. I realized that she was waiting for some kind of answer. I shrugged. I wasn't planning on staying home long enough to clean out the attic where Tea had both lived and worked. I hadn't even planned on coming home.

"She left it all to you, you know," Momma persisted. "Everything in the attic and all of this . . . " She waved at the little pots.

"Fine, Momma," I said. "I'll take care of it."

We both knew I was lying. Momma shoved the last of her premade meatloaf into the fridge, then stuffed Tea's little pots in as best she could.

"God knows, Tea was like my own," she said as she worked, "But this is one thing I really couldn't stand about her. This was too much." She waved her hands helplessly at the containers. "All these things . . . these projects and scraps."

"She was an artist, Momma," I said defensively.

"Even so." Momma shook her head. "All this mess and the junk like . . . like . . . " The more she struggled for the word, the more she waved her hands.

"Like driftwood," she ended at last.

"Driftwood?"

"Yeah," Momma said with satisfaction, her word evidently pleasing to her. "Driftwood," she repeated. "We were there to catch all the leftovers, the mess she'd already mulled over and spit out."

"Driftwood?" My voice rose an octave. My mother stiffened. She studied me warily across the pitted kitchen table where we had shared so many family dinners.

"Momma," I said finally, evenly, "I think that's the nicest thing you ever said about Tea."

"What's that?" she asked with a puzzled frown.

"You called her an ocean."

# 4

The next morning I woke in my own room in the bed I had slept in since the age of two. Abra was at the foot of my bed, sitting at the vanity table. She was watching herself in the mirror and brushing her hair, the plow of her brush turning up long fertile rows, which vanished with a small shake of her head.

I watched the procedure, a little transfixed, half asleep maybe, until Abra caught sight of me in the mirror. She turned slightly on the low-backed chair and gave me a look that made me stumble half-naked out of bed. Hastily I collected my jeans from the floor. Then, embarrassed and unsure what to do, I stood stupidly and wadded them into a lumpy bundle. I stood in my underwear and T-shirt and stared at her.

Abra set the brush in its precise position on the table and pulled a plastic container of hairpins from the drawer. "I like your vanity," she said serenely. "I've been using it each morning for a while now. I like to sit and wake up here. You have good light in your window."

I wasn't sure if what I had heard was an explanation for her presence in my bedroom, or a compliment, or something more that escaped my understanding just then. I shoved myself into my blue jeans. I tried not to watch her braid her long hair into two tails.

Abra had beautiful hair. I decided, though, that I didn't like her winding it up, taking in hand all that loveliness. Her steady twisting reminded me of the tightening of a spring. For so early in the morning, it seemed a dangerous, explosive action. She coiled the braids around her head, like a halo, and pinned them flat.

We didn't talk. I was clearly an intruder and awkwardness made me silent. My sister simply could not talk, because she held her hairpins in her mouth.

When she finished, she turned to me and said, "Momma says that you're home for Tea's things?"

"She did?" I replied in surprise.

Abra snapped the top on the hairpin container. "Honestly, I don't understand why you just don't leave it all be," she said, shaking her head.

"That's okay," I told her. "You don't have to understand." I wanted to edge out the door but was afraid to, afraid that one of her long braids would whip out and seize me like an octopus's arm. Abra wasn't done with me yet.

"No one goes into the attic anymore and Momma sure doesn't need the space," Abra continued. "Why, it could sit up there collecting dust until it rots, for all anyone cares."

I eyed my sister warily, not exactly sure what she was trying to accomplish with this conversation. Abra had a way of provoking my contrary nature and she knew it. I tried to rein in my growing irritation, to not let myself be provoked. I was not going to spend a month here, cleaning a stuffy attic in the heat of August, just for the childish pleasure of spiting my older sister. "I care," I told her stiffly, unable to help myself. "Tea wanted me to have those things."

Abra's face tightened. For a moment, I was worried that she had swallowed one of her hairpins. "Running around in the heat up there, breathing all that dust doesn't seem like much fun to me. Why don't you go to the lake or do something useful if you've got so much time weighing on your hands. Honestly, it's just all garbage up there and Tea's dead, so what does it matter? Especially now, Kat, after all these years."

I had said almost the same thing to Momma last night, but to hear Abra say it was to have something hot crammed down my throat. I felt my face go red and tight, and my rage begin to blow and turn, like a dry leaf in the wind inside me.

Abra rose and backed away from me. She looked nervously over her shoulder, as if she were looking for Momma.

I shook my head and sank to the edge of the bed. I slid my feet angrily into my flip-flops, feeling stupid, feeling embarrassed by the fear I had seen in Abra's face. What had I planned on doing? Beating her until she took it back? As if she could. As if bullying my sister would make Tea any less gone.

Abra relaxed. With efficient movements, she put the vanity table back in order, arranging the jars of cream and perfume. She smoothed her clothes, tugging at their seams. From one of the vanity drawers she drew out another ugly brown kerchief, which she began to knot around her head.

Looking into the mirror, Abra briefly touched her eyebrow and the small scar I had given her years ago. "We've never had a lot to say to each other, have we, Kat?" Before I could respond she added, "Let's just keep it that way."

I felt my cheeks burn. I guess I deserved that.

Abra finished her hair. Without another word she left the room. I sat and stared at my sandals. They had sad little silk flowers woven into the band, now crusted with dirt from yesterday's walk.

I looked at myself in the mirror. My face was more faded than I had expected. There were deep grooves of worry across my forehead, and although I had just awoken, my eyes already sagged with fatigue. Still looking in the mirror, I ran my hand through my knotted hair.

Standing, I went to the little vanity table and stroked its surface. It was cherry; the life in the wood still showed in the deep red beneath the finish. In her haste, Abra had left the vanity table drawer slightly open. I slid it all the way out. Inside was a jumble of junk: ribbons and pins, clippings and scissors. I dug around and found a familiar pair of yellow plastic barrettes. I couldn't even think how many years it had been since I'd worn them.

I turned the smooth plastic over in my hand. Then I picked up the brush Abra had left behind, enjoying its heavy weight in my hand. I looked at my hair in the mirror again, sighed and put the brush back down.

Tea used to sit me at this table and brush my hair in the early morning, before the house rose. At night, before I went to bed, it would be the same. She would brush my hair and tell me secrets or stories—about people she had known or things she had heard or read about. I preferred stories about love or death, and usually managed to combine them.

Tea had a favorite about a long-haired woman who killed her own child out of pride. The story always kept me awake at night, but that never stopped me from begging Tea to tell it. The way Tea told it, this woman had always been beautiful and was extremely proud of her long hair. "It was black like the smoke of a fire raging over the prairie," Tea would say. "Like rich turned earth, like the moment after lightning strikes."

One day, the woman came home to find her husband in bed with someone else, and her rage boiled as black as her hair. The beautiful woman grew desperate to wound her husband deeply. But she had no power over him. He didn't love her anymore. "This happens sometimes," Tea would tell me.

Everything the woman did to hurt her husband fell away from his heart, like coins sinking into a well, until finally she took the son that they had made together and threw the baby into the Mississippi. Her husband cursed her, swore that she would never be allowed to rest. She would grow old and tired and her body would rot, but she would never die. They would bury her alive. The proof of this would be that her hair would continue to grow even after her death, forever and always.

And so the beautiful woman moved on to the next town, remarried, and had another son. She lived a long time, until her son had grandchildren and those children had children. Then one day her great-great-grandson found her in the morning, sitting still and quiet beneath an elm tree, with her long gray hair all loose around her. She was never seen to move again. She was buried and forgotten, like most dead after a few generations.

Perhaps she would have stayed forgotten if the town hadn't decided to move the cemetery in order to expand the church school. The workmen had hardly dug down more than a foot before they encountered a fine web of roots. This was on flat prairie, without a tree in sight. The source of the roots eluded them, until they cut down through it all, down to the woman's casket.

For more than a hundred years her thriving hair had planted her in the earth, as solidly as a tree. The coffin couldn't be moved. They were obliged to build the new school tennis courts over her.

This was Tea's idea of a comforting bedtime story. She told me that tale the night before I started second grade. I spent the rest of the year waiting for hair to spring from the floor of Ms. Johnson's classroom. And I wouldn't set foot on the tennis courts to save my soul.

I put the barrettes and the brush in the vanity drawer and closed it. I pressed my hand to the cool wood again and looked in the mirror, hoping that deep in the glass's depth somewhere there lingered an image of Tea.

Abra had said she liked my vanity table, but we both knew it had always belonged to Tea. My father had bought it for her. For her thirteenth or fourteenth birthday, just after she had arrived at our house.

Tea had moved it to my room so that she could get us both ready for school at the same time. For years, when I was a child, the first thing I saw upon waking was Tea at that table, combing her hair, putting on her makeup, studying her face in the mirror.

For a drowsy moment this morning, for just a sliver of a second, I had mistaken my sister's presence for Tea's. Maybe that was why I could be so angry at Abra, so early in the morning. I had thought I was over waking up and expecting Tea to be there, expecting a phone call, expecting someone to come and tell me it was all a mistake.

I turned away from my worn reflection. Tea had been beautiful. I was not. Especially not this morning. My Tea, my Tea was all loveliness. From the day she first held me on our front porch steps, every inch of her was interesting to me. I gave her no privacy. Watching her brush her hair and put on her makeup was my special pleasure. I begged to be in the room. I cried for hours outside locked bathroom doors while she showered and washed her hair.

At first, I suppose, my love bewildered Tea, perhaps even suffocated her.

She banished me to corners. She forbade me to touch her. She was constantly assigning me to chairs, begging me not to move.

Inevitably, however, I would creep near her. My arm, of its own accord, would wrap around her waist. My fingers would brush her hair as lightly as a spider, hoping she didn't feel their touch. I would bury my face in her side, smelling the soapy perfume of her clothes mingled with her sweat.

It would take all my concentration not to breathe, not to jostle her when she put lipstick on. Once she finished, she would kiss me, leaving a stain on my cheek. Sometimes she would let me dab perfume on her wrists, behind her neck, and the bottle would tremble in my hands, though I never let it fall.

Sometimes, if I was pleasing and not too difficult, she would let me carry her compact in my pocket to school. The whole day my hand would be in my pocket, turning the smooth silver case over and over. And I would glow like worn silver, because I knew Tea loved me. No matter what anyone says of Tea, she loved me.

Not knowing what to do with myself, I sank back onto the bed and looked around my old room. There were shelves full of books that once interested me. There was a closet half filled with clothes that I would never wear again and shoes that had seen better days. There were pictures on the walls of people I had once known. I couldn't give a damn.

I contemplated my flip-flops some more. I pulled the cuffs of my pants down over my almost bare feet. Bent down like that, I glanced under the bed. There was a familiar bottle there, where I had known it would be, though I had forgotten it. I stared at the bottle and wondered when my own memory had become a stranger to me.

# 5

I crouched on the floor and reached through the dust for the bottle. Its neck was cool and lovely to the touch, smooth like a woman's skin. I pulled it out and smiled at the label, at the ornate red *V* in Vodka.

There was a night, so long ago now, when I had left my bedroom window open and Tea had crawled in through it. It was the bottle falling to the floor that had woken me. I hadn't remembered that until now.

The bottle was still half-full. I wondered if Tea had left it here because she had forgotten it or if she had simply thought she wouldn't need it anymore. She had certainly been drunk enough, as we stumbled from the house, holding each other and our courage up.

I tucked the bottle under my arm. Whether it was to spite Abra or please my mother, I don't know, but I decided to at least go and look at the attic.

Still holding the bottle, I climbed the two narrow flights of steps to Tea's attic and flung open the door. My sudden appearance in that quiet world, the door opening, my weight creaking across the pine floorboards, seemed to startle the dust from its slumber on ledges, in the deep grooves of the floor, and the raw rafters of the ceiling.

The dust swirled before my eyes and reflected the glare of the sunlight coming through the windows at each end of the attic. For a moment, the air seemed alive with faint golden spirits. For a moment. Then the dust seemed to sigh, to recognize my long-absent presence. The sunlight dimmed. The attic calmed. The patient regiments of dust contented themselves with another century of sleep. Dust. Dust lay in thick sheets on everything, heavy like a shroud over a body.

Tea had written Momma a letter before she died. Everything here belonged to me. Everything coated with dust, entombed under layers of forgetfulness, Tea had bequeathed to me.

I turned a slow circle. From end to end and wall to wall, the attic was crammed full. There were packing trunks; furniture covered in sheets; three desks, each missing drawers; a dozen Asian screens, some assembled, some slumped against walls. There were folding chairs and two overstuffed lounge chairs. There were lamps with no shades, cluttered shelves of ugly knickknacks, even a few crates of kitchenware, chipped plates, pots and pans. There were easels and books and boxes and boxes with no labels and bags that had crumpled under the weight of their own contents. There were a toilet and sink hidden in here somewhere, but the junk was so thick as to conceal them. An aisle cut through the middle of it all, like a mountain pass. At the other end, I could see Tea's heavy iron bed, unmade, heaped with blankets whose curved forms seemed to hump quietly in her absence.

Down at that end, there were two wood tables and cans and cans of paint, rolls of canvas, grocery bags fat with scraps of paper and fabric, an ottoman, a sofa, and three dressers, which were inexplicably taped shut.

Scattered among these mundane objects of chaos were more eccentric items: a fainting couch, a stack of curtains, dozens of curtain rods sticking out of a barrel, two canvas bags of duck decoys, a mannequin, and countless freakish blue statues that Tea had made in the hospital and brought home with her. I had trouble looking at them.

There were even things hanging from the ceiling: odd ghostly shapes, draped in plastic tarps and canvas. All of it the dust had claimed in silent, furious battles that took each object bit by bit, falling steadily, noiselessly over the room.

I reached over the bed and cranked open a window. The air was so hot outside that it made no difference in the stuffiness of the room. With my hand, I brushed the dust from a single chair. And I sat. Beside the chair was a cardboard box, half closed. I pulled it open and found myself staring at six bowling balls, four black, one pink, and one green.

I shook my head, slowly unscrewing the top of Tea's vodka bottle. I began to drink, letting my eyes drift from one item to the next, first the bed, then the bookshelves, then box after box after box.

≈

Mason came over later in the day. I could hear him moving around downstairs, watching TV, opening the refrigerator, clearly thinking the matter over before he finally decided to come up. His heavy steps creaked on the stairway. I counted the steps as he climbed them. Each one groaned beneath him, strained. I stared at the spot where he would arrive, waiting for him to fill it.

Mason had already been a man when I'd left, grown up, married, a father, thickening with determination. He was a man when I returned, maybe a little heavier—well, a lot heavier. He seemed to have doubled himself in my absence. His belly eased over his belt, natural and gentle, like the way his hands hung slack and empty at his sides. His face was easy, too. It just seemed to fall with gravity into an approximate frown that he hid beneath his thick red beard.

Mason had grease under his fingernails and dirt all over his body and clothes that I seemed to recognize from years before. His red baseball cap was brown with mud and stained with sweat. He smiled at me and pulled the hat from his head, nervously folding the brim in his hands. I could tell he needed a haircut; long, uneven tufts of hair, damp with sweat, clung to his forehead, pressed flat by the band of his hat.

I raised the vodka bottle in salute to him and kicked back in my chair, smiling at the whole bulky length of him. "I saw your girl yesterday, Jordan," I said. "She seems big."

Mason grinned goofily, like a proud papa. "She's thirteen, Kat."

"You're joking."

"Hell, Kat," Mason said, "I've got kids in elementary school that you've never even seen. I doubled the size of the farm and my dog's dead. You think the whole world stopped humping and changing just because you decided not to come home for Christmas anymore?" Mason smiled easily to let me know there were no hard feelings.

I blinked. "Mojo's dead?' I asked in surprise.

"No, not him. He's been gone a long time. I meant the next one."

"Well, shit," I said as we both shook our heads and wondered at the passage of time. It had been nine years, at least, since I'd been home.

Mason looked around at the dusty boxes and bric-a-brac, "Momma said you've come home to clean this all out."

"Momma seems to be telling a lot of people that," I said dryly.

"You making much headway?"

"No. None." I gestured helplessly. "In fact, I'm just sitting here, gathering strength, I guess."

Mason ran a hand through his sweat-matted hair, and I was surprised to see his expression grow suddenly serious. He put his hat back on, then took it off again. I held it out in front of him, seeming to notice all the grime for the first time. He swatted it against his thigh, maybe hoping to knock some of the dirt loose. It didn't do much good. I put it back on his head anyway. I stared at his boots. knocked them against each other, loosening dirt and probably manure onto Tea's floor.

"You could leave it all be, you know," he said quietly. "What are you going to do with even half the things in here? What's the sense of opening up all these boxes just to close them again. Hell, Kat, this stuff just belongs here."

For a minute, I felt that my brother was asking me for something. Not so much with his voice, but in the way his eyes fixed on mine for one brief moment, then dropped, the emotion quickly plowed under.

I stared at him, expectantly. He flushed a little and looked away. "You sure you want to do this?" he asked.

"It's been almost five years," I said.

He shrugged. "For some reason that doesn't feel like much time to me."

I said nothing.

Mason studied me carefully, then asked almost plaintively, "Why now? Just out of the blue like this? Why rush into it today? Come on over to the house with me. I'll have Constance make us lunch."

I shook my head.

Mason took off his hat and swatted it on his leg again. "Did you talk to Momma about it? About Tea?"

"Some," I felt my jaw harden like the pit of a peach.

He cleared his throat. He pulled at his sleeves, under the armpits.

"I know Momma probably told you that it was a suicide," he said. "It probably even looks that way to you. But I know, even with what all the police said, that it was an accident. She didn't mean to do all that."

"I know," I was with her, Kat, and she was happy. Real happy. Almost like . . . "

"Mason," I said looking away. "Don't. Please don't."

Mason fell silent. I stared across the room at Tea's bed. Momma had found Tea there, wrapped among the blankets. Like she was sleeping. Her sketchbook open, as if she'd been planning another painting.

It was so quiet in the room for so long that I thought Mason had flown soundlessly out the window. When I looked up, he was still standing there, watching me with this thoughtful expression that I didn't recognize.

Below us, the front door slammed. We both flinched. My younger brother, Taylor, called out for us and then took the steps to the attic two at a time. His face was red when he arrived, a little out of breath and a little sunburned.

The first words out of his mouth were for Mason. "The horses are out. I saw them along the road as I was coming here."

# 6

When Mason had gone, Taylor grinned easily at me. "Mom said you were home," he said. Then he came over and wrapped his arm around me and kissed my forehead and buried his face in my neck. Taylor, the youngest, sweet baby of my family, hugged me until I gave a little gasp of pain. He let me go and tugged my hair.

"Come down and eat lunch with me," he said. Wrinkling his nose, he added, "This place stinks."

"It's too hot to breathe, anyhow," I explained. "So that helps limit the smell."

Taylor smiled. "Momma sent a cooler home from the restaurant for your lunch. I told her I'd stop by with it. Come eat with me," he repeated.

Obediently, I followed him down the stairs, then out of the house. He pulled the tailgate down on his shiny new truck. We sat in the bed, leaning against the cab, and ate still-hot plates of potatoes with gravy, mushy carrots with pearl onions, thick slices of roast beef, and even thicker hunks of buttered bread from the restaurant in town where Momma and Abra worked. Sunday lunches from the Dinner Bell Inn were always the best.

I ate and gazed openly, gladly at my brother. If there was anyone from home, aside from Tea, that you could say I had missed, it was Taylor. For years, we had called him nothing but Baby, until his teacher sent a note home to Momma because Taylor had refused to answer to his proper name. The teacher didn't think the nickname appropriate for a boy of six.

Baby. Sweet Baby. I was five years old when he was born and considered him as much my baby as anyone else's. Today sweet Taylor Lovely was dressed in neat black jeans, straight-legged over his cowboy boots, a cowboy shirt with mother-of-pearl buttons and conchos over the breast pockets. His long black hair was neatly ponytailed and fell down his back. His thin mustache was neat and combed. Taylor caught me gaping at him. He grinned fetchingly at me and handed over a can of soda from the cooler.

"Quit flirting," I said, and gave him a playful push.

Taylor smiled down at his boots.

"How's Dinah?" I asked.

Her name said aloud changed him, softened him more if that were possible. Taylor loved this girl, Dinah Mai, from up by Gem Lake. From the look on his face when he talked about her, I hoped to hell, for his sake, that she loved him, too.

"She had a funeral. A great-aunt died. Dinah went up to the reservation last week. She thought she'd stay with her mom awhile, once she got there."

"She's staying with her momma?" I poked him playfully again. "What did you do?"

Taylor shook his head. "We didn't fight or nothing. She just wanted to see her family for a while. Some families are like that, you know."

I gave him my most skeptical look, then laughed.

Taylor fiddled with the tab on his soda can. "If you're cleaning Tea's things out, do you think Dinah and I could take some of the furniture off your hands? We're planning on getting this place together." He blushed slightly and cleared his throat. "We're moving to Denver."

"Denver?" I repeated, startled.

"Yeah, in Colorado."

"I know where Denver is. I had a job there once. Does Momma know?"

He shook his head. "No. So don't tell her yet."

"She won't take this well," I said quietly. "You've always been her baby." I shook my head. "Hell," I added, "you're the only one of us she can stand to look at."

Taylor looked away, his eyes a little bright.

"When are you going?" I asked.

"The end of summer. Dinah's uncle got us a rate on a U-Haul. Real cheap. We have room for the furniture."

"What's in Denver?"

"Dinah got into this grad program for writing." Taylor swelled a little with his humble pride. "You didn't think anyone that smart would notice me, did you? She got a scholarship, too. And I thought I might try some classes at the community college. I've been working a lot lately. Saving a lot. We've got enough money to let things ride for a while. See how it goes."

"Do you want the iron bed?" I asked.

Taylor nodded. "And some of the chairs. There's a good sofa up there, too." Catching himself, he gave me a defensive look. "I would've called you. I wasn't just going to take anything."

I reached over and stroked his long hair. "Do you want any bowling balls?" I asked. "I just found a box with six of them in it."

Taylor wrinkled up his nose. The ease of his features moving highlighted my brother's softness. He was like chamois cloth. There were three girls between him and Mason. When he was a baby we'd all loved to touch him. The gentleness was rubbed into his frame. "'Fraid I can't help you there, sister."

I leaned back against the cab of the truck and sighed. "Of course you can take what you want. What am I going to do with all that stuff? Six bowling balls. In a box. What was she planning to do with six goddamn bowling balls?"

Taylor laughed. "I remember that one. A table. She was going to make a table."

"What?"

"A table. She was all hopped up about it. She wanted a wood case to hold the balls and a glass top, so you could look down at 'em." Taylor finished his soda and crushed the can. "She got the balls for fifteen bucks at a farm auction. I was with her. We had to sneak them in past Momma."

"Then they're yours," I said grimly. "As her accomplice, you get to help clear them out."

Taylor laughed. "Tea and I were real good at sneaking things past Momma." He pointed across the driveway at the open field beside our house. Halfway into it there was a familiar old apple tree. "You know, Tea helped me sneak my first cigarette out there by that tree. Momma still doesn't know I smoke." Taylor pulled another soda from the cooler and offered it to me.

I looked over at him curiously. "Tell me about it."

"About what? The bowling balls?"

"No, about your first cigarette with Tea."

"Not much to tell."

"Tell it anyway and I'll give you the furniture."

Taylor smiled broadly. He stared thoughtfully out at the tree. "I had just got home from school that day," he said. "I went straight out to find her because I knew she'd be out by that apple tree she loved so much. She was there too, with her back up against the tree, enjoying a bottle.

"So I sat down beside her and asked her for a drink and she looked me all up and down and then said, 'What for?'

"And I said, 'What do you mean?'

"'What's your excuse?' she said. 'You gotta have a reason for drinking or it's got no point.'

"Truth is, all day long, I'd been sitting in school thinking about finding Tea and making her give me a drink. I'd worked my story out before I got there. Most of it was true.

"I was feeling pretty sorry for myself at the time. I told her all about hating school. About my teacher being a bitch who was out to nail my ass to the wall. About how I was one detention away from being kicked out of school for good. And about being so short and skinny for my age and how Daddy being a drunk didn't give me much motivation to do anything with my life except look at girls' tits.

"I poured my heart out to her, and kept at it till it was almost dark and didn't make a dent. But she let me talk and when I was done, she just smiled at me and said, 'That's a piss-poor excuse, if I ever heard one.'

"I was boiling mad then. I asked her what her excuse was.

"She pointed to the setting sun and said, 'You see that star there?'

"'Yeah, Tea, I do. What about it?'

"'Well,' she said, 'it's about to fall on me.'

"So we sat and watched the sunset together. She got drunk and gave me my first cigarette. I had to carry her to the house. All the way back and she didn't give me so much as a single drink from her bottle. And I hated her, because I thought I needed it bad then."

When he wound down his story, there was silence. Taylor sipped his soda. "You know," he finally said, a smile twitching at the corners of his mouth, "what I really needed then was a swift kick in the ass, not a cigarette or a drink." He shrugged sagely. "Dinah came along a little after that, so I guess things take care of themselves."

I laughed. Taylor smiled at me again.

"I'm glad you're doing well, Taylor," I told him happily. "I'm glad about Dinah."

Taylor gave me another hug and kissed my forehead. We sat for a long moment, wrapped together, sitting in the truck bed. For a moment, the air wasn't so much hot as warm. Then Taylor sighed and, looking down at me, he said, "You can stop beating yourself up about it, you know."

"About what?"

"About Tea dying the way she did. It's like that day I was with her out by the apple tree. There's nothing you could have done. Maybe she loved you and us. Maybe she wanted to be a part of this family, but at the same time, she was convinced the sky was falling. She was too busy watching it come down to care about us."

It just seemed easier not to argue. To say nothing. Instead, I let my head rest on Taylor's shoulder and we sat, staring off across the field before us. There wasn't a breeze that day. Just hot light. Not a leaf stirred on the trees, and for a long time, neither did we.

≈

It seemed harder to climb back up the stairs once Taylor left. I felt very old when I finally got to the top. When I opened the door, I half hoped it would all be gone. I watched the dust my return had stirred up settle back to the floor.

I hadn't decided to clean the attic yet, but had promised Taylor to free some space around the furniture he wanted so that he could haul it away. But even that would hardly make a dent.

Maybe I should run now, thought.

Halfway across the attic from me, though no one had touched it, a book fell from its shelf. It landed with a dull thud, its pages falling open and exposed. I stared at it.

Later that night, climbing into my bed, I would think about mountains and rockslides. I thought about the Rockies framed in car windows. I thought about how a boulder can sit on a ledge for a hundred years, with the wind wearing it down and the rain chewing away at its hold with insect-size bites. Not an inch in a hundred years. Not a hair moved in the time it takes rivers to cut their patterns out. Then one day a rockslide. All that motion, all that flight, running, crushing the ground and the one person in a thousand years unlucky enough to witness its birth.

The book that had fallen was *The Sun Also Rises*, one of Tea's favorites. It was a moldering copy and I threw it away. She had dozens.

I began cleaning by working on Tea's books. It would take me several whole days. I worked slowly, dusting each book off carefully, brushing my fingers along their spines, smelling the pages, reading the jackets.

I searched through each book to find Tea's notes. As near as I could tell, Tea had kept up an active conversation with Hemingway in the margins of his books since she was fifteen. She added to her notations each year, revising and reviewing earlier ideas. Nothing was organized. Most of it was illegible. The new was squeezed in next to the old, in various colored pens. The year she met her husband, Billy, was a red ink year. The year I graduated from high school was cool green.

I read her thoughts. I read everything she had to say to the old man, turning the books every which way to follow her winding script. When one copy of a book was too full, she would buy another one. All the copies were numbered and dated. On the inside cover of her last volume of *The Sun Also Rises* she had written:

"Christina Sanchez. May 25, 1996, first woman to face a bull on her feet in Spanish rings."

I knew I would have to come to a decision on the books. There were too many to keep. Most of them I had already read. None of them had any value, except for her notes. Tea hadn't bothered to write in most of the books, just the Hemingways and some stray volumes of Conrad and Brontë. She hadn't had much to say to Charlotte, but her copy of *Jane Eyre* was dog-eared and missing its cover. I began packing the unmarked books into boxes for Mason's children. I was assuming they could read, though I had my doubts about Mason.

# 7

In my dream Tea sat beside me on the bed. She opened her mouth to speak and the ring of a telephone emerged from it. When I woke the ringing continued. I opened my eyes to find Jordan, Mason's girl, there in my bed, crammed in beside me. Her face was pressed against my spine and lower on my back I could feel her hands, knotted into hard fists.

I hardly had time to feel the pressure of her when suddenly she was gone, chasing down the phone like a wolf on the hunt. I lay still, half sleeping, and listened to the murmur of her voice in the distance.

She returned to the room and, seeing me, she paused in the doorway. "You're awake." Jordan was already dressed, wearing cutoff shorts and a T-shirt. On her feet she wore my pink flip-flops. I blinked blearily at her and nodded.

I rose, searching for my clothes. I'd been wearing them for so long that it almost hurt to pull them on again. Jordan watched me carefully while I dressed. She watched me move from room to room, still a little drunk with sleep. She watched me make coffee and eat toast, sitting beside me at the kitchen table, her legs swinging freely over the edge of the chair but the rest of her still. Finally she said, "What will you do today?"

I shrugged. "Clean, I suppose. Like yesterday."

"Upstairs?"

"Yes."

"In the attic? I've never been up there."

I swallowed the rest of my coffee in one gulp. "There's not much to see," I told her.

"There's Tea's things," Jordan said knowledgeably, following me to the sink, inching closer and closer to me.

"I guess."

Jordan brushed against my elbow. "Will you take me to school?"

"It's August, you don't have school."

"I go to summer school," Jordan explained.

"Why?"

"Because. Because." Jordan reached over and turned on the water, rinsing off my dishes. "I get distracted in class. I have to take my tests in a special room. It's all white in there and there are no posters on the walls. I get to be all alone, so I can think." Jordan shut off the tap and rubbed her hands dry on her T-shirt. "Will you make me lunch?"

Jordan was hovering dangerously close, so I said yes.

Standing in front of the open refrigerator, with Jordan watching me closely, I suddenly realized I had no idea what to make for a child's lunch. I frowned, trying to remember what I had eaten at that age. I leaned into the coolness of the refrigerator. It was a relief from Jordan. There was no peanut butter or jelly. Momma's days of sending children off to school seemed to be over. Turning back to Jordan, I asked, "What would you like?"

"Six sandwiches with ham and cheese. Yogurt. Pickles. Three apples and an orange," she said precisely.

"Six sandwiches?"

She nodded solemnly.

"Isn't that a lot?"

Jordan looked down to scratch a mosquito bite on her knee. "I'm hungry all the time," she said. "I can't explain it."

"Do you want me to boil you some eggs?"

"Yes, but you should hurry. You slept late."

"I can't take you to school, Jordan. I don't have a car."

"It's in the driveway."

"No. It's off in the field. It stalled. I have to get it towed."

She shrugged. "It needed gas. I have to go brush my hair."

Once Jordan left the room, I opened the front door. There was my car. I went and made her lunch without another word.

When Jordan appeared behind me, she made me jump, startled. Her long, wheat-blond hair was now pulled back into a tail. She slid her hand into mine. "Can I wear your shoes?" she asked, looking down at her feet and the flip-flops she was already wearing.

I nodded and slipped on a pair of my mother's garden sandals. My car ran perfectly with a full tank of gas. Jordan watched me turn the key in the ignition, smiling a little. I decided that perhaps it would be best if I said nothing to encourage her.

We didn't talk the whole way to school. Jordan held the paper sack close to her chest like a doll.

The school lot was still and empty. I got the feeling we were late. Jordan paused before climbing out of the car. "You sleep like the dead," she announced. "You didn't notice when I came in last night, and you slept through the phone ringing this morning."

"I heard it."

Jordan shook her head. "That was the second time he called. The first time you didn't hear it."

"Who was it?"

She crinkled the top of the paper sack. "Shepherd McCreedy."

I stared at her, trying to place the name.

"He's the man at the gallery in Minneapolis. He handled all of Tea's paintings," she told me.

I had just remembered this myself, but nodded. "What did he want?"

Jordan shrugged. "He wanted to talk with Grandma. He's sending some papers for her to sign. I asked him why he didn't want to talk with you, since everyone knows Tea gave you all her things. He said he didn't know you were home. I told him you were asleep."

"He called back?"

"An hour later. He said he'd called back right away because he was afraid that you'd fly away before he got a chance to meet you."

"He said that?"

"Are you?"

"What?"

"Are you going to fly away?" she asked seriously.

I smiled at her. "You think I should, Jordan?"

She was uncharmed by my smiles. She studied me for a while, growing even more serious. Then she said thoughtfully, "No, Aunt Katherine, I don't think you should. Not just yet anyways."

"Well, then, do you need a ride home today?"

Reaching for the door handle, she shook her head. "You should go home," she said. "He'll call you again. I could tell it in his voice."

Jordan slammed the car door behind her a little too hard. I winced. She almost smiled at me. "I remember when I was little, you and Tea used to take a sheet off the bed and put me in it. Tea would take one end and you'd take the other and you'd swing me back and forth inside, like a hammock."

"You were very young then," I said gently.

"I remember anyways," she said quietly. Still holding on tightly to her paper sack, she turned and jogged into the school. I watched her, just to make sure she got in safely.

≈

The deep silence in the house when I returned told me that everyone was long gone. I didn't feel like going up to the attic. Since I was alone, I shucked my clothes into the machine and wandered through the house naked. I floated through the bedrooms.

None of us, save Abra, lived at home anymore. Still, our rooms were perfectly preserved; nothing moved an inch out of the position we had left it in when we each abandoned ship somewhere between the ages of fourteen and nineteen. The effect was unsettling, making me feel weightless, almost timeless.

When I entered Pearl's room, I almost expected to find her there. I peeked under the bed, thinking I might find an eight-year-old Pearl, braiding and rebraiding miles and endless miles of doll hair. I found only stuffed animals, crammed by the dozens under the box spring and carefully hidden by the quilt. In Taylor's room, I found Superman stickers still tacked to the headboard of his bed. Pearl had left school and run away from home at fourteen to live with Jerry, a forty-year-old auto mechanic. Taylor had followed a year later.

In Abra's room, the clothes my sister now wore to work at the restaurant hung in the closet next to the neat, plastic-covered dresses she had worn in fifth grade. Her room, despite the fact that it was still occupied, showed little wear from the years gone by. Everything was so unchanged that I could picture Abra clearly, sitting on her white-and-gold bed, reading fashion magazines, devouring articles about acne control and weight reduction, practicing kissing on the paper faces of the models.

I could still see her with her face pressed close to the pages, as if she believed by force of will she could enter into that magazine world, where everyone married their first love, lipstick never smeared, and not even a hailstorm could ruin the perfect mascara. Abra had never made it into that perfect world. Beside her bed, where she used to keep a stack of teen magazines, she now kept her Bible.

I was getting tired of having no underwear. Nothing Pearl had left behind could possibly fit me, so I dug into Abra's things and found a suitable bra in her bureau drawer. Tucked beside it, I found a dusty, half-used box of fifteen-year-old tampons. Abra had lost her uterus when her baby boy was stillborn. Among other things, I suspected a deep vein of morbidity in my older sister.

I helped myself to one of Abra's shirts. I preferred T-shirts, but settled for one of her innumerable button-up-to-your-chin affairs. Now partially dressed, I grabbed the afghan off my bed and wrapped it around my waist like a lumpy sari.

I floated into Momma's room. Under her bed I found the cardboard box that held our family photographs. For as long as I could remember, Momma had kept the photos here. And I had always wondered how well she could sleep, suspended above our dead, dreaming their strange black-and-white dreams.

I pulled the box out and carried it to the kitchen table. I poured the photos out onto the table's pitted surface. They smelled faintly of mildew, but mostly of glue and that curious scent of photographs that makes you wonder if silver has an odor.

They were in no apparent order, though some appeared to have been randomly shoved into envelopes. My baby pictures were mingled in with those of my parents and grandparents.

Nothing was labeled. No names. Some dates. I recognized myself. I struggled to sort out the younger faces of my numerous brothers, sisters, and cousins, but was soon lost. I spread them out across the whole table and arranged them into piles of black-and-whites, yellow-and-grays, and colors. No good. I tried sorting them by family, guessing sometimes at who belonged to who, spending long moments trying to place a particular nose with a particular family line. Despite my efforts, no coherent pattern emerged.

I decided to arrange things in a narrative strain. Some of the pictures seemed naturally to belong together, like the birthday pictures. After that, I grouped four generations of brides. With them, I mixed in the gruesome old-fashioned funeral pictures, where the open coffin was tipped forward and the family stood around.

But after those piles, things were pretty random. There were shots of adults with children, children with dolls, children with dogs, men with fish. The oldest marked date was 1920, but some of the others were older than that.

I had no reaction to any of them. There was no hum of recognition in the back of my mind. The photos only made my hands sticky. The people had familiar features. But though I recognized their noses and foreheads, I still felt as if I had walked into a room of strangers. They did not know me. I was as lost among my dead as was among my living family.

I rummaged in the kitchen drawer and found a candle, lit it and placed it next to a picture of my distant grandmother. My mother always accused this grandmother of burning the rest of the family photographs, to hide a heritage she wasn't interested in facing. With the candle and my great-grandmother keeping me company, I began to look over the pictures of Tea. I guess I was hoping she would speak to me; that maybe she was lingering around. But the only connection I felt to Tea then was the tug of memory from deep down inside, not the pull of the supernatural.

In most of the pictures she was still in her teens and not smiling at the camera. "Right back at you," I murmured.

There was a sudden, rattling pounding at the front door and I jumped. My younger sister, Pearl, yelled out, "Kat, you in there? Open up!" She pounded some more for good measure, while I rewrapped my afghan around me.

Reluctantly, I trundled to the door. I had been expecting Pearl yesterday, after Taylor and Mason came by, resigned to the idea of a day of reunions. But the afternoon and then the evening had gone with no sign of her. When I opened the door, I knew why. Pearl wore dark glasses and her skin was waxy. Her hair, stringy and artificially blond, reeked of stale cigarette smoke and staler bars. She looked at me over the top of her dark sunglasses. Her eyes were red rimmed, but she still eyed me suspiciously. "Am I interrupting something?" she asked archly. "You seem a little naked."

I shook my head. "Shut up, Pearl. My clothes are in the wash."

Pearl nodded, unconvinced, and muscled past me into the house. Her son, Blue, was asleep in her arms. He was already three, but small for his age. Pearl carried him easily, straight to my bedroom.

I trailed after her. "Why didn't you use your key?"

Pearl shook her head. "I don't have one. Momma changed the locks on the doors. I think she's got a man." Pearl laid Blue down on my bed, pulling my rumpled blanket over him. "Did you notice the TV dinners in the fridge?" she asked, turning back to me. "When I saw those, I knew for sure she had a man."

I reached over and touched the little boy on the bed. I had never seen him before, but Momma had sent pictures. I soothed his black lovely hair off his face. He had Daddy's forehead. He didn't stir when I touched him; his breath stayed deep and even and calm. Turning from him, I followed Pearl out into the kitchen.

In the narrow hallway Pearl accidentally bumped against me. I winced as her bony elbow connected with my side, then struggled to catch her before she fell. She hit the wall heavily and slid to the floor.

"Oops," Pearl breathed, crawling back up to her feet. She stepped on her sunglasses and sighed. "Piss," she said.

"Rough night?"

Pearl rubbed her thin shoulder. "You don't know the half of it," she groaned. Without her sunglasses, she was squinting painfully in the half-light of the hallway.

"Do you have anything to eat?" she asked plaintively.

I sighed and helped her to the kitchen. I sat Pearl at the table. Taking no notice of the photographs, she laid her head down on a pile of black-and-whites and closed her eyes.

Despite myself, I was taken in for the moment by my sister's delicate beauty. I stared at her, remembering her as a child. She had been a pretty girl and always Daddy's favorite. Today, her hair was a stringy mess, but even so her wide, pale face, with its high, strong cheekbones, glowed like the half moon, like a pearl. Her face was still youthful, girlish even, but now everything about Pearl was somehow wispy. Even her full mouth was somehow fragile.

The impression of fragility didn't last long. Pearl sat up again, opening her eyes. "Piss," she croaked. "My head hurts."

I shook my head ruefully. My sister had her depths, like anyone, but the water was clear all the way down. At the bottom was only sand, though sometimes, in the sunlight, it seemed to glow like gold.

"Coffee?" I suggested brightly.

≈

It took Pearl awhile to recover. While the coffee brewed, my clothes finished in the dryer. I slipped on my warm jeans and clean underwear with undeniable relief and found some sweet rolls in the freezer. Unfortunately, they defrosted in the microwave into a sticky mess. They were still pleasantly gooey and warm, though, so I cut them up and put them on plates. I sat across from Pearl and ate. Pearl picked nuts off the top of her roll and sipped her coffee slowly.

At last she seemed to notice the pile of photographs in front of her. She pushed them away in disgust and fixed me with a bleary eye over her coffee. "Why the hell are you home, Kat? You got cancer or something?"

I was about to lie, then decided on the truth. Of all the people in my family, Pearl was the least likely to have me committed. I told her about waking up in the middle of the night to the phone ringing. About driving without remembering, without conscious thought. I wound down with how I came to in the cornfield, with no gas in my car and not a single memory to show for the thousand and more miles I'd traveled.

When I finished, my sister stared at me, looking deeply impressed at how crazy I had become. "Wow," she said at last. "Nothing? You don't remember anything? Like stopping for gas? Or to go pee?"

"Nope," I said.

"Wow," Pearl said again, shaking her head in disbelief. "I wish had some of whatever it was you took."

Feeling uncomfortable, I rose and started to clear the table. "I guess while I'm home, I'll clean out the attic. Take care of Tea's things. You want anything?"

"You mean like Taylor? I hear he came by yesterday and asked for all the furniture?"

"Yeah, he came by."

"Did cheapskate even offer to pay you anything for it?"

I was surprised by the sudden venom in Pearl's voice. She and Taylor were born only a year apart, Irish twins, and usually they got along pretty well. When they were in school, as a matter of fact, they'd been inseparable.

"He told me a story. I didn't ask for more than that."

"A story about what?" Pearl asked curiously.

"Just about Tea, you know. Just a story about something he remembered."

"You should have asked him for money," Pearl said flatly. "Everybody makes such a big deal out of him these days. With his new job. He could have paid you."

I shrugged.

Pearl looked suddenly thoughtful. She broke one of the nuts from her roll in half and began gnawing thoughtfully on one of the pieces. "If I want those Roper boots of Tea's, you know, the red ones, do I have to tell you a story?"

I knew which boots she was talking about. I could picture them clearly in one of the trunks upstairs. They were battered but well enough taken care of not to have any holes. "That's the going price, I guess. If you tell me a story, you can take anything you want."

Pearl eyed me warily. "Does it have to be something nice? Do have to talk bullshit about how Tea saved children or rescued drowning kittens?"

I thought about it for a moment. Since I was home, it was inevitable that everyone would want to talk to me about Tea, about the things she left behind. It hurt to think of weeks of painful, polite conversation. I knew my cousin too well for that. "No," I said firmly. "Just make it honest. It's gotta be true."

With a smile Pearl waved me back to the table. "Cut yourself another sweet roll, then, and pour some more coffee. I think I've got a good one."

Once I was settled again at the table, Pearl hunched down over her coffee cup. Then she said bluntly, "Tea was screwing Mason."

Whatever I had expected her to say, it wasn't that. I drew back sharply, as if my cup had just exploded in my face. Several of the photographs I had been examining floated to the floor. Pearl's lips twitched at the expression on my face. Then she began to laugh.

I tried to control my face but couldn't. My eyes started to tear. Pearl laughed harder. Several more pictures hit the floor as Pearl's wild laughter shook the table. Next her cup went flying. "Shit," she swore, as the black water spread over the photographs. Pictures of Tea, of myself, of birthday parties began to submerge in the liquid. Pearl dove for the paper towels and started dabbing ineffectively. "Shit," she groaned again. "Mom's going to kill me."

Coffee started to dribble off the table onto my clean jeans. I pushed myself away slowly, watching Pearl struggle. At last she swore again and scooped the whole mess up into the sink. "Damn it!" she yelled. She cast about the room, looking for something to help her clean. Her eyes fixed on the dishrag, hanging from the refrigerator door handle. She seized it and shoved the rag into the sink on top of the ruined photographs. Frantically, she grabbed more paper towels and thrust those on top, too. Then suddenly, she turned away from the sink, looking pale and sick. The next instant she was on her knees, vomiting violently.

I felt sick myself. Shakily, I rose and went to my room. My head hurt so much all of a sudden that I was certain it must be vibrating. Blue was still sleeping in my bed. I closed the door and sat at the vanity table, trying not to listen to my sister vomiting and swearing in the other room. I closed my eyes and tried to think about nothing for a while, to find that clear, clean feeling in my head and drive out the pain in my throbbing temples. Behind me, on the bed, I could hear Blue's calm, restful breathing. I focused hard on that.

Eventually the house grew quiet around us. The pain in my head subsided. When I went out to the kitchen to look for Pearl, I found her gone. She had left the mess in the sink. On the floor, she had hastily piled paper towels over her vomit.

I peered out the screen door. Pearl's car was gone from the driveway. I rested my head against the cool of the metal door and sighed. I thought about Blue in the other room, wondering if I should call my mother at work. Pearl had left no note, and I wasn't quite certain what to do.

Feeling numb, I went back into the kitchen. My foot touched something cool and papery. I looked down to find a photograph, staring up at me from the floor. It was thankfully free of vomit, so I picked it up. On the back it said, "Montana." There was no date on the picture. Tea was standing arm in arm with a boy, grinning at the camera. She couldn't have been more than twelve. The boy was maybe fifteen, but no older. He was wearing a cowboy hat and a nervous smile. The picture gave you a sense of open spaces and blue skies. There was a tiny bit of a cabin in the background and the glimpse of some mountains. I stared at my cousin, loving her freckles, loving her smile.

# 8

The phone rang and I set Tea's picture down on the counter. Out of the corner of my eye I saw it flutter to the floor as Constance's voice spoke over the line. She invited me over for coffee. I closed my eyes. Mason's wife was the last person I wanted to talk to. I wanted to hang up the phone. "Is Mason there?" I asked, unable to help myself.

"Mason?" Constance repeated. "Yeah, he's out working on one of the cars."

"I'll be over," I said and hung up the phone. I was almost to the door when I remembered Blue. I sighed and dialed Mason's number, hoping it would still be the same after all this time.

Constance answered after just one ring and I told her about Blue. She didn't seem surprised and said she'd watch him until Pearl surfaced again.

I woke Blue as gently as I could. He wasn't startled to find himself waking up to a stranger, just watched me silently with his wide, blue eyes as I put on a pair of Momma's tennis shoes.

Together we walked to Mason's house. Blue's legs were small but sturdy. He walked the whole way by himself and didn't say much. He held my hand, though, gripping it tightly whenever a car passed by on the road, as if the noise startled him. If I had to carry Blue the whole way, I still would have walked it. The day was hot, but it felt nice to walk. I enjoyed the sense of covering real distance, even if only the space between our house and my brother's. It seemed to clear my head.

Walking up Mason's driveway, I could see him down by the barns, leaning into the engine of a car that had been propped up on cinder blocks. There were several vehicles in similar shape scattered around the immediate yard and I knew there were more down in the pastures. We used to play in them when we were young. On warm summer nights we would sleep in the old truck beds.

Several of Mason's children ran over at the sight of Blue and swept him away from me into the backyard. I continued on down to Mason by myself, feeling a little numb in the legs. He used to pound me flat when we were kids. I had a feeling that today would be no different.

Mason grinned when I approached. His forehead was smudged with grease. "Did Constance call you?" he asked, ducking his head back under the car hood. "Are you here for some of her coffee?"

I nodded. My throat was too tight for talking just then.

"After we eat, I'll take you around the place," he said. "Show you everything that's new."

I nodded again.

Mason glanced up at me. "Something wrong?"

Feeling annoyed with myself, I shook my head. Forcing myself to talk, I said, "I took your daughter to school this morning. I hope Constance wasn't worried." That wasn't what I intended to say, but at least my voice was working.

Mason grinned again. "Constance spends half her life worrying about Jordan. But," he shrugged, "Jordan just needs a little room to run. Like her dad." He nodded over to the barns, to the corral where the horses were kept. "That's her horse there." Mason pointed to a tall earth-colored horse bellied right up to the edge of the electric fence. It watched us with intelligent eyes. The horse snorted and tossed its head angrily at us. "Can't you tell?"

The horse continued to stare at us. It inched closer to the electric fence.

Mason puttered with the car some more.

"Wanna hear a joke?" he asked finally, closing the car's hood.

I looked at him apprehensively.

Mason scratched his beard and grinned. "Well, there was this old farm couple. Old Swedes. They didn't have any children of their own, so one day they went to town and got a boy from the orphanage. He was a good kid, but a little strange. He'd never been on a farm before. One day the farmer looked out his window and he saw the boy heading down to the pasture with some chicken wire.

"'Where you going with that chicken wire?' he called out.

"The boy yelled back, 'I'm going to catch me some chickens.'

"Well, that farmer had himself a good laugh, because he knew there was no way in hell that kid was going to catch chickens with chicken wire. But soon enough, the boy came back with a string of chickens on his wire.

"The next day the boy came out with a roll of duct tape and swore he was going to catch some ducks. The farmer had another good laugh, but the boy came back in a few hours with a string of ducks.

"The next time the farmer looked out the window he saw the boy heading off across the pasture with some pussy willows. He called out, 'Boy! Wait for me!'"

Mason laughed at his own joke until he was weak in the knees.

I stood and stared at him, until he finally said, "Let's go up to the house. Constance'll be waiting." He moved to throw his arm around me, but I flinched. Surprised, Mason fixed me with a long, hard look. I felt myself going numb again.

Mason tried to grin but failed. His face hung in a weird sort of nervous grimace, half smiling, half frowning. "Kat, ain't you going to tell me what's wrong? You're making me edgy. You find something up in the attic?"

"How long?" I finally just came out with it.

"How long what?" Mason asked, glancing up at the house.

"How long were you sleeping with Tea?"

Mason went very still. Then he smiled and shook his head. I felt a brief flutter of relief, hoping he would deny it. This wouldn't be the first time Pearl had lied to me.

Mason scratched his beard. "Since she first came here. Since we were kids."

My stomach dropped. I closed my eyes. "I don't believe this," I murmured.

I opened my eyes again to find my brother grinning unapologetically at me. "I'm a sonofabitch, ain't I?"

"Screw you, Mason," I hissed and turned away.

Mason caught my arm. "Oh, come on, Kat. Don't go acting like this. What did you think was happening? Wasn't like we grew up together. Wasn't like we were family. Not really. We were both teenagers when her mother dumped her on our doorstep."

I pulled my arm free with a jerk that almost sent me tumbling on my butt into the dirt. Mason tried to catch me and I struck out at him. The flat of my hand collided with his thick, padded chest. Mason laughed, brushed my arm aside, and picked me up like a rag doll. He set me straight on my feet. We glared at each other for a minute. Then he let me go.

"Wasn't like I forced her or anything. Wasn't like . . . ," he faltered, trying to explain. "It just was. That's all."

All of a sudden, I started to feel in need of something steady to keep me on my feet. I sat down on the bumper of the car, more leaned against it, I guess.

"What about Billy?" I asked, looking up into Mason's big, meaty face.

Mason raised his eyebrows at me, as if I were being stupid on purpose. He scratched his elbow, then spat into the dirt of his driveway. "Billy never held Tea back from doing anything she wanted, even when they were married. You know that. Hell, half the time he wasn't even there."

"Tea was in love with Billy." I heard my voice waver a little. "She was crazy about him."

"Kat," Mason said gently, "it didn't take much to make Tea crazy. Sometimes it didn't take anything at all, she just was."

"Constance?" I almost whispered. "What about her?"

Mason looked away, up at the house. It took him a full minute to answer. "Constance doesn't know," he said. "She should, but she doesn't." He shook his head and leaned against the car beside me. Uncomfortable, I moved away, putting a few more safe inches between us.

"When Tea first came to live with us," he rumbled, "I knew exactly what I wanted and so did she. She came up to me one day after school and asked me to drive her down by the lake. After that, all I could ever think about was screwing her."

Mason made a face. "I thought it would end when I married Constance. Then . . . do you know old Shelby Road? It's down by Comfort Lake, so it's always nice and cool in the summer. There's these two fields of hay on either side. It's a dirt road to get down there. No lights. Way out in the middle of nowhere. Well, about a week after my honeymoon, Tea called up late and said she had a flat down there. She wanted to know if I could come help her.

"I found her car by the side of the road. It was empty, so I figured she was farther on, down by the lake. I guess I was mad about her calling so late and always acting like I damn well better just do what she said. So I thought I'd scare her a little.

"I killed the lights on the pickup and drove real slow, trying to sneak up on her. I found her hip deep in the hay a little ways on. She had her arms crossed around her, and she was staring out at the lake, looking at the moon's reflection. She looked real peaceful. So, all of a sudden I threw on my headlights and hit the horn."

Mason laughed. "Boy, that startled her, but it also startled these deer, a doe and her yearling, that had been sleeping in the hay. They jumped out of nowhere and charged right past Tea. It scared the shit out of her. She ran for the truck and practically threw herself in my arms.

"I was a lot more agile then. I yanked open the door on my side, right as she came in the passenger door, and pulled both of us out onto the gravel. We landed on our asses and made love right there in the middle of the road."

I held up my hand. "That's enough," I said, feeling unsteady.

Mason shrugged, "That's pretty much the end of the story. After that, I went back to Constance like nothing had happened. Things were pretty regular with me and Tea from then on. We never had a fight. She never threatened to tell

Constance. Most times, she'd come visit me at work or I'd go over and work on her car." He smiled broadly. "I did a lot of work on that car. She'd smash it up anytime I made progress, so I'd have an excuse to keep going over."

"Why are you telling me this?"

Mason blinked at me. "Didn't you just ask?"

"I wasn't asking for details," I said shakily.

Mason spat again. He stared at me, standing there with his big arms crossed, and started to feel uneasy. I looked over at Jordan's horse, who seemed to be watching us.

"Taylor told me that you gave him and Dinah all of Tea's furniture," he said finally.

"Yeah, I did."

"He said you gave him all that furniture because he told you a story about Tea."

I felt a prickle of warning in my neck and looked uneasily at Mason.

"You could of gotten a couple hundred bucks for that big old-fashioned iron bed. It's an antique. I helped Tea carry it up there myself." Mason continued, "He must have told you a hell of a story."

"What do you want?" I asked flatly, tired of this entire conversation.

"Tea's car," he said. "I want her old Belair."

Suddenly, from behind us, I heard Jordan's horse scream. It reared, then stomped around in a circle, shaking its head wildly. It reared again and charged off, disappearing over the hump in the pasture.

"It's the fence," Mason explained in disgust. "I just put that stretch of electric fence in. All of the other horses caught on right away, but it takes that one awhile to get things through its stubborn head."

"No," I said flatly.

"I know it's a lot to ask," Mason said quietly. "The car's worth some money, I know. But Constance needs a car. Hers broke down for good and we can't afford a new one just yet. She needs it for the kids. And it's only fair. I spent a lot of time over the years repairing it."

A suspicion dawned in the corner of my mind and spread over me like an early winter frost. I hadn't seen Tea's car up at the house, though until now I'd just assumed it was parked in the garage, out of view.

"Where is the car?" I asked, trying to keep my voice low and steady.

Mason ran his hand through his beard. "In our garage. I told Constance she could have it over a year ago."

"No."

"Look, if I'd left it outside in the winter it would have been ruined by now anyway," Mason wheedled. "I just got tired of storing it, that's all. No one was using it."

"No." It felt good to say that to him.

"Constance already thinks you gave it to her. How are you going to ask for it back?"

Ah, defeat. Constance, whether she knew it or not, had enough problems. I couldn't strand her without a car, too. Defeat. Defeat. The word chimed like a church bell in my mind. "Screw you, Mason," I said and turned to go.

I'd walked about three steps when Mason said, "She came to see me the day she died, you know."

I stopped, even though I wanted to keep walking. I didn't want to hear anything else Mason had to say, didn't even want to look at him. I felt battered. My ribs ached, as if we'd been wrestling like kids. Mason scratched at his scraggly beard. "She was happy. That day at least, she was happy. Came to see me at the garage. We went and had lunch down by the lake. Messed around a little." Mason shrugged. "You know."

Silence.

"I just wanted you to know that," he continued. "I know a lot of people say . . . well, just want you to know that it was an accident. The way she died and all. It must have been. Because Tea was happy that day."

"Fuck you, Mason," I said. "Fuck. You." I began to walk away.

≈

Before I could escape Mason's yard, Constance's voice called out from my grandmother's front porch and I froze guiltily. "When Mason told me you were back," she said, "said I'd have to see it to believe it. But here you are, clear as day."

As she spoke, Constance pulled a comb through my grandmother's tangled hair. Grandma, sitting in a lawn chair with bare, purple-veined legs and naked feet, showed no signs of recognizing me.

Constance had weighed a little over ninety-five pounds when she married my brother. She was the boniest, tiniest thing ever seen back then. But like her house and the kids, she'd added on in my absence. Somewhere along the line, Constance had blossomed into a bright, ripe apple of a woman. Above the line of her halter-top, a shocking expanse of pale pink skin spread with the serenity of a sand dune. Her breasts, her shoulders and thighs, once stick thin, now possessed the smooth, generous curves of a gelatin mold. Her face was very round, piled with an expanse of familiar, curly blond hair that she held in place with a plastic clip.

After what Mason had just put me through, it took an effort even to look at Constance. I stood my ground, though. I could feel my toes curling into the dirt of the driveway, trying to anchor me like prairie grass.

Constance climbed heavily down from the porch. She hugged me and said wryly, "You know, I ran away from home once too. I was thirteen and came home after half an hour. But you," she laughed, "when you left home I had five fewer kids."

When Constance pulled away, I was surprised to see tears running down her face. I had forgotten how easily she could cry. I felt myself blush.

She squeezed me even harder this time, then pulled back to look at me again. "It's good that you're here, Kat," she said. "Better late than never. It's wreal good to see you."

Not knowing what to say, I stood and stared at her, while Constance continued to beam at me.

Slowly, I began to smile back. I pushed the secret I was keeping for Mason and Tea to the back of my mind and reached up to brush one of her round cheeks. Backbone or not, I liked Constance. We'd never had much to talk about, but she had always been kind to me.

Constance moved me onto the porch, steering me by the elbow. "Sorry," she explained, "I need to work and talk at the same time or I feel like I'm falling behind."

My grandmother shifted position as we approached. She fixed her eyes on me for the first time. "Constance," she said, "thirsty."

Constance smiled tolerantly, squeezed my elbow to say she'd be back in just a minute, and then disappeared into the house. My grandmother continued to watch me warily. I leaned against the wall and watched her back.

"I heard about you on the TV," she said at last.

I looked at her in surprise.

"Shame about your father. I liked that Willie Nelson. He sang some good songs."

"Willie Nelson isn't dead, Grandma. Daddy is."

"Well," Grandma blinked at me, "that's a relief."

I was about to reply when a movement down on the road caught my eye. I looked up to see a car slowing down near the drive, as if it were trying to read the name on Mason's mailbox. The car turned slowly into the driveway. I squinted. The driver was a woman I didn't recognize. The car was new and brown.

I was turning to call Constance when the woman hopped out of her still-running car. She was clutching a brown paper sack and covered the ground between the car and porch in three steps. She flew up the porch steps and was reaching for the door handle when I put myself in front of her. She clearly hadn't seen me until that moment. The black cloud of anger on her face rippled. "I'm here to see Constance," she bit out.

"She's not here," I lied blithely, not ready to let this woman launch herself on my sister-in-law.

When she saw that I wasn't going to move, she drew back a few steps. She stared hard at me, her face growing a deep, angry red. "I didn't know you were home, Kat," she said at last.

I didn't recognize the woman, so I just shrugged. "Would you like to leave a message for Constance? I'll make sure she gets it when she comes back."

The woman thrust the crinkled bag into my hands.

I opened it. Inside was the lunch I'd prepared that morning for Jordan. Bemused, I glanced back up at the woman.

"Tell Constance that I send my son to school with his own lunch," she hissed. "I do not need her daughter to feed him."

"Jordan?" I asked.

"Yes, Jordan," she spat out the name. "I don't expect that girl has had much raising, considering this family and the way you all carry on. But that girl had better just leave my son alone or I'll see to her."

For a moment the threat hung in the air between us. "What did you say your name was again?" I asked coolly.

"Lily Tippleson," she snapped.

"Well, tell me, Lily, exactly what kind of example does my family set for our children?"

Lily Tippleson flashed her teeth at me. "I went to school with your cousin Tea," she said. "I know what she was. She slept with half the men in this town."

I tried to keep my expression as bland as possible. "Half the men in this town slept with Tea as well," I said.

The woman stared at me blankly.

"In my experience, it takes two people to make love," I explained. "Although, I've heard that some make do with just one."

The red that was already in the woman's face deepened.

I frowned at her, narrowing my eyes thoughtfully. "You look familiar. What did you say your name was again?"

Silence.

"Tippleson," I answered for her as if had just remembered. "You're Darrell Tippleson's wife, aren't you? You live just on the other side of town, don't you? How is Darrell doing?"

"Do you know my husband?" the woman asked tightly.

I tilted my head, trying to look like I was considering the question. "You know," I said finally, "I'm not real sure, but I'm pretty sure Tea introduced me to him once. Doesn't he hang around at Riordan Chagall's bar sometimes? Tea used to work there, you know. She knew everyone that came in there."

More silence.

"I have already spoken to the director of the summer school program," the woman breathed at me. "She expects Constance and Jordan in her office tomorrow morning at nine o'clock. We're going to settle this then." She smiled. She drove off.

≈

Glancing back over my shoulder, I saw Constance, peering out of the screen door with a glass of melting ice cubes in her hand. She looked terrified. Constance had never been known for her nerve. "Did Tea really know that woman's husband?" she asked, wide-eyed.

I shrugged. "More than likely."

"Oh, Kat, you shouldn't have said that. Not if it wasn't true."

"She deserved it," I said flatly.

Constance now eyed me warily.

I sighed, settling onto the steps. "Constance, it's no secret that Tea liked men. But that doesn't mean I'll let just anyone call her a whore."

Constance stepped timidly out onto the porch. She kept peeking at the road, as if she was expecting Lily Tippleson to return any minute with heavier ammunition. "What a horrible woman," she shuddered. "Last time we went to the director's office, she yelled like a madwoman."

I glanced back at Constance. She was real pale and the ice cubes in the glass rattled as her hand shook. "What are we going to do now?" A note of panic had crept into her voice. "This will be my third conference with the director already this summer."

"They always say the third time's a charm," I joked halfheartedly.

The glass, slippery to begin with from sweating in the hot August air, slid from my sister-in-law's nervous hand. It landed with a sound that made me think of mirrors cracking and plain old bad luck. Sighing, I went over to pick up the pieces.

Constance grabbed my arm, struck by a sudden alarming thought. "I can't go to the meeting tomorrow. I have to take your grandmother to the doctor."

Constance had cut her toe. It wasn't deep, but the blood trickled onto the porch. Her grip on my arm tightened when she saw the blood.

"Call and reschedule," I suggested.

"I can't," Constance gurgled nervously. "Jordan's on probation. They might throw her out of summer school." She swallowed hard. "She might have to repeat a grade."

Constance's grip on my arm tightened and tightened, like a vise. The only way to get loose seemed to be to volunteer to take Grandma to her appointment.

Hearing this, my grandmother squawked indignantly. To say that I was not her favorite was an understatement. I sighed. The next thing I knew I was making arrangements to pick Jordan up for her nine o'clock appointment.

Sweet relief flooded into Constance's anxious face. I felt like kicking myself.

"I want a glass of water," my grandmother said. "Kat drank all of mine. Look, she's got the pieces of my glass in her hands." The old woman gave me the evil eye.

Constance ducked back in for more water. Mason came up to the house to see what the commotion was about, and I decided to leave right then and there. I dumped the shards of broken glass into Mason's hands and jumped down off the porch.

As I walked shakily down the driveway, I was a little light-headed, as if I hadn't eaten in awhile. I felt something else that I didn't want to think about just then. As I left, I sensed that my grandmother was watching me closely. I glanced back. The woman stared at me with eyes that meant that, somewhere inside her, a house fire was still burning. I felt her eyes follow me all the way down the driveway and farther down the road until I was out of sight.

# 9

There was a little dip in the road. That's when I felt her eyes leave me. The absence of my grandmother's regard was like a sudden coolness. I slowed down. I wasn't as dizzy. The tension left me, and I took a good look at the late summer afternoon unfolding around me.

That's when I saw the calf. It was lying almost in the ditch, but more in a little stand of anemic pines that marked the borders of our property from the cornfield. It was obviously dead, its eyes open, its head unnaturally tilted up towards me, following the slope of the earth as it curved up from the ditch to the road. The calf's mouth gaped open and its tongue lolled out, stained a brilliant grass-green. It lay too far away from the road to have been hit by a car. I stumbled down the ditch, extending my arms like wings to keep my balance. The calf's soft, all-white hide was streaked with rich black earth. Its belly was noticeably swollen. Other than that, I could see nothing wrong with it. I nudged it a little with my foot, just to be sure.

The honk of a car horn made me jump and spin around. My car. Jordan had pulled my car over to the side of the road. She leaned out the window, watching me.

Carefully, I climbed up the steep side of the ditch.

"Stupid thing," Jordan said when I drew close. She thrust her chin out at the calf. "Ugly thing probably ate itself to death out in the corn."

"Probably," I said. "It's been missing for a few days, hasn't it?"

Jordan made a face that I couldn't read. "Stupid thing," she repeated, shaking her head. "You let a horse into the corn and it'll eat until it's full. It knows when to stop. A cow's so stupid it'll eat and eat until its stomach blows up. That one's Grandma's. All the white ones belong to her."

She reached across the seat and opened the car door for me. "I'll have to come back later with the truck and clean it up."

"By yourself?"

Jordan regarded me calmly. Feeling chastised, I climbed sheepishly into the car.

She restarted the engine.

"Do you know how to drive this thing?" I asked.

"No," she said, but I think she smiled. The corners of her mouth twitched at least. She maneuvered a U-turn on the narrow road, edging a little into the ditch to do it. She got us turned towards home and smiled at me, tolerantly.

"We have a meeting with your summer school director tomorrow morning," I said.

The smile melted off her face.

"Do you know why?" I asked.

Jordan nodded. "The hell bitch," she said calmly. "This'll will be the third time this summer."

"Hell bitch?" I asked mildly.

"Bitch," she repeated.

≈

When we reached the house, it was obvious that Momma and Abra had just got home as well. They hadn't gone in yet. Their identical big, ugly handbags sat by the door, waiting side by side. Next to them was a paper bag filled with take-out containers of food. Probably our dinner.

Abra and Momma were down in the garden, picking tomatoes. I squinted down at them. They were still in their restaurant uniforms.

To my surprise, I saw Pearl there as well.

Momma and Abra wandered along the rows of tomatoes, each plant drooping under the weight of its fruit. They reminded me of those statues of Kali, her heavy breasts growing redder and redder in the summer heat. There was a growing stack of tomatoes by the edge of the garden, where Pearl sat sipping meditatively from a can of beer. From the looks of it, my sister was on her way to being deeply stoned. She giggled when she saw me and wiggled her tongue.

Momma glanced over frowning, and saw Jordan and me for the first time. She nodded at me and then fixed Pearl with a stern look. Squirming uncomfortably, Pearl quickly stifled her laughter. Momma went back to work, examining her tomato harvest.

"Are you going to tell them?" Jordan whispered quietly.

"Tell who what?" Momma asked calmly, without looking up from her work.

"I found your white calf," I said simply. "It's down in the ditch by the three pines. Dead."

Momma twisted a tomato off its branch. The branch snapped audibly. Abra reached down and picked a thick green caterpillar off a plant. She dropped it to the ground and smushed it with her foot.

Pearl looked confused. "The cows got out again?"

"The day I got home," I explained. "Momma's been looking for it."

"You found it down by the pine trees?" she asked, troubled. She looked over at Momma. "Isn't that where you found Tea?" she asked. "Right there in the ditch?"

A sudden tense silence descended on us all. Abra straightened and stared, another green caterpillar in her hand. Momma glanced quickly up at me, then away.

Unable to take the quiet, Pearl giggled again. "Why's everyone looking so serious? What'd I say?"

Momma darted a fierce look at Pearl, who started to complain, her voice high. "I don't understand why—"

"Shut up, Pearl," Abra said abruptly. Pearl fell silent, looking hurt. Abra suddenly remembered the squiggling caterpillar she held between her fingers. She gave a little jump and threw it to the ground.

Momma went to the edge of the garden and began piling tomatoes in her arms. "I think we're done here for today, Abra," she said calmly, not looking at me. I, however, stared at Momma so intently that I felt as if my eyes were being pulled from my head by some magnetic force she had mastered.

"Can you two handle bringing the rest of these tomatoes up to the house?" she said to Jordan and Abra, already walking away.

"Is that true, Momma?" I asked, as Momma moved to walk past me.

Momma dropped a tomato. It split open at her foot.

I bent over and scooped the tomato up. It was still warm from the sun. "Is that true?" I repeated, my voice sharp.

I felt my sisters' and Jordan's eyes on us. I could sense Abra's nervousness. When Taylor was eight, he had accidentally driven a nail through his hand and had sworn at Momma as he stumbled, bleeding, into the house. Momma had calmly taken him to the emergency room and then, after he'd been bandaged, smacked him hard across the face for daring to speak to her in that tone, whatever the situation.

We had all felt the hard slap of our mother's hand from time to time. Maybe too much. My sisters' eyes grew wide and alarmed as the fight between Momma and me brewed in the air.

The tension grew too much for Jordan, who turned away, heading for the garage, galloping off like a horse.

"You told me you found Tea's body in the attic. Not out in the ditch like that." I was trying to keep my voice calm and steady, even though I could feel my heart pounding in my chest. I knew that if I showed the slightest tremor of naked anger, my mother would clam up.

"Honestly," Momma said, "I don't see what difference it makes."

"It makes a difference that you lied," I spat back at her.

Momma had clenched her jaw so tight she had to work hard to get the words out. "It was one of the hardest things I ever had to do in my life," she said. "To tell you Tea was gone. Over the phone. To not see you when I said it. When I called, the lie just came out. I was afraid you would take it so hard."

"The point is—" I insisted. My anger seemed bigger than myself. I felt it standing behind me, facing my mother down.

I'd gone too far. I sensed the crack in my mother's face before it appeared. Her eyes reddened and her chin tilted up. Her voice got a little ragged when she spoke. "The point," she said, "is that I thought you'd take it better if you thought she'd died there in her attic, painting. I thought it would be, I don't know, a good image for you to hold on to. You sent all those brushes that summer."

"She needed materials."

"She never used them." Momma's voice cracked like a whip. "From the time she left the hospital until the day she killed herself she never painted a thing."

"Tea didn't kill herself," I yelled, losing all vestiges of control.

"She didn't so much as move a finger to save herself either," Momma returned, her voice rising as well.

"That's not true! Tea told me she was painting," I practically shrieked.

"She lied," Momma said flatly. "She was good at lying."

I felt every muscle in my body clench. An animal howl rose up inside me. I wanted to scream and throw myself at Momma. Instead, I turned my back on her and started walking. My cousin died in a ditch alongside the road.

I climbed in my car and sat for a long while, my hand ready to turn the key in the ignition. Slowly, it got dark all around me. It was all too much. I felt like Jordan's damn horse, backing into an electric wire it should have known was there. I felt weak and tired, as if a current had been shot through me. I shook my head, suddenly more angry with myself than anyone else, even Momma. I should have known better. I should never have come home.

≈

When I climbed up the steps to the house later that night, the house was empty. Momma had gone over to fix a meal for my grandmother. Abra's church people had picked her up at the end of the driveway again. Jordan and Pearl had simply disappeared.

Momma had taped a note to the front door for me. It said that Shepherd McCreedy had called again asking for me. Wearily, I peeked into the kitchen. Someone had cleaned up Pearl's mess from this afternoon. For a moment, I stood, considering several courses of action. Then I climbed the steps to the attic and started to clean.

# 10

The dusty light bulb in the attic worked fine, so I kept going until late in the night. It wasn't so hot in the attic once the sun went down. It was even a little chilly. I found Tea's sweater on the chair by her bed, waiting there, as if she'd only stepped out just a minute before. I put it on. I wanted to smell her just then. Feel her. But the sweater only gave me mildew and age, stagnant air and abandoned places.

I found some empty boxes and started packing knickknacks into them, carefully wrapping everything with the newspaper I found piled in a great stack by Tea's easel. As I worked, I found eight or nine of her sketchbooks in with the newsprint. I put them in boxes, too, not feeling up to paging through them yet. I sorted through crates of miscellaneous dishware, all, most likely, bought at auctions along with the bowling balls.

I tossed into the garbage several years' worth of musty magazines. I tried the locks on Tea's trunks.

When I couldn't get them open, I searched for the keys. Not finding them, I took one of Tea's hammers and smashed them. Tea's clothes were folded neatly inside. When I opened them, her scent wafted into the room like heavy lavender perfume.

It was well after three in the morning when I began to feel tired. I stretched and looked around me. The place was still a mess, but there were areas of order appearing in the corners. That, at least, was satisfying. I could leave when I finished this. Once everything was organized, I would go. Maybe not back to Louisiana, but perhaps someplace else far away down the highway. I would call my landlady and have her send my things.

Once I had decided that, I felt ready to go back downstairs. I had just entered the kitchen when the phone rang. I felt my heart sink. Slowly, I went over and answered it.

"Hello?" I said into the receiver.

There was a strange clicking on the other end. Then nothing. I waited. Still nothing, and then faintly, a soft, ragged breath, almost like a sob. Someone was crying on the other end, quietly, with their hand pressed to their face.

"Where are you, Pearl?" I asked wearily.

"Daddy?" the voice croaked hesitantly on the other end of the line.

"No, honey," I said gently. "It's me. Kat. Where are you? I'll come get you."

Still weeping, Pearl told me. It took awhile before I understood her.

Just as I hung up, the light in the kitchen flooded on. I blinked painfully into the brightness. Momma and Jordan stood together in the frame of the door. Momma wore her robe, but Jordan was still in her T-shirt and shorts, one of Tea's paperback books clutched in her hand.

"Who was that?' Momma asked, sharply.

"No one," I said, turning away, looking for my car keys. "It was just a wrong number."

Momma knew better. "Where are you going, then?" she demanded.

Still looking for my keys, I glanced back at her. Momma's mouth grew thin and hard. She jutted out her chin. "Your keys are on the cabinet by the sink."

I nodded appreciatively and grabbed them. They were cool and wet in my hand. "I'll be back in a bit," I said.

Momma shook her head, turning away in disgust. "Tell me, do you think I'm blind and deaf or just stupid?"

I stared at her.

"This isn't the first time Pearl has called in the middle of the night." Momma disappeared down the hallway to her bedroom. "Take her back to her place," she called out. "I don't want her here. I've cleaned up enough vomit for one day."

I heard Momma's bedroom door close. I looked over at Jordan.

"Where are we going?" she asked.

≈

Having Jordan along saved some time at least. I'd been gone too long and lost track of half the backcountry roads. Jordan, however, knew how to get to Lindstrom without having to go all the way out to the highway first.

The address Pearl had given me was for a large boxy house. She was sitting on the front steps when we arrived, wailing piteously, hugging her knees tight to her chest, as if she were an animal about to be kicked. She was drunk out of her mind. She cried out loudly and incomprehensibly when she saw me and let me pull her to her feet. She clung to me and somehow we managed to stumble-walk to the car, where she collapsed into the backseat with her legs hanging half out. Jordan watched the whole operation from the car's front seat, her face neutral. She studied the now whimpering Pearl with a clinical eye and then asked calmly, "Do you think we need to take her to the emergency room?"

I shook my head, panting from the exertion of moving Pearl to the car. I stood for some moments in the dirt yard, looking around, trying to find the energy to shove her the rest of the way in.

"Maybe if you pull on her arms from the other side," I told Jordan, "we can get her in."

Jordan got out and went around the car. After a few minutes of pushing and pulling, we had her in, still conscious but useless, spread out across the back seat.

Jordan slammed the door and Pearl began to sob again, deep, hollow sobs.

I climbed into my seat and called to Jordan, "Let's go."

She shook her head, looking thoughtfully up at the big house. The front door stood half open, revealing a gaping darkness within. There was a light on in a window above, but little else. From the lower front windows, a pulsing brightness erupted occasionally. The flickering didn't so much dispel the dark as accentuate it.

Jordan stared up at the house, a considering look on her face. Then she sighed and started up the steps. "I'll be right back," she said.

"Jordan," I called out.

"I'll be right back, Aunt Katherine," she said again, disappearing into the dark hole of the door.

I swore and went after her.

I practically knocked her over bumping into her in the shadowed living room. The TV was there, flickering uselessly at the empty couch. Towards the back of the house, a light was on and there were lower, muttering voices. The sour, heavy stench of cigarette smoke was everywhere, so thick that it stung my eyes and nostrils. A slight chill of apprehension crept up my spine. "Jordan," I said urgently, "let's go." But Jordan shook her head. Turning away from the light in the back, she began to climb the dark stairs to the second level. I followed nervously, squinting frequently into the darkness behind us.

The second level was illuminated only by a thin beam pouring out from a half-open door. From inside the room came the sound of a man grunting, deep and guttural, and the all too recognizable rhythm of a bed rocking back and forth. I blushed in the dark and grabbed Jordan's arm.

Jordan shook her head and whispered, "Blue."

I let my hand fall from Jordan's arm. I nodded in the dark.

The hallway had several doors. Jordan silently turned the knobs on each one and pushed the doors slowly open. Each time she poked her head into a room, I got queasy with fear.

At last, Jordan waved at me and disappeared into a room. I went after her. The room was pitch black, but Jordan moved steadily and soundlessly in the dark. Somehow, she found a nightlight on a little table and turned it on. In the dull gray light, we found Blue fast asleep. He lay on a bare mattress in his underwear, curled up with two other sleeping children. There wasn't a blanket in sight. Above the bed hung a thick cloud of cigarette smoke. I looked around the shadowed room. It was dull and bare. The table and nightlight were the only furniture in the room. The mattress itself sat on the floor.

Jordan shook Blue gently awake. He made no noise when he saw us. He simply held up his arms, and Jordan lifted him from the bed.

In the hallway the grunting and rocking continued. I motioned to Jordan, asking her if she wanted me to carry Blue. In the dark, I could see his wide eyes on us. Jordan shook her head, hitching him up higher on her nonexistent hip, before we tackled the stairs. Together, we passed through the house, as silently as three ghosts.

≈

When we reached the car, we found Pearl sitting up once more, leaning heavily against the frame of the open door. She only glanced dully up at us, not really seeming to register me, Jordan, or her son. She half hung out of the car, her feet in the dirt and her head in her hands.

Jordan got into the front seat with Blue. I shucked off my sweater and handed it to her, before turning my attention to Pearl. "Where do you want to go, Pearl?" I asked. "Do you want me to take you home?"

Pearl looked up at me, tears streaming silently down her face. She shook her head. "This is my home," she whispered, glancing blearily up at the lighted window above us. "Steve is such a bastard," she choked. "I can't believe he'd do this to me."

I glanced up at the window too, comprehension suddenly dawning.

Pearl buried her face in her hands again. She was shaking all over now. "He's such a bastard."

I looked helplessly at Jordan. She had wrapped Blue in my sweater and the little boy was asleep again, tucked safely under Jordan's chin. She rubbed his back soothingly. "I guess we could bring her back to Momma's," I said.

"No!" Pearl shrieked. "No! No! Not Momma!"

Startled, I stared at my sister, who had once more dissolved into maudlin weeping. I glanced up at the lighted window, then back at Pearl. I felt myself losing patience. "Where do you want to go?" I asked her.

"Taylor's," she sobbed. "Take me to Taylor."

≈

Following Pearl's lead, Taylor had dropped out of school when he was fourteen. When Momma found out, Taylor preferred to run away from home rather than face her. At first, he lived for a while with Pearl and her boyfriend, Ronald, the forty-year-old bait store owner. When Pearl broke up with Ronald, Taylor had been all set to come to California and live with me and Bob in our cramped college apartment. But those plans were interrupted by some trouble that Pearl and Taylor got into. Taylor spent almost two years in juvenile detention. After that, he moved back in with Momma briefly, but that hadn't worked out too well. Since then Taylor had been the caretaker at Paradise Resort on Comfort Lake. He lived in a little Quonset hut down by the docks, so he was always on hand to help the fishermen off in the predawn.

Paradise Resort was more of a campground than anything else. It had several ramshackle cabins, but most of the fishermen who used the place preferred to rough it. In the summer they slept out in tents. In the winter, they brought in their own RVs or stayed in their fish houses out on the ice.

Friends of Momma owned the place, and Taylor managed the grounds for them. He trimmed the grass where it was needed and kept a watchful eye on the resort's ever-shifting population. Mainly he lived there for free, which was good, because while his hut had electricity, it had no indoor toilet. In the winter, he heated the place with a tiny stove that burned wood he cut himself.

With his new job, Taylor could have afforded a little house of his own somewhere, but he liked the lake. He liked the fishermen. Instead of a house, he'd bought himself a small fishing boat and a fancy snowmobile. He ate fish all summer. In the winter, when the water froze over, the whole lake was his backyard.

I had never been to Taylor's place, but Jordan knew the way there. The only noise in the car was Pearl's soft, breathless sobs. At last Jordan grew impatient and flipped on the radio.

Paradise Resort was way back in the woods, and the road was so dark we missed the sign and had to backtrack. A narrow trail, two parallel tracks made by countless passing vehicles, was the only road down to the lake. I drove slowly, feeling every bump as the car jolted this way and that on the uneven ground.

Down by the lake, at least, there was light. The parking lot was illuminated by two caged bulbs on tall posts. In the woods, at a few campsites, low fires still burned. I parked next to Taylor's truck but didn't turn off the engine. Squinting hard in the dark, I could make out a trail, showing only faintly in my headlights. Here and there, along the path, plastic camp lanterns, pink and green, yellow and blue, floated like fairy lights.

When I opened the car door, Pearl looked at me. For a moment, she seemed to regain herself. Then her face crumpled.

"I miss Daddy," she sobbed. "Daddy always took care of me."

"I'll be right back," I told Jordan in a resigned voice. Even bumping around in the dark was better than listening to Pearl whimper.

≈

It didn't take long to find Taylor. I just followed the feeling of cool and the smell of water down to the lake. The path was steadily, if faintly, lit by the pastel lanterns. They swayed in the unexpectedly cool breeze from the lake.

I was just wondering how I would wake Taylor when the sound of music reached me. The dirt path curved sharply and I found myself suddenly standing on the shore, just feet from a steep, muddy bank. The moon wasn't full tonight, but it was large and bright anyway. Its reflection on the water was so clear and brilliant that it almost seemed as if the lake were lit from within. The surface rippled in the breeze and the light seemed to dance.

There were three docks, packed with boats bumping lazily into one another with hollow thumps. Tonight, the docks were brightly lit, and at the very end of the middle dock stood my brother.

He was looking out across the water. He wasn't alone. Dinah was with him, and they had a little radio on. Taylor had his arm around Dinah's slim frame. Then, he spun her slowly, swaying in time to the music. I heard her laugh as she stepped lightly away from him, then danced back into the circle of his arms.

In the moonlight, they, like the lake, seemed lit from within.

Taylor spun her again. She danced out, then in, her long hair lifting slightly in the breeze. When he pulled her to him, he spoke, but couldn't hear any of the words.

Not wanting to be seen, I stepped back into the dark of the path, beneath the sheltering trees. My heart ached with a dull, curious pain I hadn't felt in some time. I watched Taylor and Dinah for a moment longer, until the announcer on the radio broke the spell. I shook myself and walked quickly through the dark. It was a lot harder to see on the way back. The cheery camp lights bobbed drunkenly before my eyes, and I was mystified to realize that my eyes were wet with tears.

≈

By the time I made it to the car, I was more composed. Blue was still fast asleep in Jordan's arms. Pearl, in the backseat, was completely unconscious.

"Problem solved," I said grimly, glancing at myself in the rearview mirror. I decided that didn't look too suspiciously soggy. There was enough crying going around tonight. "We'll just drive home and let her sleep it off in the car."

Jordan cast a contemptuous look back at Pearl, then said, "Dumb shit."

I nodded in agreement, staring off at the distant lights leading down to the lake. In the quiet, without the radio or Pearl's sobs, you could almost hear the water lapping the shore. Almost hear the music. I took a heavy breath and glanced over at Jordan. She was watching me with concerned eyes.

"What are you thinking about, Aunt Katherine?" she asked.

I put the car in reverse. "I was just thinking about all the things I used to do," I said. "They just seem so far away these days."

Jordan frowned at me.

I looked away, embarrassed. Jordan was hardly a child, but she wasn't an adult either. It wasn't that I didn't think she could handle all that I wanted to say just then about mistakes and loss and grief. It was just that I'd been gone for most of the girl's life, and if there was one thing I didn't want her to remember me for, it was creepy, half-coherent conversations in the dark, by the lake.

"How did you know Blue was in that house tonight?" I asked, changing the subject. "I thought he was with your mom."

Jordan shrugged, looking down at her cousin. She held him a little tighter. "I brought Pearl over to Mom after—" she broke off, sounding uncomfortable.

"After my fight with your grandmother?" I suggested.

Jordan nodded, still looking anxious.

I smiled encouragingly at her. "Don't worry too much about that, okay?" said. "Your grandmother and I have been fighting for years. We're old pros at it. We don't take it personally anymore."

Jordan tried to smile.

Thinking about the fight earlier that day, I asked her, "What do you remember about Tea?"

To my surprise, Jordan's face grew troubled again. She hastily turned her head.

I reached over and touched her shoulder. She looked back again, her face tense with anxiety. She bit her lip and stared at me.

"It's okay. You can tell me."

Jordan gazed out the window again, but I could see her reflection in the glass. She seemed more sad than tense now. "The last few months were rough. Dad and Mom went to pick Tea up from the hospital. When they got her to Grandma's house, Dad had to carry her up the steps. She was real thin and sick. I heard them all talking. They said the doctors wanted to put Tea in an institution, but Grandma made them bring her home instead. She didn't think Tea could get better in a place like that."

# 11

I put Blue and Jordan to bed in Taylor's old room, but the other half of my bed was still warm from Jordan when I woke. She was in the shower already when I stumbled into the kitchen for breakfast. My back hurt. I rubbed the sore spot gingerly while I heated water for tea and thought of Jordan's bony knees digging into my spine all night. I had done the same thing to my cousin for years.

Strange, I thought, how life never ventures into the original. Everything just turns out to be the same pain over and over. Still very tired, I sat at the table and stirred sugar into my cup. As the spoon went round and round in my cup, I remembered that Tea always talked in her sleep but never said anything I could understand. Sometimes she cried too, and I'd wrap my arms around her tighter, though it never seemed to make any difference.

I went into Taylor's bedroom and checked on Blue. Momma was sitting by his bed, watching him sleep. She almost smiled when she looked at me. Then she said, "You better get dressed if you're going to make your meeting at Jordan's school."

I blinked. I had forgotten.

Jordan popped her head into the room just then. She was sleek and wet like a seal, smelling of soap. "We don't have to go, if you're too tired," she suggested quickly. "We were out with Pearl until almost four last night."

Grumbling, I went to take a shower.

≈

Since Abra wasn't home, I borrowed one of her dresses. It fit too tight in the shoulders and bust, so I practiced taking shallow breaths. I was just debating whether I should help myself to a pair of her low-heeled, boxy-looking shoes when Momma came in to drag me away. I poured myself a thermos of tea, then Momma and I practically carried Jordan to the door. It was only when we stepped out onto the porch that I realized that both my car and Pearl had vanished.

Jordan looked at me and said hopefully, "Guess we can't go, huh?"

With a sigh, I went back inside to ask Momma if I could borrow her Chevette and found Blue standing hopefully at the door. He was already dressed, watching me with wide, silent eyes.

"He wants to come with," Momma told me, handing me her car keys. I was already beginning to feel a headache coming on.

≈

All the way to the school, Jordan slumped low in her seat. At first she was just sullen, but by the time we reached the parking lot, she was actually pale. I didn't blame her.

The school was the same place I had attended for thirteen years. I could see they'd added on to the back, but all in all, it was the same squat structure I remembered. In general, my feelings toward the place were mixed at best. I remembered making a kite out of bright wrapping paper in first-grade art and gleefully shrieking my whole way home, running full speed, trying to make the kite fly behind me. I also remembered being asked to sit at the back of the kindergarten class while Mrs. Larson read aloud to us, because I kept hugging her legs and she was afraid I would ruin her nylons. Once I wet my pants and Mrs. Larson made fun of me in front of the whole class. And once a teacher flushed Taylor's pet mouse down the toilet, and Tea had appeared like a storm cloud and threatened to smack that teacher silly.

Taylor and Pearl had both dropped out of this school of their own volition and never come back, though Taylor later got his GED. Abra hadn't graduated from here either. Senior year, she'd been asked to take night classes for pregnant girls instead. Billy Chagall, Tea's husband, had been a favorite teacher here, before he met Tea.

Jordan and I stared at the building. "It'll be okay," I told her unconvincingly.

Jordan squared her shoulders and said glumly, "Thanks for coming, Aunt Katherine. Mom never knows what to say. She gets too nervous."

"I don't know what I'm going to say," I said, still eyeing the school warily.

Jordan made a face. "Mom always cries. Sometimes that works."

"I may try that."

Over to our right, on the blacktop of the fenced-in playground, some children were playing kickball. The game involved a lot of shouting and shrieking. As a child rounded one of the bases, the yelling got louder. Jordan and I exchanged nervous glances.

We climbed out of the car. The blacktop was too hot for Blue in his sandals, so I carried him to the front door, his head turning every which way, trying to see everything. The door closed behind us with a whoosh, abruptly cutting off the children's voices.

Inside, the air was unnaturally cool. The halls seemed to vibrate slightly with the faraway noise of the central air-conditioning. I put Blue down, but he stayed close to my legs, sensing our nervousness. All along the wall, a butcher paper banner had been tacked up. It read "Welcome To Summer Session." We didn't feel welcome. A long empty hallway stretched before us. It looked dirty. Here and there it was littered with forgotten papers from the last day of classes. The janitors must not come in as often in the summer, I thought.

To my surprise, I felt Jordan's hand slip into mine. I squeezed her hand and remembered that there were days when Tea had begged me to go to school. Other days she bribed me. Mostly, though, she hauled me crying and kicking and abandoned me at the front door. "You don't have to go in," she'd say with a shrug and a tight smile. "But I'm not coming back for you until school's out." Then she'd drive away. One time, I threw a rock at the windshield as she pulled out and then ran into the school as fast as I could while the windshield cracked and spiderwebbed.

Jordan's hand felt cold and clammy.

"You know, Jordan," I said, suddenly sure of myself, "let's not do this."

She nodded. I scooped up Blue. Then Jordan and I turned around and walked quickly back to the car. Like Lot and his daughters fleeing into the desert, we didn't look back.

"Do you want to see him?" Jordan asked me, when we were safely back in the car.

There was no need to ask who he was. I couldn't think of anything else to say, so I agreed.

≈

The boy that Jordan loved was around the back of the school. I slowed the car down when Jordan asked, but we didn't stop. We just rolled slowly past. Jordan pointed him out to me. He was sitting alone on the bleachers, staring off across the empty ball field. I'm not sure he saw us.

He was perhaps the roundest child I had ever seen. He was apple-shaped and pale, like a porcelain Buddha. His hair was cut short and was blond white, sticking out in short spikes all over his head. He was probably thirteen or fourteen, but seemed so much younger. All in all, he was a strange creature. His belly was big like a woman about to give birth, but his legs were scrawny, emerging oddly from his body like the stick legs of a marionette. He wore spectacles; they helped me locate his eyes, which were small and buried deep in his unhappy face.

"Should we stop?" I asked Jordan.

"Nah. He's too scared of his mother to talk to me now."

We continued to roll slowly past him. "Do you think he needs a ride home or something?"

Jordan shook her head. "He has to run his laps. His mother won't let him come home until he finishes six laps around the field. It used to be ten, but one night he didn't come home. He has to pause a long while between each lap. He's asthmatic."

"How does she know if he's run them or not?"

Jordan pointed off somewhere in the distance. "He says she watches him with binoculars. Not every day, just some days, so he never knows if she's really watching or not."

"What's his name?" I asked.

Jordan smiled contentedly. "Engel Tippleson."

≈

Neither of us felt like going back home just yet, so we drove out to the highway instead. I rolled down the windows, and Blue giggled as the wind tickled his face. We followed the highway until we found a fast-food restaurant.

Jordan and Blue chased each other around the air-conditioned play area. Blue ate a whole hamburger, fries, and a milkshake. He fell asleep on the ride home, one hand clutching a French fry, the other resting on his full belly.

When I dropped Jordan off, I asked her why she liked Engel so much. She shrugged. "I don't know. I was just sitting in class one day and looking at him. I started to feel real bad that no one ever talked to him. He's so soft. He cries a lot because he gets hungry and his mom says he's too fat."

She paused thoughtfully, rubbing her hands together. "He has poor circulation," she continued. "Sometimes his hands and his feet turn blue. Totally blue."

That seemed to me a good enough excuse to love someone as any.

Jordan and I smiled at each other. Then her smile cracked a little at the edges and her reserve crept back in. "You know those flip-flops you let me wear yesterday?" she asked.

I looked down at my bare toes, poking out of my mother's sandals. "What about them?" I asked.

"Can I keep them?"

I nodded.

Jordan's smile returned. She got out and slammed the door a little too hard. With a wave she loped up the driveway, bypassing the house and heading straight for the horse barn.

I watched her closely as she ran. Jordan was tall and narrow, though sturdy. Her long wheat-blond hair was almost to her waist. She kept it tied loosely back, but wisps of it fell around her face, softening her usually frank expressions. Suddenly, I had a feeling Engel Tippleson's mother was merely the first in a long line of mothers my niece was going to anger.

≈

I drove the rest of the way home to find that Pearl had returned but that my car was still missing. She was sitting off to the side of the garage, sheltered from the view of the house. She slouched on a cement block, smoking a cigarette, beside the battered steel drum Daddy had used to burn garbage.

Scraps of charred junk lay all around and ashes leaked out of a rusty hole in the barrel's bottom. I don't think anyone had used it since Daddy died, but the detritus remained.

Burning things had been one of my father's special pleasures. He'd sit out here for hours, cradling a beer, watching tires, garbage, leaves, anything really, reduce to cinders.

It was still early, but a six-pack of beer sat by Pearl's foot. She waved me over when she saw me get out of the Chevette.

I peered into the backseat to check on Blue. He was still sleeping. Reluctantly, I went over to her. She handed me a beer.

"You ever notice Jordan?" I asked, staring at the beer in my hand and wondering what to do with it.

"Of course I've noticed her."

"I mean, do you think she's strange?" I asked, slipping the beer into the pocket of Abra's dress, where it bulged awkwardly.

Pearl let out a short sharp laugh. "You're one to talk, sister of mine. One to talk. Sit down." She patted the ground beside her. "Come on, sit down. Drink with me." Drinking with Pearl was the last thing I wanted to do, especially after last night.

"Pearl—" I began.

"Shhh," she interrupted me. "Don't talk. I get dizzy when I'm talking and drinking. Just sit and look at the damn corn with me."

I sighed and sat. Pearl drank and I watched her sadly out of the corner of my eye, feeling my heart sink lower and lower in my chest as I looked at her.

Finally she said, "You know, I hate it when the corn gets this high. Every year I'm scared to let Blue out of my sight. That corn's too high. Oughtta cut the tops off it or something. If Blue got lost out there, I'd never see him again."

I glanced over at the car. Blue still hadn't stirred, but it was getting hot. "I should take Blue into the house," I told her gently. "The sun's a little much for him to be in the car. And he'll sleep better in a bed."

Pearl gave me a confused stare. "What's Blue doing in Momma's car?" she asked.

I gave her the simplest answer. "I took him out to eat."

"Oh," she said and popped open another beer. Her eyes strayed back to the corn. I left her there.

Blue woke up and smiled at me when I pulled him from the car. Some of his french fries had spilled out across the seat, and I helped him put them back in their greasy sack.

As we walked towards the house, Pearl called after me, "Momma went to work in your car. But she said to tell you that man, Shepherd McCreedy, called today."

"Again?"

"Momma told him you'd come in tomorrow morning to look at things, because she didn't think you had much to do anyway and she was sick of him calling all the time."

"She really say all that?" I asked, surprised.

Pearl shrugged and took a long sip of her beer. "You never really know with Momma," she said and didn't smile at all.

# 12

I rose early the next morning to find a neat stack of brand-new underwear, T-shirts, and socks at the end of my bed. There was also a knee-length skirt in a sort of sage green and another in denim. I sighed. Evidently, Momma was planning on me staying longer than I was. Either that or she'd gotten tired of seeing me wear the same clothes over and over.

I also found Blue sound asleep beneath my bed. I had put him down in Taylor's bed the night before, but now his white stocking feet were sticking out from under the dust ruffle. He'd pulled a sheet down over his whole body, even his head. Before I went to take my shower, I tucked him into my bed.

Blue was a good sleeper. He didn't so much as stir when I moved him. I was a little envious. The day had barely begun, and already my insides were roiling. Momma had made an appointment for me, just like when I was little and had to go to the doctor's office. I felt faint. I didn't want to go meet Shepherd McCreedy. In the bathroom, I ran the shower as hot as it would go and climbed gratefully into the billows of searing steam. When I was done, my skin was a bright, clean red. It clashed horribly with the sage skirt and lemony yellow T-shirt I slid on.

I moved towards the kitchen, trying to be as quiet as possible in the pre-dawn. I might have saved myself the trouble. Momma, Pearl, and Abra were already waiting for me at the table. I paused and stared at them.

Abra was dressed in one of her ugly Sunday dresses, with her hair almost completely hidden under a gray cloth. Pearl was grudgingly sober. She wore jeans and a sleeveless, black T-shirt that read, "Tell Your Boyfriend I Said Thanks." Pearl had roughly cut the shirt off at the midriff, baring her navel. It was clear that they both intended to come with me, though for the life of me I couldn't guess why. Neither of them liked galleries and both had hated Tea. I argued with them until Mason arrived with Jordan and I was rendered momentarily speechless. Jordan was neatly combed. She had done her hair in elaborate braids, then pinned them close to her head in a neat bun at the back. She wore a navy blue skirt that fell just below her knee. Her shirt was white and buttoned all the way up, only open at the neck to reveal a gold cross on a necklace. She wore nylons and a pair of low-heeled shoes.

Jordan saw me staring and tugged nervously at the skirt. "Is it all right?" she asked. "I wore it to Great-Aunt Deana's funeral in June."

It was the first time that I'd ever seen Jordan act even remotely girlish. I felt myself relenting, then gave myself a shake. I turned back to Abra and Pearl. "No way. You're not coming with me."

"Kat," my mother said, without turning from the stove where she was cooking us bacon and eggs, "take your sisters with."

And that was that. I heaved a loud sigh of frustration and threw up my hands. Momma pretended not to notice.

I gave her back a disgruntled look and turned to find Mason standing much too close to me.

He grinned at me. "Did you sleep well, Kat? All ready for your big girls' day out on the town?"

I looked away.

"Daddy, don't," Jordan whispered.

Mason patted his daughter on the shoulder and grinned. "I'll see you all later," he said, as he moved to the door. "And Kat," he said, pausing, "let me know if you want to hear another story."

He left. Jordan looked at me curiously. The others just stared. I glared back at them. "Let's get going," I said. "I don't want to spend all day at this."

≈

In the car, the four of us maintained a morose silence that only thickened as, on our way out of town, we drove past the cemetery where Tea was buried. I stepped on the gas, hoping to get to the gallery before my self-control gave out.

The tension in the car rose as we neared the Twin Cities. My sisters didn't talk much, and Jordan watched me furtively as drove. I thought about her funeral clothes and realized suddenly why my sisters had come with me today.

They were curious. They were like people rubbernecking an accident. I hadn't come to Tea's funeral, so they never had a chance to see me weep over a cold grave. But they were determined to have their dose of soap opera today. I shook my head in disgust. They miss Tea more than they know, I thought grimly. Life must have been pretty dull for them after she died. Tea was the only one who ever said what needed to be said and got down to whatever needed to be done.

"Aunt Katherine," Jordan said softly. I looked at her, pulled out of my reverie. "I think you just missed the gallery."

I nodded tersely and made a U-turn at the next light.

We parked the car down the street from the gallery and walked the half-block back. My sisters eyed me nervously as we paused outside the front doors. Their awe of this event amused me a little and then it saddened me. Tea was gone, and like my sisters I missed her more than I knew. There's a limit on pain. After a certain level the mind just shuts it off and leaves you driving in the dark.

≈

Shepherd McCreedy's gallery was in an old brownstone building in the warehouse district of Minneapolis.

Across the street was the chain-link fenced front yard of a massive brewery complex and what looked like a nightclub, now dark and abandoned for the day. Once a factory, the gallery's building now seemed also to be home to a dance studio and an insurance agency. Above the door the words "Fulk & Tatter Starch Initiative" were engraved in deep Gothic letters. The outside didn't prepare you for the cold white within nor for the gallery's owner.

When I first saw Shepherd McCreedy, memory flickered like a candle within me. I had seen him before. Not in person, but in a photograph only days before. An old one that I had picked up off the floor. Tea and this man, standing arm in arm, grinning at the camera. There was a glimpse of mountains in the background, and Tea's freckles glowed like copper pennies in the sun. He couldn't have been more than fifteen then, but it was clearly the same person walking toward me. His eyes and tentative smile were unmistakable.

Our eyes met and he hesitated before offering me his hand. His hesitation gave me a moment to study him fully. I decided he wasn't the sort of man I imagined would own a gallery. He was too weathered. His black hair was too graying and his eyes too devastated. The first few layers of him were calm, as gray as his suit, but below things were shifting, like deep-sea currents. I would have put his age at much older than he probably was, except that in all his movements and in the curious heat I felt when shaking his hand, he seemed to be much younger. The effect was unsettling, almost irreconcilable.

I realized that his hesitancy was probably my fault and tried to collect myself. I gave him a lopsided, apologetic smile and said, "I was just thinking that

I had seen you before in a picture."

Shepherd looked startled, then his features relaxed into a slow, easy approximation of a smile. "Funny," he said, "I was just thinking the same thing." Then before I knew what was happening, Shepherd's arm slid easily around my waist. Separating me neatly from the tight cluster of my relations, he pulled me deep into his gallery.

I squirmed uncomfortably, but he seemed unaware of my efforts to disentangle myself from him. I cast a desperate look back at my sisters, but they apparently were too in awe of the surroundings to speak. As for Jordan, she had drifted away and was now looking intently at a painting on the wall of a family having a picnic. Before Shepherd swept me away completely, I had a brief glimpse of her standing so close to the picture that I worried she might set off some alarm.

Shepherd and I rounded a corner into a small white room. Abruptly, I found myself staring at a familiar image.

The frame was new, heavy and ornate, but I recognized the painting. It was a small canvas, a portrait of half my face drawn in long, black lines. The black was too severe. All around it wild, light hair flowed, making the whole seem unbalanced. Parts of the canvas were exposed. Other parts had been treated with resin and blotted with paint.

I felt my face wrinkle into a grimace. I looked around for other works. It was strange that he would have given this odd little canvas such a place of honor. It was the only thing hanging in the glowing space.

"I thought you might like to be alone with it for a while," Shepherd said quietly. "I'll have Lionel bring you a chair."

He was so serious that I tried hard to suppress the smile creeping onto my face. I shook my head. "That won't be necessary."

Shepherd looked puzzled. He smiled politely, but his eyebrows knit together.

I couldn't help myself and laughed outright. "Shepherd, I hate this painting. Tea hated this painting."

He blinked and stared at me for a long while. Pretty soon I began to hear other noises in the gallery distinctly. My sisters were moving around in the other room, discussing the paintings in hushed voices. I heard Jordan's low-heeled shoes clicking from room to room. Somewhere a clock ticked. My discomfort grew with the lengthy quiet. I shifted uncomfortably as my own eye stared at me from the canvas. It seemed bored with me.

Slowly a wry, self-deprecating expression spread across Shepherd's face. "Well," he drawled, "this is a little anticlimactic for me." I realized that I liked his smile.

"Why is it anticlimactic?" I asked him.

"I guess it never occurred to me that you wouldn't like the painting." Shepherd reached out and took my hand. His was very warm to the touch. "At the exhibition, everyone was curious to know who you were. I've been waiting for you to come."

My hand in his felt hot. I was relieved when his eyes flicked back to the portrait.

"I've never understood this painting," Shepherd continued. "My business partner insists it's not sellable, but something about it makes me curious." He tilted his head, studying the picture still more closely. "It's you, but it's not you. There's no date—I think it must have been an earlier work. The lines are too hard and exact. It wasn't until after you left her that Tea let herself loose. I think painting from memory freed her."

"I didn't leave Tea," I said, abruptly pulling my hand out of his.

Shepherd turned back to me, startled. For a moment, there was such an expression of stark pain in his eyes that I felt my heart falter. Tea and Shepherd had the same eyes, but on him, even their blue was gray. I looked away.

"I didn't leave Tea," I said, relenting. "It was more . . . " I hesitated. "It was more like I relinquished her."

To my surprise, Shepherd reached out and touched my cheek. Just for an instant his fingertips brushed against my skin. "I'm so glad you came, Kat," he said softly. "Since Tea . . . " He paused, then continued with difficulty. "Since Tea died, I've been waiting for you to come."

My throat was painfully tight, but I needed to talk, to say something casual and easy. I smiled brightly at him, a little too polite, and spoke as if he hadn't said anything. "Where are the rest of her paintings?" I asked, stepping back from him, trying not to look as anxious as I felt.

He stared at me. A new feeling entered the room. I couldn't quite read the change in his expression. I glanced over my shoulder, wondering where Jordan and my sisters had disappeared to. I looked back at Shepherd, who was looking quite anxious himself.

"What is it?" I asked, stepping towards him, in spite of myself.

Shepherd shook his head, then said quietly, "I thought your mother had told you. The paintings are all gone."

I needed to sit down. The room was too white, and I found myself reaching for whoever caught me before I fell.

≈

Shepherd calmly guided me into his office and eased me down onto a tiny sofa. It was all artful angles and black leather. He left the room briefly and returned with a glass of water. The water did nothing to ease the hurt in my chest.

Shepherd sat down beside me. He took one of my hands in both of his. "I'm sorry. Tea left specific instructions. She wanted there to be a show and all the paintings to be sold. She requested that several of them be destroyed, the unfinished pieces mainly. The night before she killed herself, Tea went through and marked everything clearly."

"It was an accident," I said almost mechanically.

An emotion I couldn't identify darted, like a fish, to the surface of Shepherd's eye, then submerged again into deeper waters. It was gone too soon for me to understand it, but I suspected it was pity.

"Tea's life was a mess," Shepherd said calmly, "but it was no accident. The same with her death. I have enough respect for Tea's memory to accept the choices she made. Even though it might hurt like hell."

"They're really all gone?" I asked weakly.

"Yes."

I folded over, resting my head against my knees. I simply was not prepared for this. Shepherd let me work it out on my own. He sat beside me, his hands hanging open at his sides.

When I finally looked up, I asked him dully, "How many were there?"

"Over three hundred."

"How many of them were of me?"

Shepherd hesitated. "You were in all of them."

Above Shepherd's Spartan black lacquer desk was a framed portrait of a nude woman with her back to the viewer. The woman's dark brown hair was straight and long, falling raggedly to the small of her back. A childlike dandelion crown lay off to one side, forgotten. Shepherd followed my gaze. "I bought that for my private collection," he said softly. "You know, I never would have imagined you'd cut your hair."

"Are they really all gone?"

Shepherd's hand curled into mine. "I have something to show you. It's a secret, really. I have to ask you to respect that."

≈

Maybe there was an elevator to the vaults, but we didn't take it. The wooden steps were creaky, the stone walls cool to the touch. The faint lights and the distant hum of the machines that controlled the climate made the whole chamber seem eerily womblike. Hanging from sliding panels of chain-link fencing were several dozen works that the gallery was currently brokering. Beyond all of this, toward the back, on the very last panel was Shepherd's secret.

The painting was obviously unfinished. Spots of bare canvas glared out. In some places there were still visible pencil marks. The lines were indistinct, hastily and carelessly laid out on the canvas as if the artist had just begun to loosen her gestures. Still, the form of two women was unmistakable. I recognized myself, but the other woman was a mystery. I stared at her. Her hands had been clearly established, folded like a Pietà, but the face was an indistinguishable blur of soft orange. Tea's presence in the painting was unmistakable. I felt her in this canvas. "Can I touch it?" I asked, compelled to whisper.

Shepherd took my hand and held it against the canvas.

"This was one of the works that Tea wanted destroyed, but I couldn't bear to do it," he explained softly. "The others meant nothing. They were exercises. Abandoned projects. But this," he nodded at the canvas, "this had something of Tea in it. It's unfinished, but it has life. I couldn't burn it."

The canvas almost felt warm to the touch. Perhaps it was the orange, which seemed to suggest a deep and settling pink, like a sunset. "It's lovely," I said breathlessly. I touched the orange blur of the second woman's face. "Who is this?" I asked.

Shepherd seemed surprised. "Your mother. Tea painted a whole series of her, holding a locket or a picture frame with your image in it."

I pulled my hand back as if that strange orange were suddenly hot to the touch.

"There must be some mistake. My mother would never sit for Tea."

"But she did," he insisted. "Many times. Tea's last six paintings were all of your mother. Look here." He lifted the canvas from its hooks and flipped it over. "Your mother's name is even on the back."

It was there, "Kat & Naomi," written in pencil in Tea's angular script. Impatiently I turned away. "You don't understand," I argued, feeling something like anger growing in me. "For Tea to paint a portrait took weeks, even months at a time. I sat for one painting on and off for two years. My mother couldn't stand to be in the same room with Tea for five minutes, let alone sit for six paintings."

Shepherd carefully replaced the canvas on its hooks. "Would you like to see the catalog of the exhibit? I have it in my office. Inside are photos of all six paintings."

I shook my head, more at the rage burning inside me than at him. Momma had lied to me again.

"It's interesting to see all the paintings together," he went on. "Tea started out using fairly dark tones and thicker, more severe lines. But the paintings began to lighten as the series progressed. She started to use clearer colors."

Shepherd tapped the canvas. "This orange first appeared in the third painting as a tiny patch in a quilt draped across your mother's shoulders, and it grew more and more dominant in each painting. In this last painting this orange and the softer pinks seemed to be the only colors Tea intended to use." Shepherd gave me a sidelong glance. "It seems almost tender, like forgiveness, don't you think, Kat?"

"You can tell all that, just from a painting?" I said, my voice sounding raspy in my own ears.

Shepherd's fingertips brushed my cheek again. "I knew Tea for a lot of years," he said simply.

≈

It was hard to stay down there alone with Shepherd for long. The walls were too close. He was too close. He never gave a hint that he was planning to leave anytime soon. Eventually I just turned and began walking up the stairs. Shepherd followed.

Once back with the others, the five of us chatted vaguely and then my sisters hustled me off to the car. Their boredom had peaked half an hour earlier. Shepherd followed us all the way outside and stood on the curb. For four blocks, until I took the turn, I could see him in my rearview mirror. He stood dark and mute in the street, watching us beat a hasty retreat.

# 13

During the ride home, my sisters were chatty. Whatever spell had bound their tongues this morning had obviously been broken. Pearl took over Jordan's place in the passenger seat. She spent the whole trip pushing the buttons on the radio. Not too happy with this arrangement, Jordan stared quietly out the back window.

We stopped at the Norwegian Inn in Lindstrom for lunch. I was feeling very tired and disoriented. Pearl and Abra talked to cover my silence and eyed me warily when they thought I wouldn't notice. Both of them tried persistently to draw Jordan into the chatter, but she resisted. At last, Jordan pushed her chair back and headed for the video game at the back of the diner.

I watched her go, feeling envious, as my sisters redoubled their efforts at conversation. I listened vaguely and looked around the diner. Nothing had changed much since I was a child. The tables were all plastic laminate and steel. The chairs were orange vinyl. At the very front of the restaurant was an iceberg lettuce salad bar and a long metal counter. We used to eat here on Sunday nights. Daddy would always order the steak. This was even our old table.

It was strange to suddenly find myself sitting in the circle of my sisters at a table we must have eaten at a hundred times as children. I felt the frail bonds, like spider webs that stretched out from me, tying me to them. It was a learned connection, more habit than love.

Looking at their faces around the table, I was shocked by the weight of memory. I used to read Pearl bedtime stories. Her favorite was *Where the Wild Things Are*, and she would kiss all of the monster faces, then giggle. Abra and I were five years apart, but it had always felt like much more. The reasons why we could no longer look each other in the eye were too numerous to list.

Strange that this was enough to knot their lives into mine. I knew them like I knew my mother's house. Their faces were in my memory, like my own.

There was nothing that I loved about them, but to have altered a single atom of their being would have stirred something in my depths.

"This is nice," Pearl chirped, interrupting my thoughts. She was peeling the label off the long neck of her bottle while she spoke. "I mean, I don't remember the last time all of us went out together."

"I do," Abra said crisply. She stirred sugar into her Coca-Cola and swirled it around with her spoon. "Tea was there. She called me a whore."

Pearl giggled. Abra gave her a look that ought to have ripped her in two and stirred another packet of sugar into her glass. "Pearl is right, though. This is an exciting occasion. I do believe this may be the first time in our adult lives we've ever sat down in a restaurant together. Seems odd, doesn't it?"

No one answered her.

Abra smiled bitterly. "Of course, we always had plenty of other things to do together. Hospitals, emergency wards, bars, lunatic asylums to visit. Regular family fun."

"Abra," Pearl said sharply, "stop it."

But evidently the day had affected Abra deeply as well. Her voice was overflowing now, like a swollen river. It would allow no obstruction. "Yes, it's enough." Her voice rose an octave. "I've had enough. I'm tired of it. Momma, too. Life shouldn't always be chaotic and miserable."

Framed in the window behind Abra I could see the main street leading through Lindstrom. A blue car moved past, as if looking for a parking spot. It was only then that I realized how much of a toll the day had taken upon me. I was too worn out to care much what Abra had to say. Shepherd and Tea and that damned white gallery had already drained my anger. I knew I could still feel it if tried. It ran around in my blood like a freight train, but the tracks to that secret place where I hoarded my rage had all been pulled up. I sighed and let my eyes slide from the window and the blue car back to Abra. "You got something you want to tell me?" I asked Abra levelly.

We stared at one another.

The silence was broken by the appearance of my brother. Taylor breezed into the diner, cowboy hat in hand. "I saw your car out front," he said, nodding at me. "You guys gotta come, Mason's horses are loose in the corn. Again."

"What?" I said dumbly.

Taylor waved his hat at me with an impatient gesture. He was looking a little wild. "Mason's going crazy. He thinks they've been out since last night. He can't find half of them."

Jordan returned from the video game at exactly that moment. She looked around at us. "What's wrong?" she asked. "Aren't we going to get lunch?"

"The stock is out again," Taylor told her. "Looks like they've been gone so long they made it to Highway Eight."

Jordan didn't seem particularly surprised. She scooped up her purse and turned to me, expectantly.

The rest of us all rose, our chairs scraping against the floor. All of us, that is, but Abra; she sipped her cola and stayed put. We shifted around impatiently, waiting for her. Taylor shot an inquiring glance at me. I shrugged.

"I'm getting married," Abra announced.

≈

I could hear them off in the distance, somewhere out of sight in the corn. My whole family was beating pots and pans with spoons, trying to drive the horses forward out of the fields. I stood on the receiving end at the edge of the corn, waiting for whatever stumbled out.

More often it was Mason's boys that came whooping out, screaming and running, rather than the stock. Jordan stood waiting with me, her arms crossed, her lips pressed closed. She was better with the horses than I. When the strays burst out from the corn, they invariably stopped at her whistle and let her take hold of their bridles. They seemed to calm in her presence.

Unfortunately, she seemed to have no such effect on her brothers. Two of the younger boys had been assigned to stay with us. They clung to Jordan's legs and wrestled around her feet. They were not much use to us. If anything, they were an outright nuisance, but we kept them close because Constance had been afraid to let them loose in the corn.

Jordan ignored the boys. In fact, she ignored me. Everything.

Mason's sons tumbled over in my direction. One was making the other eat dirt. Eventually they both seemed to tire of this game and separated. They sat some distance apart, chests heaving, and began throwing clods at one another. Even this lost its attraction after a short while.

The boys took to sitting side by side, staring at me petulantly and angrily heaving dirt by the handfuls at the corn. One was maybe four, the other closer to six. They were both hulking children, like all of Mason's boys, too big for their age.

"I should be able to go in," the six-year-old announced belligerently, still staring at me. "I'm not a stupid girl like you. I'm not afraid of the corn."

I never saw Jordan make her move. Suddenly she was there. She flew at her brother with such rage that he had no time to react. The first punch, and I mean a square, hard-knuckled punch, stunned him. The second knocked him flat. The third blinded him to the world.

Trying to wrestle Jordan away from him was like fighting the Mississippi's currents. I went under pulling her back. We rolled on the ground. She struggled and roared to be free, like a bear in a trap. Vaguely, as we tumbled around, I was aware of the boys fleeing to the house.

Suddenly, though, I seemed to have more than Jordan to worry about. The horses broke free of the corn en masse. Hooves pounded the ground around us. Jordan and I stuck out like nail heads. I rolled on top of her and heard her shriek beneath me. I held my breath and tensed my body, waiting for the pain to come. Not a single blow fell on us. Then, in a heartbeat, the horses were gone.

It was Jordan who got to her feet first. I was trembling so bad I could hardly stand. But my niece was smiling.

Standing a few paces off, watching us, was the horse I recognized as Jordan's. Jordan clucked at it reassuringly. It pawed the ground, stepping a few nervous paces toward us. Like a snake, Jordan's arm darted forward, catching the horse's bridle. Smoothly, she threw herself onto the horse's bare back. When she had seated herself comfortably on the beast, she paused, looking over at me. "You saved my life, Aunt Katherine," she said mockingly and did a half bow from her high seat. She grinned at me wolfishly and then, taking hold of the horse's mane, she was gone, easily galloping after her herd.

I was shaken. Deep in me, I felt as if something had been knocked loose. Slowly, almost painfully, I made my way to Momma's house, then up to Tea's attic. "Lord," I said, "I can't take this."

≈

Except for a soft glow from the kitchen, the house was dark by the time I was through cleaning for the day. Coming down from the attic, I found Momma at the kitchen table eating ice cream. I dug a bowl out of the cupboard for myself. The clock above her head said three o'clock.

"How long have you known about the wedding?" I asked casually.

Momma spooned ice cream into her mouth. "About a month now."

"You know this guy?"

"Not well."

I pulled up a chair across the table from Momma and helped myself from the carton. "Abra says he's got two sons already."

"Yeah. Guess so."

"Where's his first wife?"

"Gone."

"Gone?"

"Dead gone. Long dead."

"What'd she die of?"

"Don't know."

"She was young?"

"Yes."

I thought about it for a moment. "You don't find that strange?"

Momma let her spoon clank loudly against her dish. "For heaven's sake, Kat," she cried, "It's not like Lovell killed her. It was cancer or something. Abra told me once, I just forget. Why do you always have to think the worst?"

"I didn't say anything like that."

"Abra's getting married. She's been looking forward to this her whole life. Can't you be happy for her?" Momma collected her things and rose from the table.

"I saw the paintings," I said quietly.

Momma sank back into her chair. She couldn't quite look at me. "Shepherd McCreedy told me they were on exhibit someplace. He said that they were already sold," she said softly.

"There were photos in the catalog."

"I see," Momma said, turning pale. Absently, she reached out and caught a drip of ice cream on the side of the carton. She licked it from her finger.

"When did Tea paint them?" I asked.

Momma shrugged. "After she got out of the hospital that last time. It broke my heart to see her looking so lost, like she was searching for something, but not really knowing what it was. When she asked me, I couldn't say no. And I suppose I was a little curious. No one had ever painted me before. Only at first I didn't know how hard it would be—sitting still all those hours, I mean." She glanced up at me hastily. "But I guess you'd know all about that. All those years you sat for her." Momma pulled her robe a little tighter around her. "After awhile it wasn't so bad, because we started talking to make the time pass." Momma paused like she expected me to say something. We stared at each other. "We talked about you a lot," she continued calmly as if the pause had not existed. "She told me about you when you were growing up. About school and stuff. She told me that you used to have a crush on Piper Olson's boy. That he's the reason why you fainted that day in the fifth grade. How come you never said anything to me about that?"

Suddenly I wasn't hungry. I pushed the bowl of ice cream aside. "I didn't think you'd be interested."

"Maybe I wouldn't have been," she said with simple honesty. "Seems like I wasn't paying attention to much back then." Momma shook her head. "It all went by fast." She pulled my abandoned ice cream towards her and started working on it with her spoon.

"Tell me about you and Olson's boy," she said.

"Not much to tell."

Momma waved her spoon. "Tell it anyway. I got time. " She glanced at the clock. "Actually," she said, "what I've got is insomnia."

"Been to the doctor?"

"Yes, but it's no business of yours. Tell your story, Kat."

"It's not much. I was in class with Canaan Olson for years. I had a crush on him that must've lasted from kindergarten to fourth grade. And then it was just over."

Momma leaned across the table. "What about that day you fainted?"

"It was silly, really. One day on the playground, some kid shoved him down and he hit his head on the concrete real hard. I was so upset I fainted. I fainted dead away when I saw the blood on his forehead. I thought he was going to die right there.

"The teacher carried me away, down to the nurse's office. I never saw that Canaan got up a few minutes later and knocked the other kid flat. He didn't even ask for a Band-Aid. But not knowing what had happened to him ate at me. I kept getting dizzy every time I thought about it, so the nurse called you and you came and took me home. And kept me at home for the next week."

"You should have said something."

"I didn't tell anyone. I was too scared to speak of it. It took Tea days to wheedle the truth out of me. And even then, I wouldn't believe her when she told me a cut like that couldn't kill a person. She kept telling me that there was a lot of blood in the body, gallons of it maybe, and that a person can bleed and bleed for days sometimes, before it hurts them. But I clung to my grief.

"Finally Tea just got sick of it, I suppose. When you weren't looking, she pulled me out of bed and locked us in the bathroom. She took Daddy's razor and slit her hand clear across her palm and calmly watched me watching her bleed into the sink.

"I fainted, but when I came to, there she was, still bleeding. She kept me in the bathroom until I'd admit to her that bleeding to death was too long of a way to die."

"That was the end of your crush on Canaan?" Momma asked.

"Yes."

"You should have told me that," Momma said. "I wouldn't have taken you to all those doctors then."

I shrugged, watching Momma finish off the ice cream. "Like I said, I didn't think you'd be interested."

Momma set her spoon down with a final chink and pushed the bowl away from her. "That specialist I took you to told me it probably wasn't physical. He said I should take you to a psychologist. I told him to go to hell, of course, but sometimes I look at you and think maybe I should've."

"Am I that messed up, Momma?" I asked wryly.

Momma pursed her lips, debating with herself, and then she said, "Pearl told me about how you got home. About you driving all those miles and not having any memory of it."

"Pearl has a big mouth," I said.

Momma frowned. "So it's true then."

I looked away, my face feeling hot.

Momma sighed. "I always meant to sit down and have a talk with you. You know, about all of it. It always seemed to bother you so much more than it did the others. But by the time I got around to it, you didn't want to talk to me anymore. So I just kinda let you go. Off with Tea, mostly. There was all five of you and then your father . . . " Her voice trailed off a little. "I just don't know where all the time went."

"Maybe it's not so bad that it's gone," I said quietly.

Momma hugged herself. "You wanna know why I didn't want to tell you about the paintings? I sat for all those pictures for Tea and there wasn't a single one of them that I could stand to look at." Momma stacked the bowls and carried them over to the sink. She leaned against the counter, resting herself. "I'm not saying anything bad about Tea," she continued. "I'm not saying she painted me wrong. I know it's the truth. I just never thought I could look so aged, like that."

Momma turned and rinsed out our bowls. "I know you probably just think it's vanity." She shrugged. "It's not that. I don't mind wrinkles. I look around me. The girls I went to school with are just as wrinkled as am—some of them worse. I don't mind looking old, Kat. It's looking so used up that I can't stand."

The ice cream was melting. I watched water from the sides of the container make a puddle on the table. I wanted to tell Momma about the unfinished painting. About the orange that Shepherd had liked so much. About the softness painted into the hands and the delicate pink blurring of the mouth that was so like a kiss. I wanted to comfort her, but in the sharp light of the kitchen, there were deep shadows of blue and black. I couldn't see what Tea had seen in her.

So I said nothing. Whatever else could be said about Momma and me, there was something honest about the distance we maintained. It was too late for tenderness now.

After awhile we went to bed. I undressed and lay in the still, hot quiet. I wasn't particularly tired, but it felt good to lie down and spread my body out across the cool bed. My back ached, so I rolled over and looked at the ceiling. Across the silence of the house, I heard a soft noise, a snuffling whisper. I rose and found Blue under the bed, sleeping on the cold floor in nothing but his underwear. I pulled him out and put him in my bed with the sheet over him and lay down beside him.

# 14

Momma's scissors cut through the cloth of Abra's wedding dress the way Moses must have moved through the waters of the Red Sea. Her face rippled with concentration as she cut out the sections of the skirt. The bodice had already emerged. Pearl and Jordan sat with the pieces of it in their laps, pinning the lining and the outside together, right sides facing. Abra sat beside Momma, her hands still, her expression tense, watching Momma's every move.

Abra had recently graduated from kerchiefs to a more elaborate form of head covering. Today, she was wearing something that looked like a cloth shower cap. To the back of the cap she had sewn another long piece of fabric that hung all the way down her back. It looked hot.

I was untangling Christmas lights I'd found in a box in the attic. It was no easy task. I wasn't even sure how many different strands were knotted into the bird's nest of wire. I worked beside Momma's chair, sitting on the floor on our porch, stretching the green wires out across the weathered wood of the floor and down the steps and sidewalk.

"Tell me again why we can't be in the wedding," Pearl asked Momma.

Momma snapped her thread neatly and rummaged in her box. "You'll have to ask your sister," she said without looking up.

Pearl took a long sip from a soda can that I suspected contained something near eighty proof. She was the only one drinking to stave off the day's cool and halfhearted sun. It smelled like it would rain soon. "How come you don't want us to be bridesmaids at your wedding?" she demanded directly of Abra.

Abra calmly handed Momma a spool of thread. She pressed her lips down into a narrow line until all the pink almost disappeared and said nothing.

"And how come you wear that stupid thing on your head all the time now?" I asked, giving the Christmas lights a vicious yank. Something in the pile snapped and a little shower of delicate glass fell onto the porch.

Abra rocked back in her chair, serenely folding her hands into her lap. "Lovell's sisters offered, and Lovell thought it would be great since they were the bridesmaids at his first wedding. They can wear their same dresses."

"But we're your sisters," Pearl said, plucking at the edge of the skirt in Momma's lap.

"I know that." Abra's fingers drummed softly on the arm of her chair. "You'll still be at the wedding, Pearl. It's not like I didn't invite you."

"You don't really have a choice," I observed coolly. "If all of Lovell's people saw that we didn't come to the wedding, they might think you're hiding something. I don't know why you worry about it. Everyone already knows who we are, Abra."

Abra fixed her eyes on some point in the distance, something I'd noticed her doing a lot lately. I felt like she was leaving us. That the spirit was lifting out of her body. "A wedding is a sacred thing," she explained calmly. "God is joining two people. Every aspect of the wedding is symbolic of God's will."

We all stared at her blankly, wondering when Abra had become this scary. She saw us staring and added with a touch of exasperation, "For heaven's sake, Pearl has a kid already. A bridesmaid needs to be a maid." Seeing Pearl's confused look, she added, "You know, a virgin."

Pearl turned a deep shade of red. "You think Lovell's sisters are?" Pearl sputtered a little when she spoke. "Just because their brother's found God doesn't mean they aren't the biggest sluts around. Ask your own brother. Before he met Dinah and got to be such a tight ass, Taylor dated at least two of them. Half this town has. The only way those girls are maids is if they've been letting boys take them up the ass all these years."

Abra sprang from her chair. In a minute she was tearing the bodice of her dress from Pearl's hands. Pearl held on. The sound of ripping cloth split through our afternoon.

The two struggled mightily, almost knocking Jordan to the floor. Abra's face had compressed into a bright feather of anger. The passivity, the peace that had resonated in her face a moment ago, was gone now. At the edge of my panic, as my sisters squared off, I felt something like relief.

Abra finally pinned Pearl to the floor across my Christmas lights and held her there for a moment. Abra's eyes burned into Pearl like a sharp hot needle. "You know," she hissed, "not everyone lives in a family like this. Some people actually have normal lives."

"Fucking is normal," I interjected calmly. Striding over, I pulled Abra off Pearl. "Anyone who says that they don't or that they wouldn't like to is lying."

Pearl giggled. Abra whirled around, looking ready for another round. Pearl was a little tipsy from drinking. Apparently she didn't notice the danger she was in because, still giggling, she said, "Tea used to say that all the time."

Abra's fists clenched.

"Is that Lovell I see?" Momma interrupted, staring out the window.

A blue Chevy rolled into the driveway. It was the man I recognized from the day of my arrival. So this is Lovell, I thought.

"I won't tolerate any more of your filthy talk," Abra hissed and ran down to meet him.

"Kat, tell me again, why we can't be bridesmaids?" Pearl demanded.

"Because we're whores," I told her and went back to my Christmas lights. No matter how much I worked to free them, the cords twisted tighter.

Momma reached over and took the remains of the bodice from Pearl. "Jordan, Pearl, go in and check on Blue. Go see if he's still watching TV in the living room," she said firmly. Pearl was about to argue, then thought better of it. She allowed Jordan to pull her to her feet and hustle her into the house just as Abra and Lovell started back towards the porch.

This left Momma and me alone, waiting for my sister and her beau. Momma rocked slowly in her chair. "Behave, Kat," she murmured softly. "Just for half an hour maybe. It won't hurt you."

≈

Lovell Lake, the man who was to marry my sister, wasn't anything special. He was long and thin, with skinny arms covered in thick black hair. He wore short-sleeved, button-down shirts, like a salesman, and he was pale. A fine network of veins decorated his cheeks. His eyes were blue. The veins on his temples were blue, as well, and stood out starkly.

He and my sister walked side by side, their arms hanging loosely. I noticed that they didn't hold hands. At the porch steps, they stopped. Lovell smiled at Momma and nodded at me. Abra eyed me warily.

A smile crept onto my face. I turned back to my Christmas lights to hide it. I hadn't realized what a dangerous person I had become. I felt Abra's eyes boring into the top of my head as I went on with my work.

Momma offered Lovell a seat. Abra went and stood beside him. Momma wrung her hands, nervous, and tried to clear the sewing away. With a shock, I realized that this was probably the first time Momma had ever met Lovell.

"I'll bring my boys by next Thursday," he said by way of making conversation. "They had Bible camp today."

"What are their names?" Momma asked.

"Abednego and Samuel. Abednego is the oldest—he's ten. Samuel is eight." The rest of the conversation floated off around me. I worked on my knots. Lovell's voice droned on not unpleasantly, his hands hanging still and empty between his widespread legs. He talked without looking at Abra or my mother. His eyes fixed straight forward as if he were practicing some lines he had rehearsed. Lovell Lake, I decided, was not a nervous suitor, but perhaps he was contemptuous. My attention drifted farther away until the noise of his conversation with Momma became smaller than the buzz of a fly circling my head. I think Momma showed him the pattern of Abra's wedding dress. Abra spoke infrequently.

Lovell said something about the Lord, several times. I unraveled string after string of lights until, from somewhere off in the distance, I felt, like a cool breeze, like a damp draft in an old house, that Lovell's eyes had settled upon me. At first I tried to ignore him. He continued. Finally, I set down the lights and returned his stare.

"Who's this, Abra?" he asked, interrupting my mother's question about his suit for the wedding.

Abra fidgeted a little, as if a mosquito had just bitten her. "My sister."

"Ah." His gaze had never left mine. "Abra speaks of you all often when it's time for our prayers. I know your names but not your faces. Which sister are you?"

"Jezebel," I answered.

"I see," Lovell nodded.

≈

After that incident Momma said she sure wished I would go find an attachment to her sewing machine. She thought it was stored somewhere out in the garage. Momma did most of her sewing on her grandmother's treadle-powered machine. She described in detail several places where the attachment might be stored and asked me to search them. So off I went, feeling relieved.

Into the floor of our garage, Daddy had built a rectangular pit, maybe six foot deep. Most of the time there were boards over it, but sometimes he would position our cars just so and work on them from underneath. It was cool and usually filled with salamanders. When the light was let in, their black bodies remained invisible against the oil-stained floor, but their yellow spots stood out.

Momma now took her car to Jiffy-Lube and stored some folding chairs and junk down in the pit. They were heavy and metal, over two dozen of them. Momma claimed the attachment for her sewing machine might be down there.

Somehow I doubted it, but I was down in the pit when Shepherd McCreedy arrived, unexpected and unannounced.

He stared down at me. Surprised, I stared up at him. He smiled a little nervously. "Your momma said you'd be here."

"You're welcome then," I said, not really knowing what to say. Our words tended to echo and rebound, playing out several times in muffled tones.

Shepherd toed the edge of the pit. "Seeing you there like that reminds me of one of the paintings. It has a gray background, gray like this cement. You're sitting near a window, but not looking out of it, and you have this expression on your face that's difficult to understand. It's got sadness in it, but that's not all. There is such a stillness in you, as if every muscle had been positioned just so, but your eyes have something wild in them. They seem to say, 'Sing, burn, flee, like a belfry at the hands of a madman.' "

I stared at him for so long that I felt my eyes go dry. "That's very poetic," I said at last.

Shepherd smiled a lopsided smile. "It should be. Pablo Neruda wrote it."

I was suddenly conscious of how badly the garage reeked of gasoline. The fumes were acting on me, making me a little dizzy. "He was Tea's favorite poet," I said and found myself faltering when spoke. "She used to read him to me."

"I know," he said comfortably. Shepherd tilted his head to one side, studying me. "Now your face seems to say—"

"Stop, please," I interrupted.

He seemed genuinely surprised by my discomfort. "I've embarrassed you?"

Not wanting to look at him, I shook my head and hoisted myself up out of the pit. I rose unsteadily and Shepherd took my hand, helping me to my feet. Even on level ground he was taller than me. I'd always been short but, standing close to him, I was more conscious of it.

He continued to hold my hand. "You don't like to talk about yourself, do you?" He wasn't really asking a question. I could feel self-consciousness heating my face. With Shepherd, I sensed that I'd stepped a little too close to a fire. It irritated me the way he so unsettled me.

"Maybe I'm just not very interesting," I said, trying to keep my voice low and steady.

Shepherd smiled. "I think you are. I've been curious about you for a long while. And now you're here."

"You said that before," I said, and gave my hand a little experimental tug to see if he would let go. He didn't. I pulled a little harder. When I spoke, I heard a thread of panic tangling itself around my words. "I'm not here for long," I said. "Only a little while. To put Tea's things in order. Then I'll be leaving."

Shepherd folded his other hand over mine. His eyes were teasing when he said, "Before you vanish then, can I ask you a question?"

"Only if you let go of my hand."

He dropped it instantly. Once he let go, though, he seemed at a loss for what to do with his own hands. He rubbed them together a little self-consciously, then jammed them into his pockets. "What was it like, being in all those paintings?" he asked. "You were Tea's life's work. You hung in the Minneapolis Institute of Arts all last autumn, you know. People wonder about you. What's it like?"

I thought about it for a moment. Through the open garage door, I could still see Lovell and Abra sitting on the porch. They were alone, although they made no move towards each other. "It's a lot like most things, I suppose," I answered slowly, watching my sister. "At first blush it looks more interesting than it really is. It's like some families, they look a lot better from the outside than in." I looked back at Shepherd. "Being Tea's model all those years meant a lot of sitting still. A lot of cramped muscles. Not being able to scratch an itch or slap a mosquito. I remember that most times I was too cold or too hot. It was work. I cleaned her brushes. I washed up after her. I stretched her canvases."

I couldn't read Shepherd's expression, but I could see myself reflected in his eyes. I looked away quickly. Once again, I could feel the heat rising in my face and was very conscious of how alone we were together. "Maybe that's not what you wanted to know," I said awkwardly into his silence. "Maybe you wanted to know what it's like to see yourself on canvas, hanging on a wall. What it's like to be external to yourself?"

Shepherd half smiled. It was almost encouraging, so I continued. "At first you wonder if that really looks like you. And then you feel distant. And then you get used to it. I'm used to seeing myself as someone else. It's easier that way, you know."

When I finished, Shepherd's face remained unreadable, but he said, "I'm sorry I touched you earlier. It seemed natural to me."

"Why?" I asked. "We don't know each other."

"But it's not like we're strangers," he insisted. "Tea . . . " he began, then hesitated. "Tea talked about you a lot," he said gently. "Every painting had a story. I know so much about you that we might as well be . . . friends."

I stared at him.

Shepherd smiled almost shyly. "Besides, Tea must have talked about me too . . . about things . . . "

I shook my head abruptly. "No, she didn't," I said honestly. "I saw a picture . . . and Momma told me in her letters that you were selling Tea's paintings . . .

but no, Tea never talked about you. She never talked about things that happened before she came here."

"Oh." Shepherd blinked, then looked away, but not before I saw the expression of pain that crossed his face. Almost against my will, the tide within me changed and I felt a swell of sympathy for this strange, weathered man from my cousin's past. I didn't know anything about the time they'd shared, but it was clear what she had meant to him. I cast about for something comforting to say.

"Why don't you come into the house," I suggested awkwardly. "I'll make some coffee."

My words had some effect. Shepherd looked back at me, his eyes a sad gray blue. A familiar sadness. For a moment, I thought he might be right, we might just know a lot about one another. My heart contracted painfully and I had to look away. It had been a long time since I'd had anything that could be called a friend.

Silently, we turned towards the house. "Why did you come out here?" I asked, trying to find something to say.

Shepherd paused. "At the gallery yesterday you said you had Tea's sketchbooks. May I see them?"

I didn't remember saying that, but then I had done a lot of babbling towards the end of the visit, trying desperately to get away.

"If you want to donate them," he continued, "I talked to some people at the university. They're interested and would take good care of her work. My mother was an artist, and when she died I gave a lot of her things to them. She was a sculptor. I used to put a piece of plywood across the top of our washer and dryer, and she'd work there standing up. That was her studio."

He seemed about to touch me again, so I turned to lead him from the garage. I wasn't ready for that yet. "I have the books in the attic. It's this way," I said quickly.

On the porch Lovell was standing, leaning over my sister. Abra was talking, glancing over at us occasionally.

I turned abruptly back to Shepherd. "Would you like to go somewhere?" I asked him. "We could go down to the lake."

Shepherd seemed surprised, but he smiled his easy smile and nodded.

"My sister is marrying that man in a week," I said quietly as Shepherd led me back to his car.

"Congratulations," he said.

"I've only known him for about half an hour," I shrugged. "He's an asshole."

≈

Down by the lake, the dock was a lot more overgrown with weeds than I remembered. The water was high that year, and reeds and cattails swallowed the shore. "My dad used to come here to drink in peace," I told Shepherd. "Tea used to take me to a beach near here in the summer to swim."

"Would you like to swim?"

"Now?" I asked, surprised.

"Now."

I shook my head. The water was murky and shifting with hidden life.

"Come on." Shepherd had already begun to shuck his shirt.

"There's weeds." The idea of being bare with him was too uncomfortable. Shepherd hesitated a little in the face of my resistance. He seemed embarrassed almost, but his shirt was already off. Then he kicked off his pants and handed me his watch. I turned and settled his clothes onto a hump of clean grass. Behind me, I heard his feet on the wooden dock and then the splash as he plunged in.

A pair of dragonflies zoomed by, locked together. I waved my hands in front of my face and turned. Shepherd was swimming out towards the center of the lake, his arms pumping steadily. I watched him for a while. Then he dove under the water, flipped, and headed back to shore. It wasn't long before he reached the weeds and disappeared into them.

I kept waiting for him to surface. Instead, a redwing blackbird erupted, its scarlet wings on fire.

"Shepherd," I called out.

No response.

"Shepherd!" A few frogs helpfully added their voices to mine.

"You know," his voice emerged from the stalks. "I knew Tea when she was a baby. I've always known her. All my life, it seems like." I peered into the weeds, but the moment he was silent, I lost him again.

"I always wondered what she was like when she was young," I answered, edging a little closer to the lake and the weeds, feeling the mud squish beneath my feet. I was mainly talking to hear his voice and reassure myself he was still there. "She was practically grown up by the time I met her."

"The first time I ever laid eyes on Tea she was already an old woman, and she was only two years old then," Shepherd said wryly.

I found a drier place on shore to sit. Even so, when settled down, I could feel the damp creep into me. "How did you meet Tea?" I asked the wall of green reeds.

"My father's name was Moses. Moses McMonagle McCreedy. He was a friend of Tea's mother, though no friend of mine."

"I've heard of him."

Shepherd let out a short laugh. "He was a sonofabitch. I can't say I was too sad when he and Tea's mother split for good for Alabama, though Tea took it hard. Did you ever meet her mother?"

I shook my head, though I wasn't sure if he could see me.

"She was a beautiful woman," Shepherd said from inside the weeds. "Did Tea ever talk to you about her mother?"

Again I shook my head.

"Like I said, Tea's mother was a beautiful woman and that's really the only kind thing to be said about her. She had this tattoo of an Apollo butterfly on her back. Its red-and-black wings opened across her shoulders. One summer, when I was living with Moses and Tea, her mother would lie out in the sun and tan for hours, turning brown, covered in oil. Tea and I would climb up to the roof of the trailer we were living in and we'd lie up there the entire day just watching her. Tea would stare at the butterfly. And when she turned over, I'd stare at her breasts. She was a beautiful woman. Moses was wild about her."

I couldn't tell if it was the wind moving in the rushes or him.

"Hell of a life, huh?" he continued. "But really that's what we would do. Climb onto the roof and stare at her mother. Moses worked all day, or at least pretended to, and there was nothing for us to do in the trailer park. Eventually Tea's mother got tired of us staring at her and she enrolled us in this Bible camp run by the Baptists down the street."

I laughed. "I can't picture Tea at Bible camp."

"Everyone in our trailer park sent their kids to that camp," he explained. "It was run by a woman who had visions. Sister Odile could tell people their license plate numbers and stuff. Once she helped a neighbor lady locate a missing social security check.

"Every morning we were supposed to go to this camp. We stayed until late afternoon. Tea hated it from the first day. She didn't like having her mother too far out of sight. After the first few days she started hiding out up on the trailer roof.

"Every morning she'd kiss her mother good-bye and then walk a little ways with me. Then she'd double back and climb up to the roof. She could see her mother tanning outside, and there were these air vents on the roof that you could open up, so Tea could stare down at her mother while she was inside, too.

"Every day after camp, I waited for Tea on the corner. She'd climb down and join me and I'd tell her what we did at camp that day so that she could fake it over dinner. We'd walk home together holding hands. I always covered for her.

"Then one night Tea told her mother and Moses at dinner that she shouldn't have to go to camp anymore, because she had visions that were better than Sister Odile's. Then she repeated to her mother everything she'd done that day. Tea told her what time she'd walked the dog and who had called and that she'd taken the garbage out at three o'clock and stuffed a bottle of vodka down at the bottom of it where Moses wouldn't see. It scared the shit out of her mother.

"Tea kept it up for a week. Her mother didn't know what to do, but for the first time she started sending quarters along with us to leave in Odile's offering plate. I bought candy with them. One day she gave me a whole dollar and told me to keep an eye on Tea and see what she did during the day. I reported back to her that everything had seemed fine to me, and I bought myself a stack of baseball cards.

"That night at dinner Tea told her mother that in a vision from God she'd witnessed her drink exactly six beers and watch the *Glen Campbell Goodtime Hour* on channel nine. She'd also smoked exactly nine and a half cigarettes. Smoked only half of one because the landlady had dropped in unexpectedly and she'd had to stomp it out quickly.

"I think that finally did it. Tea's mother followed us to camp the next day. She watched Tea double back and climb up the elm tree and drop down to the roof like a cat. It must have gotten up to a hundred degrees that afternoon, but Tea's mother let her stay up there the whole day watching. When I got home from camp, she beat us both within an inch of our lives and sent us to bed before Moses got home."

Shepherd laughed harshly. "She never told Moses the truth, though. I think she convinced him that Tea had visions of him, too. She told him that Tea had seen him flirting with the waitress down at the Hammerhead Bar. I guess she thought it might keep Moses in line."

"Did it work?"

"Moses?" Shepherd shook his head. "Not by half. And if Tea's mother couldn't do it, no woman could."

It seemed to me that his voice was drawing closer and closer. "Were your parents divorced?" I asked and then was surprised at myself. It was easy to talk to Shepherd, especially like this, when his too-gray eyes didn't bore into mine.

"No. There was a lot of love in my parent's marriage. My mother loved Moses and Moses loved himself. He could never let her go, even when he didn't want her anymore. He could never let her be in peace."

Shepherd emerged from the weeds while he spoke, dripping and slimy like he'd just been born. Duckweed and grime clung to him. He slapped at a few mosquitoes that were biting him.

"I've been watching you," he said. "You couldn't see me, but I could see you." He stretched the length of his long body out onto the shore next to me. "I like you like this. Your face seems relaxed. Unhurt. You were calm while we talked, maybe a little drowsy even."

It hurt to look at him. I kept staring at my hands, the water, the weeds, but despite this, my eyes kept wandering back to him. Shepherd seemed oblivious to my discomfort.

"I sold a painting of you once, where you're sleeping naked on blue cushions. It was one of my favorites because you seemed calm, like you are now."

"It's a lot of work," I said.

He half smiled, maybe a little amused. I cleared my throat. "It's difficult to lie still and close your eyes like that," I informed him. "To pretend you're sleeping for hours or days at a time."

"It must be terrible."

"Yes. It is."

He smiled softly. "You are formidable, aren't you?"

"Yes," I agreed softly.

Reaching over, he gently stroked my hair, then my cheek. "Can I touch you now?" he asked.

# 15

Abra's wedding was suddenly only three days away. I woke that morning to find Blue under my bed again. Despite the hardness of the floor, he seemed comfortable enough. I noticed he'd even dragged a stuffed animal with him this time.

I shook him awake. At first he eyed me groggily, then smiled. "Hide," he said, pointing at himself. Then he slid out from under the bed and trotted happily off to the kitchen. I put on my jeans and a T-shirt and followed him. I made coffee and watched Momma make French toast for breakfast. She talked while she worked. She and Constance were going to start cooking today. She wanted me to go to the Red Owl in town and pick up a few groceries for the wedding. She handed me a list the length of my arm.

I took it absently. "Momma," I asked, "why do you think Blue keeps hiding under my bed? I always find him there in the morning."

Momma looked surprised. "I didn't know that," she said.

"Has he done this before? Hide under beds?"

Momma shook her head, looking over at the boy. He was amusing himself, rummaging through the can cupboard. Momma's expression grew thoughtful.

"I just think it's strange," I said.

Momma shot me a look. "You're the last person to talk about strange."

I made a face. I seemed to be hearing that a lot lately. "I just meant there's got to be some reason why he sleeps under my bed."

Momma's face grew grim and her lips very, very thin. "I don't know, Kat. Maybe it's because his mother is a selfish drunk who doesn't spend five minutes a day thinking about him."

I stared at her.

Momma nodded at my list. "Now, will you please go take care of the shopping like I asked? I've got a lot of work to do today."

≈

The Red Owl was kitty-corner from the ball field of Jordan's school. Since it was midday, I wasn't too surprised to find my niece leaning against the dumpster in the parking lot smoking a cigarette. Grinning unapologetically, She stomped out her cigarette and loped over to me.

Squinting off behind her, I could make out the little Buddha on the far side of the field. Engel seemed to be running at full speed, though at a pace no faster than an invalid walks. "Has he lost any weight this way?" I asked by way of greeting.

Jordan tucked her cigarettes into her shirt pocket and made a face. "Maybe fifteen pounds in the last three months. His mother weighs him twice a day. Before and after school. Why are you here?"

I showed her the list. "Abra's wedding."

We walked into the store together. I offered to let Jordan sit in the cart. She gave me a withering look.

In the end we needed two carts. The store was cool. The air-conditioning hummed loudly. It was almost soothing to push my heavy cart up and down the aisles alongside Jordan.

When we reached the checkout counter, there were three packs of cigarettes not on the list and a hibachi complete with charcoal and a dozen skewers. As I pulled the heavy hibachi box out of the cart, I shot Jordan a questioning look. She kept serenely piling bags of sugar onto the moving belt. "I didn't think you'd remember to buy Abra a wedding present," she explained.

"A hibachi?"

She smiled blandly. "It's on sale for nineteen ninety-nine."

I plunked the grill down on the counter and added the cigarettes.

The bag boys helped us load the car. While they worked, Jordan settled on the front bumper. Engel was still running his laps. Jordan chewed thoughtfully on a piece of her hair.

"How long does it take him to finish those laps?" I asked.

"Sometimes it's dark before he gets home."

"Does it bother him when you watch?"

"I'm not watching him."

"Looks like that to me."

Jordan scowled at me. "I'm looking at that crow," she said. She pointed off across the lot. A crow the size of a cat was there, sitting on the yellow painted curb, its intelligent head tilted at us. "I know that crow," she said. "It sits outside the school window. I watch her every day during class."

"You sure it's the same one?"

Jordan nodded. "Yeah, it's her. She's real big like that. Every day she's there. It makes me wonder why she has wings and I don't."

Almost as if it had heard us, the bird shook its wings. It opened its mouth to squawk, but strangely no sound came out. It shook its wings again and then launched itself into the air. The crow circled above us, than took off on the road heading for home.

"What bird flaps its wings and covers the sky with a single feather?" Jordan asked, climbing into the car. It was an old riddle that Tea would tell.

"Night."

≈

Lovell visited one more time before the wedding. As promised, he brought his sons. I was sitting on the porch when they arrived. It was raining softly. The boys didn't seem to notice as they filed dutifully out of their father's car and up our front steps. They were thin, sunless children.

My mother invited them into the house for lemonade. They turned their large moon eyes to Lovell for approval. He nodded. They nodded back. Samuel buried his hands in his pockets. Lovell gave him a firm but encouraging push on the shoulder. I wasn't exactly sure what was being said, but I bet if written down it would have consumed whole chapters. They spoke that secret language that people who share sadness or secrets have. It was probably in a dialect similar to the one I had learned at my own mother's knee. Still, their noddings and silences and shuffles mystified me. Each family, I guess, is like a foreign country.

Abra and Lovell followed the children into the house. Lovell emerged several minutes later with a glass of lemonade for himself and one for me. He set it beside me on the floor, where I sat sorting through a box of Tea's old letters.

Most of the letters were from me, written in my years of absence. It was almost like a catalog of my old addresses. Sometimes there was less than a week's gap between new and old residences, even though I often moved across state lines. Sitting in the calm stillness of my mother's porch, with the soft rain all around, I found it hard to imagine such restlessness.

Lovell settled into a chair and sipped his lemonade, watching me. Finally he said, "Sister, I believe we began on the wrong foot, though I can't for the life of me tell where we went wrong. Perhaps you could let me know, so I can correct my mistake."

I kept my features carefully blank. He continued anyway.

Lovell's voice took on the same tones as a minister working at his sermon. "I wanted to tell you how sorry I am for your loss." He paused unnecessarily between words. "Abra tells me you came home to finally set Tea's things in order. I think it a shame her going like that. My own wife died some years ago. I understand how you must feel right now. I understand some of the questions you must be asking yourself."

It didn't take much imagination to see where this conversation was going. Lovell was hoping for my conversion.

"I'm sorry for your loss," I said shortly.

Lovell put his glass down and leaned forward in his chair with his hands folded out before him, his elbows resting on his knees. When he was close like that, I could smell the soap and bleach he used on his clothes. "I haven't lost my wife," he said, lowering his voice as if he were telling me a secret. "My wife loved God. She's with God at home in heaven and we'll meet again, according to God's plan. But sometimes," he leaned even closer to me, "I worry about people who don't have that assurance. Who don't know where the souls of their loved ones will land. So few, we are told, will make it into heaven."

"I see you knew my cousin Tea," I said neutrally.

Lovell smiled broadly, easing back into his chair. "Most people did."

"Its a small town." I said evenly.

"Even so, Tea was hard to miss."

I scooped up the letters and dumped them back in their box, throwing a day's organizational effort into chaos with a single irritated gesture. "You know," I said impatiently, "I've always been amazed by people like you, Lovell. You act as if you've done some great thing by believing in God. But really, you just plopped your money down on a bet you can't lose. How much balls does that take?"

Lovell sipped his lemonade. "I'm afraid I don't follow you, Sister."

"You can't lose," I repeated. "If you die and there is a God, you'll go to heaven. If you die and there is no God, well, you're dead. You won't care. People like you don't have to spend a lifetime suffering, knowing that there's nothing else after this life. That once you say good-bye to someone, you've lost them forever." I laughed shortly. "We're supposed to believe you're the martyrs? You've got it easy."

Lovell wasn't ruffled. "You sound a lot like Tea."

"You could say worse to me." I looked him over. "How did you know Tea?"

Lovell's hand anchored itself around his sweat-beaded glass. Surprised, I watched his knuckles grow white. When Lovell noticed the direction of my gaze, his eyes slid self-consciously down to the fist he was making. Slowly he soothed that hand with the other. He cast me another look, a long look, from far away. Then he swirled his lemonade around a little. "You know," he said with a little hitch in his voice, "I'm a man saved by Jesus."

Just that moment Abra appeared on the porch, letting the screen door slam behind her. We both started, feeling a little guilty, though I wasn't really sure why. Abra eyed us coolly, suspiciously, the same way I'd seen Momma size up my father a million times.

"What were you talking about?" she asked directly, calmly.

Lovell chuckled a little nervously. "The wonders of the Lord, Sister, the wonders of the Lord."

Abra snorted. "With Kat?" She shook her head. "Kat doesn't believe in God. She can't keep him in her pocket. She doesn't want anything she can't have completely."

I folded the flaps of the box over Tea's letters and stood to leave.

"Of course," Abra continued, peering out through the gray rain, "that's not all her fault. She didn't learn that by herself."

Before I said anything, Momma said through the screen door, "Constance is on the phone for you. It's about Jordan."

≈

"Kat? Kat, is that you?" Constance cried when I picked up the phone. I could tell she was trying hard to keep the waver from her voice. The rain beat on the window just beside me. I felt as if the glass that separated me from the elements was thin and getting thinner.

"Hello, Constance," I sighed.

"Kat, the director of Jordan's school called," Constance said in a rush of words. "She said that if I don't come in, she'll consider throwing Jordan out of the program and Jordan will have to repeat a grade."

"Why is that?" I asked, frowning.

"Because that horrible woman calls the director every day. She says Jordan won't leave her son alone. Yesterday Jordan wrote him a love letter, and his mother found it in his backpack."

"What did it say?"

"There were just some silly hearts drawn on it and Jordan wrote 'I like you' or something like that. The director read it to me over the phone. I was so embarrassed."

I could picture Constance clearly on the other end, her face getting puffy with tears. I had to search in myself for patience. I'd learned a lot of it, sitting all those years as Tea's model. I took a deep breath. "Did you tell the director that it's a perfectly normal thing for a thirteen-year-old girl to have a crush on a boy and write him notes that say 'I like you'?"

A wail escaped Constance. "I tried to! But the director said given our family history and all the troubles we had with Tea, that she thinks Jordan needs special attention." Constance's voice had acquired an edge of panic. "Kat, she said she's considering calling in a social worker."

I didn't really hear much of what Constance had to say after she spoke my cousin's name. Of course, I seethed. Of course this is about Tea. They must pick up her scent on Jordan, I thought. It must drive them wild. I felt suddenly very light. My anger made me feel like I could fly over rooftops.

"What should I do?" Constance demanded.

The rain had intensified its assault. Momma's roses were collapsing under the beating. Our dirt driveway was becoming a slick trail of mud. As I was watching the driveway dissolve, Shepherd's car pulled in. "She said to come in today?" I asked.

"Yes. Four o'clock, after classes."

I glanced at the clock. "That's fifteen minutes from now." Shepherd climbed out of his car, making a sprint for the porch. The rain darkened his overcoat and made him seem even taller and thinner, like a dog with wet fur. Constance was speaking, but my mind was no longer translating what she said into words. "I'll take care of it, Constance," I assured her, and abruptly hung up.

Shepherd let himself in before I got to the door. He smiled at my startled mother and then wrapped me in his wet arms and squeezed.

"Can we go for a drive?" I asked, trying to worm my way loose.

"In the rain?" He glanced out the window. The lightning was just beginning.

"Yeah. It's kind of necessary," I said as I gathered up my purse and shoes.

# 16

We were sitting in the school parking lot. Shepherd turned to me and said, "I'm not sure what you want me to do."

"Just come in with me. You know, for moral support."

"What has Jordan done?"

"Nothing." I must have spoken a little too vehemently, because Shepherd drew back. "Nothing," I repeated, trying to sound calmer, "except be born in a small town. They're only doing this because of my family. Because everyone knows who we are. My father was a drunk and Tea . . . "

Shepherd gathered my hand into his and kissed it. "Tea was different," he finished for me.

Gratefully I gave his hand a squeeze. Shepherd soothed my hair. "I have an idea," he said. "Why don't you let me take care of this, then we'll go out to dinner. You might fly off the handle in there."

"I should go in . . . " protested.

Shepherd smiled. "Let me handle this. Trust me."

I squirmed. "What will you tell them?"

He winked. "I'll think of something. Who do you think taught Tea how to talk her way out of trouble?"

≈

Shepherd emerged twenty minutes later. He ducked through the rain, head bent low. The drops ricocheted off his back. The rain that didn't hit him fell to the pavement with such force that it seemed to shatter, like glass. He landed in the car, a little battered by the storm, but intact. "Done," he announced with satisfaction.

"What did you say?"

He grinned lopsidedly. "I told them I was Jordan's lawyer and requested that they stop harassing my client. I used a few fancy phrases like 'infliction of emotional harm.' " His grin grew a little vicious. "I think it scared the shit out of them."

"They believed that you're a lawyer?"

Shepherd laughed, touching my cheek. "Kat, I am a lawyer."

I stared at him and then started to laugh.

"My father was an unsuccessful con man. My mother was a dreamer, an artist. I became a lawyer." He shrugged. "It seemed like a logical response at the time. Now I sell art."

"How did that happen?"

Shepherd stared out the window, watching the little town drown in the rain. He took my hand and pulled me closer. "You can't change people," he said finally, "but people change in their own time, given good enough reason. That's what happened to me, I guess."

"That's vague enough."

He smiled gently. "Did you live here the whole time you were growing up?" I knew he was deliberately changing the subject.

"Me? Yes. My mother moved here when she was six. My grandfather bought a farm near where Mason lives now, and they moved out from the city. That was maybe fifty years ago, but we're still considered strangers.

"This whole area, Comfort Lake, Lindstrom, Center City, was settled by Norwegians and Swedes, farmers mostly. It's been a tiny, isolated island for a long time. When Momma first showed up at school, everyone kept touching her eyebrows. The kids in her class thought she was coloring them with makeup, because they'd never seen dark eyebrows before. Everyone but Momma had blue eyes and blond hair."

"I can't imagine Tea here," Shepherd said, starting the car.

"Tea couldn't imagine herself here. That was part of the problem."

We drove out of town. "I suppose your family is a little anxious about the wedding," he said carefully, glancing at me while he drove. "This is the first big family event without Tea. I suppose it will seem strange without her."

"My family?" I shook my head. "Abra would probably dance for joy at not having Tea there, if dancing wasn't against her religion. Family gatherings and Tea were like gasoline and matches—they didn't mix well. Weddings and funerals were Tea's battleground. When she drank, she'd beat up the bridesmaids and piss on the corpses."

Shepherd laughed.

"I'm not joking about the corpse part," I said, then added seriously, "I'm the only one who will miss her." My mood suddenly went black again. We drove in silence. The rain seemed to be battling with the dirt roads and winning. They had been pummeled into mud. Between the muck and the rising fog, driving became almost impossible. The thick walls of corn on either side of us were all that kept us on the path. I hunched down in my seat and shivered.

Suddenly, a horse erupted from the corn in front of us and streaked across the road. A rider clung to its back, crouched low, like a second skin. Her hair was plastered flat against her body. They saw us too late to alter their path. I screamed.

Shepherd swore and then the brakes shrieked. We spun out of control. I lost sight of the horse and rider. Suddenly all I saw was green streaks as the car crashed into the corn.

Just as quickly as we lost control, the brakes caught and we shuddered to a stop.

Shepherd and I stared silently at one another, taking in during the first minute that the other was all right, but needing to keep reassuring ourselves for several more minutes. Then, slowly we turned and looked behind us at the path of destruction. Corn bodies were littered everywhere. We were so far into the field that the road was no longer visible. The path our vehicle had cut was at least twice as wide as the car. Shepherd's hands tightened around the steering wheel. "What the hell was that?" he asked shakily.

"I think that was my niece," I said, feeling weak. "That was Jordan."

Once again, Shepherd turned to gape at the churned-up ground and the flattened corn. "There is something sincerely wrong with that child." I don't think he meant to yell, but he did anyway. He hit the dash for good measure. I cradled my head. "Let's get out of here before the farmer sees this and we get shot or something." He tried to back out. The tires spun in the mud, unable to find a grip. The rain continued unabated, deepening our problems.

Eventually Shepherd gave up trying, and rested his head against the steering wheel.

"At least we're dry in here," I ventured.

He turned and stared at me. Then he opened his car door, got out, and slowly walked around to the passenger side, picking his way through the mud and corn debris. He yanked open my door and pulled me out.

All it took was one minute in that downpour for me to be soaked to the skin. I slipped in the mud. He steadied me and I clung to him. The hood of his car was covered in corn, but he laid me across it anyway. His mouth was insistent, his hands probing.

I felt my hand clench around a fallen ear of corn, like a weapon. My fingernails cut through the rough outer skin and the softer silk inside.

Shepherd's lips found their way to my breast. I wrapped my arms around him. The heat from the car's engine made the hood as warm as any blanket. We peeled off our clothes.

The rain beat down against us, against the earth around us. In the onslaught, only the stalks stood unwavering. Their strong, red roots held them upright, while the world dissolved into mud around them.

"Your sweet kiss," Shepherd murmured. "Your sweet kiss."

# 17

It was nearing dark when Shepherd left me in our yard. The rain had stopped. Everything smelled of mud. Abra had the living room windows open and the lights on against the fading day. Standing on the porch, I leaned into the screen on the window and watched her sewing the hem on her wedding gown.

"It seems to me I remember that man," Abra said by way of greeting.

"Shepherd?"

"He was at Tea's funeral," she said. "He cried real hard. He and Tea must have been close?" Abra frowned at her needle, than snapped the thread. She reached down, rummaging in her sewing box for another spool.

I nodded.

"But that doesn't bother you too much, does it?" she asked.

"What?"

Abra licked the end of the thread, before putting it through the eye of the needle. "Maybe it's just got so that you're used to it."

"You're speaking in tongues, sister. I don't understand you."

Abra glanced up at me impatiently. "I tell you, even after all this time, I still find it amazing that no one in this house could ever have a man that Tea hadn't gotten to first or was going to get shortly. Seems to me that Tea never had an interest in a man until somebody else wanted him."

"Shepherd and Tea grew up together," I explained.

"Oh, Kat," Abra said pityingly, "don't you ever get tired of defending her?"

"No."

Abra tested her newest stitches with a vicious pull. "You can stop being so smug. Lovell says he told you he and Tea were friends. And we both know what 'friends' means when we're talking about Tea."

I felt a mosquito sink its sting into me. "What does it mean?"

Impatiently Abra tossed aside her dress. "It was a long time ago. Lovell has made his peace with God. He's a new man. The man Tea had was the old man. I want the new one."

"Is that how you've got it all worked out?"

"Yes," she said flatly. "He was a drinking man then."

"But he's not now?"

"No, he's not."

"You're sure?"

"Yes."

Another mosquito found me. "Because," I told her, "sometimes it's hard to spot a drinking man when he doesn't drink. He may drink only lemonade and still be a drunk underneath."

"You know," Abra said acidly, "I believe you honestly try not to make any sense. You and Tea always acted like it was a sin to have an intelligible conversation with anyone. I really hated that about her. "

"Is that the only reason?"

"The only reason what?"

"Why you hated Tea so much. I've never been able to figure it out. What'd Tea ever do to you?"

Abra laughed harshly, rocking back in Daddy's chair. "You know perfectly well, Kat, you know perfectly well."

"Does it change anything to know that Tea was right?"

"No."

"She only told you the truth, Abra. What everybody else knew already. She was trying to protect you. He did exactly what she said he would, didn't he? He ran the minute he heard about the baby. He never even admitted it was his, did he? Not even after the poor thing died and it didn't matter anymore. But Tea helped you out. She was the one that talked Daddy out of—"

"No!" she shouted. "No! I don't know what you're talking about. That never happened." Abra fled from sight, leaving behind her white wedding dress, collapsed across the chair like a wilting flower.

The worst part is that I think maybe Abra believed the things she said.

The night was warm, comfortable. Evening was settling in. Momma's chair beckoned. As I rocked, I started wondering what other parts of my sister were gone. What else had she given over to Jesus?

≈

Abra stayed locked in her room for the rest of the night. I climbed the stairs to Tea's attic. I wasn't able to stay there long, though. When I pulled on the cord of the attic's main light, there was a sharp pop, a flash, and then darkness. Resigned, I trudged back downstairs. I couldn't find any spare bulbs in Momma's cupboards and soon it was too dark to work up there. There were too many things to stumble over. I had already stubbed my toes, several times, before I tripped over the carton with Tea's china. I recognized the box instantly, because it was the same one the dishes had arrived in years before. Tea's mother had sent them for Tea's birthday, the year she began living with us. Tea had never used the dishes because she said she didn't want to jinx herself. She wanted her mother to write again, which, of course, she hadn't, not once.

I picked up the box and made my way downstairs. Finding the china covered in grime, I ran hot water and, one by one, plopped the delicate cups and saucers and teapot into the sink. A ring of dirt began to form around the edge of the sink. The water turned a reddish brown.

Momma was beside me before I noticed her approach. She stared down at the sink and wrinkled her nose. "What a mess," she sighed, then added, "I would have thought you'd have given up by now. I certainly would have."

Gently, Momma moved me aside and began rummaging under the sink. She emerged with a pair of yellow gloves and some soap.

"The cleaning's not so bad," I told her, watching her pull on the gloves with the studied air of a surgeon.

Momma barked out a laugh. "It's a disaster up there."

I shrugged. "It gives me time to think."

"Think about what?" Momma began dumping liberal amounts of soap into the water.

I leaned against the counter. "I think about Tea. Lately, I think a lot about Abra. Her wedding. About how strange life is or, at least, it's not like we expect it to be."

"You waste your time thinking about things like that?" Momma shook her head.

"I think about love, too."

"What did you decide?" she asked dryly.

"You know, most people have a wrong idea of it. We think it's something exactly opposite of what it is. We think people who love us are the people who would never hurt us. But the truth is, the people who love us are the ones that always hurt us, because they're the ones who have the balls to tell us the truth. People who don't care so much don't bother to tell you things."

"I think you're exaggerating the importance of the truth," Momma observed. "Saying it out loud doesn't always help." She handed me one of the newly washed cups. Water dripped all over my arms. She handed me another. I started lining them up on the counter on paper towels. Once the grime had been removed, the cups glowed a deep and brilliant blue. The inside of each cup, however, was china white. At the bottom was painted a butterfly with red-and-black wings. Momma held a cup up to the light, studying it. "What a strange present to give a child," she murmured.

"Tell me about Tea's mother."

"I hardly knew her," Momma said as she carefully placed the cup back down on the counter. "I only met her once, on my wedding day. She was your father's only sister."

"What was her name?"

"You know, I don't even remember now. Neither Tea nor your daddy ever wanted to talk much about her."

"Shepherd said she was beautiful."

"The ones that break your heart usually are." Momma grimaced. "Your father's whole family was handsome."

For a moment we were silent, working on the cups together. The persistent moths gathered in ever deepening layers on the screen of the kitchen window. Then Momma said, "How come you never ask me about your father? We talk about Tea all the time, but you never mention him."

I went very still. Slowly, I placed the cup I was holding on the counter. At last I tried to say matter-of-factly, "I guess because I don't ever think of him. He doesn't mean that much to me."

"He has to have meant something to you," Momma said, a small crease of disapproval forming on her forehead. "You knew him your whole life, Kat."

I shuffled uncomfortably, not answering.

Momma stared at me, waiting.

I suddenly felt impatient. "What am I supposed to say, Momma? Most of my life he sat in his chair and drank."

Momma poured water into the brilliant blue teapot, then emptied it. The water that sloshed out was almost black. Momma squirted some soap into the teapot and swirled the water around with her hand.

"You know what I think about your father, Kat?" Momma asked.

I said nothing.

Momma took her scrubber up and started working on the inside of the pot. "I think the way he grew up was a hard way to come into life. His mom came and went. His dad stayed gone. He and his sister got bounced around from family to family. No one ever loved him. In all those years before he met me, no one ever loved him.

"But I loved him. Like you loved Tea, I loved your daddy. I was seventeen when I met him and he was already thirty-five. A man. A real man who laughed and swore and drank and made me his own." Momma chuckled. "I never met anyone as powerful a man as your father. He was almost like whiskey himself."

I blushed and looked away.

Momma studied her work on the teapot. Satisfied, she rinsed it in clear water. She handed me the pot to dry and said, "I loved your father and loved him and loved him and he just didn't know it. He couldn't see it. He couldn't see me.

"It was like I was invisible. That love was such an important part of me. It was all of me. And he couldn't see it. And he didn't even know enough to care. And that just about drove me wild with anger. First hurt. Then anger."

I stared at Momma, swallowing hard. In my whole life, she had never talked like this. "When did you start thinking about all of this?" I asked.

Momma stared out the window, at the white-winged moths clustered there. She seemed to consider the question and then she said, "When your Daddy died, the house got real quiet. Everybody moved on and out, everyone but me and Abra. That left me with a lot of time to think. A lot of quiet that I hadn't had in years."

"Until Tea came home," I amended.

Momma looked up at me in surprise. Then she nodded.

Momma wasn't satisfied with the job I was doing on the teapot. She took it from me, plucked the towel from my hand, and started drying it herself.

"Why did you take her back, Momma?" I asked. "You hated having her here in the first place."

Momma's hands slowed but didn't stop. She rubbed the pot until it shone. Then she set the pot on the counter and fit the little lid on with a soft click. Momma's mouth looked grim. "I never saw anyone so sad as Tea after Billy died," she said. "And she just never seemed to get better. She went to the hospital, but pretty soon she wasn't talking or eating. Her doctors wanted to move her to a different kind of hospital—not a rehabilitation home like she usually went to when she drank too much, but more of an institution. I couldn't let her go there. I couldn't abandon her to a place like that.

"So I went and visited her and asked her to come home with me. And I promised her that I wouldn't bother her. I told her she could have her old room in the attic back and I would see to meals and all that.

"And she agreed. So that's what we did. We got on pretty well for a while there."

"So you brought her here because you felt sorry for her," I asked quietly, feeling a painful pull in my chest.

Momma shook her head. "No, I brought Tea here so that I could feel better about my damned quiet house, and my dead husband who couldn't see me, and the kids I was too angry to love, and all the things I had started to think and feel about my life being mainly over with."

I didn't know what to say, so I fiddled with the lid on the teapot. A spot in my chest hurt just then, as if something hot were trying to work its way out of my body.

"What are you going to do with all this?" Momma asked, carefully picking up one of the fragile cups. "It'd be a shame to close it up in another box. It's beautiful."

I reached down through the filthy water and pulled the plug out of the drain. "I was thinking maybe you'd like to keep them."

Momma glanced at me, startled. Then a hesitant smile spread across her face. "Yes, I would love to keep them," she said softly.

For a moment, it seemed that the distance between us lessened by a few miles at least.

I turned back to the sink. The hard ring of dirt showed clearly against the sink's white interior. I sighed, reaching for the scrub brush. "You know what I think, Momma," I said, pouring soap into the sink. "I think love involves a lot of cleaning."

She laughed. It was a good, true sound.

# 18

The day before Abra's wedding, Momma asked me to wrap the gifts while she finished our dresses. The gifts were hidden in Mason's barn. I would have begged off, except for Momma mentioning that Constance was in town having her hair done and Mason had taken the kids to do some errands.

I was walking up Mason's driveway when a car honked behind me. I jumped. It took me awhile to make myself turn around, because I expected to see Constance. Instead, Shepherd leaned out of his car and waved at me. "I was just heading to your house," he called out, smiling his easy smile.

I was getting used to his unannounced visits. I stepped aside and let him turn into the driveway. He rolled slowly down to the barn, holding my hand through the open car window as he bumped up the dirt driveway. "I haven't been on a stock farm for quite a few years," he said, turning off the engine. His nose wrinkled. "Glad it still smells the same." He climbed out of the car and pulled me tight against him. We kissed and then he grinned. "Let's go check out the hayloft."

Together we pried open the heavy barn doors. I hesitated at the ladder to the loft. "I don't know how stable it is."

"Only one way to find out," Shepherd said as he hauled himself up. Anxiously I watched him disappear through the trap door in the ceiling above. The floor creaked beneath his feet. Dirt showered down onto me.

"Wow," I heard him say from above. I scrambled up after him. He stood framed by blue sky in the open door of the loft. "Great view," he murmured, turning a little and smiling at me. "I think see your crazy niece down there."

Looking beyond him, I saw Jordan in the far pasture, riding in furious circles. "She's not crazy." I must have spoken more sharply than I intended, because Shepherd gave me a wary glance. He put his arm around me anyway. "You're right, of course," he sagely agreed. "It's not craziness. It's just something about the will of the women in this family." He kissed me, but even while we touched his eyes were still thoughtful. I squirmed in the circle of his arm.

"You know, it's been years and years since the last time I was on a farm," he said again. "I guess it was more of a ranch. I was still a kid. Fifteen maybe. Tea was there."

"In Montana," I said softly.

Shepherd looked surprised. "Tea told you about it?"

"No, I found a picture. You're standing together, with the mountains behind you. Tea is smiling, and you're wearing a cowboy hat."

Shepherd looked sheepish. He hesitated, then said, "That was during one of the summers I was with Moses. One day he showed up at my mother's door, loaded me into his truck, and we just picked up and left Tennessee. He didn't even tell me where we were going until we were halfway to Montana. I should have guessed, though." His lips curled. "Tea's mother was living with a rancher out there. She put us up in one of the shacks for the hired hands. The old rancher had so much land, he never even knew we were there. We stayed a whole week, fishing and doing whatever. Every night Tea's mother and Tea would come down and visit and bring us supper." Shepherd glanced down at me. "Ever been to Montana, Kat?"

I shook my head and looked away from him. I felt a curious pressure growing in my chest. It spread to my fingertips and toes. I felt numb, but still all right somehow. I leaned into Shepherd while he spoke, pressing my face into the smooth cloth of his clean, pressed shirt. I liked the solid feel of this man.

"You'd like it," he said. "Montana is this wide open place. Even more big and open than here. I remember one night we had this cloudy sky. You could hardly see the moon. Up above us the sky was like black water, one huge expanse of ocean. It was almost pitch black, but there were these lightning bugs floating up over our heads like stars.

"Tea and I took off running after the bugs, letting them lead us farther and farther across the fields, trying to jump up and catch them in our hands.

Sometimes in the dark, Tea and I would collide when we jumped up. We'd hit in midair and kind of land all tangled and laughing together in the tall grass. Then we'd kiss and roll around, until one of us ran off after bugs again. We chased those bugs almost the whole night, but it seems to me that we must have been the clumsiest kids alive, because we collided every five minutes." Shepherd grinned. "Not on purpose, of course. We'd fly through the air and somehow always just land together.

"That was the best part about Montana," Shepherd continued, with the quiet ache of longing in his voice. "We could just keep running like that on and on. I loved that. That was the last summer I ever spent with Tea like that. Just being free."

Shepherd looked down at me. He'd been smiling, but his expression grew concerned when he saw my face. "Kat, you're crying."

It was true. But I wasn't just crying. My chest hurt so bad that I felt as if the air were being squeezed out of me. I couldn't breathe. My body began to shake. I hadn't really cried in years, and now it was coming out of me like an earthquake.

"Kat," he said gently, "does it still hurt that bad?"

My voice cracked. "Yes, it does. Of course it does."

≈

Eventually, the storm of tears passed and we sat in the quiet of the barn. The hay smelled good and dry all around us. Like summer. Shepherd smiled down at me. Exhausted, I rested my head against his chest.

We were like that when Jordan found us half an hour later. I must have been a little red-eyed still, because Jordan seemed suspicious. When she spoke, she looked at accusingly. "Grandma Naomi called," she informed me. "She wants you to come and get your dress hemmed for the wedding."

I rose very slowly, brushing hay from my clothes. "Do you remember Shepherd, Jordan?" I asked.

"Of course I do," she said, disappearing down the ladder.

When I turned back to him, I could see that he was trying hard to keep a straight face.

"Don't say it," I warned.

Shepherd pecked me on the cheek. "She's the spitting image of Tea, you know."

"That's exactly what I didn't want you to say."

Shepherd drove me home and walked me to the front porch. He kissed me before leaving. When he saw Momma watching us through the screen door, he winked at her and waved. "'Evening, Naomi," he called out easily as he turned to go.

Momma looked at me and then at Shepherd's departing car. "Did you get any of the presents wrapped?' she asked, already knowing the answer.

"Not even the hibachi."

Momma sighed and disappeared into the house. With some trepidation, I followed her inside for my hemming. I wasn't sure if I trusted her with pins just then.

≈

The dress Momma made me was demure and yellow. I had just slipped it over my head when Pearl emerged from the depths of the house, carrying a box of her things. Blue trailed behind her with a grubby stuffed animal.

"Where are you going?" I asked, then yelled, "Ouch!" as Momma pricked me.

Pearl shot me a look of pity and practically sang, "I'm moving back home."

"Home?" I tried to say as I shrank from Momma, who was brandishing another pin.

"Home," Pearl chirped merrily. "I'm moving back in with Steve."

"Steve?" I repeated, feeling bewildered. I glanced at Momma. She was looking resolutely at my hem and didn't meet my eye.

"But what about . . . " I began, thinking of the darkened house and the ominous creaking of bedsprings. Then I thought better of it. I stared at my sister, utterly dumbstruck. Pearl smiled back, perfectly content. She was looking better than when she'd first come home. Her hair was clean and her skin clear. The dark shadows under her eyes had evaporated. She'd even put on a little weight around her middle, where she was usually dangerously thin.

I looked at Blue, holding his battered toy. My throat constricted. Whose bed would he hide under in that smoky house?

"Bye," Pearl burbled happily.

"Okay," I stammered feebly. "I guess I'll see you at the wedding tomorrow."

She sketched a wave, turning towards the door.

"Don't forget your dress, Pearl," Momma said from my hemline. "It's on the table. We'll see you tomorrow at nine."

It was clear that Momma was concluding a prior argument, one held outside my hearing, because Pearl rolled her eyes. She gave the top of Momma's head a furious look, then stomped across the room and retrieved her pale pink dress. She jammed it carelessly into the box with her "Tell Your Boyfriend I Said Thanks" T-shirt and, probably, some of Abra's hairbrushes.

Momma stuck me again.

"I'm out of here," Pearl said firmly. She seized Blue by the arm and dragged him with her. Right before the screen door slammed behind her, Pearl called back, "I'm serious, Momma. I might not be there tomorrow. I could feel real good about that."

Soon after we heard Pearl gunning her car in the driveway. I thought about Blue again and looked down at Momma. She shook her head, her lips pressed into a tight, white line. The places where she had poked me began to throb like bee stings.

# 19

The next morning Momma and I were eating oatmeal when we heard swearing and voices from the porch.

"What was that?" Momma asked.

We watched the door, like two people waiting for a storm to break. Then I heard Taylor: "Just calm down, Pearl, we're almost there."

The next moment the door banged open, and Taylor and Pearl stumbled in. Pearl wore only one shoe and was so drunk she couldn't stand on her own. She wore the pink dress Momma had sewn for her, but it was ripped on one shoulder and the hem was black with mud.

I jumped up to help Taylor, who seemed to be losing his grip on Pearl. I got her slung at me for my efforts and almost fell to the floor. Pearl seemed to lose consciousness just then. Under her dead weight, I began to sink. Taylor leapt forward to help me, and we struggled to get Pearl into a chair. Desperately, I looked over at Momma for help. She turned away and went back to her breakfast.

Pearl regained semiconsciousness and we finally managed to put her into a chair beside Momma. She flopped loosely there, like a rag doll. Her eyes fluttered opened and then closed, but she seemed generally all right. Just drunk. Chests heaving, Taylor and I exchanged rueful glances.

"Nice clothes," I observed, wiping sweat from my brow. My baby brother was looking handsome this morning.

Taylor was freshly washed, a little damp and smelling of soap and aftershave. He was dressed in black slacks and a pressed cowboy shirt with silver buttons and pale green trim. He wore black cowboy boots with silver tips and fancy stitching all across the arch. He grinned at me.

Our eyes slid back to Pearl. "Where did you find her?" I asked.

"Walking along the ditch about a mile away from here," he answered, casting a sidelong look at Momma. Momma was now buttering her toast with a fierce sort of calm. She didn't so much as glance at Pearl sitting inches away.

I reached over and touched my sister's forehead. She flinched. Pearl felt damp and feverish. She smelled strangely of mud and tar. I felt her hair. That was damp, too.

Taylor looked around apprehensively. "We better not let Abra see her. She'll pitch a fit."

"Lovell's sisters came before dawn. She's already left with them," Momma said calmly, taking a bite of toast.

I went over to the sink for a damp cloth. When I tried wiping Pearl's face with it, she began to giggle. Eventually she giggled and squirmed so much that she slid out of her chair onto the kitchen floor and wrapped her arms around my legs. "I'm a little dizzy," she said apologetically.

Momma took a final sip of coffee. She slammed the cup down and it shattered. The noise was so sudden that we all jumped and stared, as if someone had fired a gun in our Sunday morning kitchen. We stared at her in shocked silence. Pearl began to giggle again. Momma swept the pieces off the table into her hand. She rose and discarded them in the trash can under the sink. Nobody said a word until she broke the silence.

"Taylor," Momma commanded, as if she were telling us to clean our rooms, "will you please pick your sister up off the floor."

Cheerfully, Taylor scooped Pearl up. "Don't worry, Momma. Pearl just started celebrating Abra's wedding a little early, that's all."

Pearl began to cry deep, maudlin sobs. She wiped her hand across her eyes. "I'm not crying because I'm sad," she sobbed. "I just can't help it when I'm drunk."

Someone knocked at the door. Almost glad for the distraction, I ran to answer it.

≈

Standing on our front porch was Lily Tippleson. Now that I had seen her son, I could tell the resemblance between the two. Lily, however, was much, much thinner. Her face was a serious pink and she was twisting a Kleenex to death in her hands. I stepped out onto the porch, not inviting her in. She watched me warily.

"Am I interrupting something?" she asked, beginning with a slight nervous flutter.

"Yes," I told her coolly. "Today is my sister's wedding."

"I see," she faltered. "What I have to say won't take long."

"Fine."

"I've come to apologize," she said simply. "Your lawyer said maybe we could clear this up if I came over in person and said how sorry I was."

"My lawyer?"

She nodded. "Mr. McCreedy."

"Shepherd McCreedy?"

"Yes, he said that if I apologized you'd understand that I wasn't making any accusations against your family to the school. I had no intention to slander your niece. You just have to understand that I care very deeply about my son."

"Shepherd McCreedy told you to come over here and apologize?"

"Yes."

I pretended that I was scratching my nose so that I could hide my smile behind my hand. Before I could say anything, however, Pearl pushed past me, almost knocking me over on her way down to the sidewalk, where she vomited noisily into Momma's rose bed. Momma must have been trying to change Pearl's clothes, because she only wore a bra and a muddy slip.

Engel's mother drew back so far she pressed against the porch wall. Her face grew redder, like some unseen person was choking her. My sister continued to empty her stomach.

Momma appeared on the porch. At the sight of Lily, Momma froze. She looked from the woman to me, her eyes boring into mine. As for Lily, she edged herself off the porch and without another word turned and hurried down the sidewalk to the driveway.

I wanted to say something biting, hurl some insult after her, but a sudden thought distracted me. I stared at Pearl, still heaving into the flower bed.

I ran down the stairs and jerked her upright. "Pearl," I demanded, trying to look straight into her bleary eyes, "where's Blue?"

She tried to pull away, but I held on and shook her. She groaned.

"Blue," I repeated, "where is he?"

Pearl wiped her mouth with her hand. "I dropped him off at Jackie's last night. My girlfriend. He's fine."

Relieved, I let her go. She staggered and almost fell.

It was only then that I felt my mother's eyes drilling into the back of my head. Steeling myself, I turned to face her.

Momma's voice trembled with rage. "Why are you all trying so hard to ruin your sister's wedding? Do you want her to be ashamed of us? Is that what you want?"

Of course there was no response to that. I stood frozen, like a deer being shined by a hunter. Pearl retched dryly behind me, finally empty.

Taylor appeared in the doorway. "Constance just called," he said. "She needs someone to come over and help with the food."

"I'll go," I volunteered quickly.

# 20

I was so anxious to get out of Momma's way that it didn't hit me until I reached the end of the driveway; spending the morning with Constance would be an equal but separate sort of discomfort. My step slowed a little, but inevitably it carried me down the road and up Constance's dirt driveway.

The two houses looked particularly rundown today. So much white paint had chipped off my grandmother's house that its true color was now gray. Constance's house seemed to be heading in the same direction. Sitting in the driveway, though, a clean and jolting red, was Tea's old car. Constance was leaning into it, making room in the backseat. Every time I saw her, I had a sick feeling that I was going to go mad and blurt out the truth. I hated keeping their secret for Mason and Tea and wondered if Constance knew—if she could sense it. And wondered if it gave my brother some secret kind of pleasure, seeing his wife in that car. I wondered if he was laughing at her. That revolted me the most. I considered slinking off, Momma be damned, but Constance straightened just then and saw me. She smiled and came right over and hugged me. She didn't seem to notice that I shrank away. Part of me, in my head, was running, fleeing as fast as I could, disappearing like a lunatic into the corn.

The rest of me followed Constance up to the house, while she patted my arm and smiled. "That woman, Lily, was over today. She apologized for everything."

She squeezed me one more time and released me. "You really did take care of everything." The simple gratitude in Constance's eyes made me want to seep right into the earth.

"I'm so glad you're here," she said, steering me by the elbow into her kitchen. Inside, every surface was piled high with food in various stages of preparation. Constance had a veritable wall of casseroles stacked near the table. She smiled ruefully at the scene and said, "It's amazing how one happy bride can make such a mess for everyone else. You wouldn't believe the hamburger I went through the day my youngest sister, Regina, married."

I felt Jordan's presence before I saw her. She was in the living room, and I could tell she was supposed to be supervising several of her brothers. She wasn't doing a good job of it, since two of the younger ones were crying and the five-year-old appeared to be chewing on the carpet. Jordan didn't seem to notice. Cartoons were playing on the television, but Jordan just stood there staring off into space. She was so tall and thin, so remote, she reminded me of an antenna of some kind. I wondered what she was picking up.

Mason emerged from the bathroom just then, his hair combed and damp. He looked awkward in the clean clothes that he was already sweating through. He grinned at me. I turned my back on him.

As Constance brushed past him, he reached out and caught her hand. He squeezed it a little. She stood on her tiptoes and pecked him on the cheek. My stomach tightened. I was surprised that things didn't blow up more often in Mason's house. That the horses didn't run off, straining for the horizon, every day. I glanced over at Jordan. She was still staring blankly, a few feet away from her brothers and the television, receiving transmissions from deep space.

Smiling, Mason turned to me and said, "Wanna hear a joke about a wedding? I figure it's appropriate, considering the day and all."

"Sure," I said, conscious of how tight my smile was over my teeth.

Mason sat down at the table and pulled his coffee cup towards him. He leaned back in his chair. "See," he began, "there were these two Swedes, a man and a woman. They'd been shacked up together for years. They must have had a dozen kids. One day they decided they really should get around to getting married.

"The minister was real happy they'd finally decided to tie the knot, but he told them that in cases like this, where the man and woman were already living together, the Church asked that they live apart until the marriage. But since they had all those kids, they could keep living together if they agreed to give up sex for a month.

"The minister said he'd call every week to check on their progress."

Mason always gestured expansively when he told a joke. He seemed to take up the whole kitchen. Constance pulled a bunch of carrots from the refrigerator and began to trim and peel them for the vegetable tray.

"After the first week," Mason continued, "the minister called and asked them how they were doing. The man says, 'Well, you know it's been real hard. But I think we can hold out.'

"Two weeks later, when the minister called, things looked a little more glum.

The minister told them to keep up the good work.

"By the time the third week came around, things didn't look good at all. When the minister asked what had happened, the big Swede explained. 'Well, you know, we was doing real good. We went three weeks without sex and then the other day Ma was leaning into the freezer to get some ice cream. It was one of those floor freezers, and she had to bend down real far, all the way to the bottom, and when I saw her there like that, boy, I just couldn't help myself.'

"'Well,' the minister sighed and shook his head. 'I'm afraid this won't do. I'm afraid you're no longer welcome in our Church.'

"The big Swede heaved a huge sigh and said, 'I don't think we're welcome in that grocery store anymore either.'" When he finished laughing, Mason winked at me. I felt like throwing something at him. All around us on the counters were jars of Constance's homemade pickles. They looked nice and solid. Her father's laughter caught Jordan's attention. She seemed to notice us for the first time and studied us carefully.

"Taylor told me that one earlier." Mason whistled. "He was high as a kite last night."

"Not anymore, he's not," I said wearily, thinking back on the scene at Momma's house.

Mason scratched his beard and raised his eyebrows.

"Momma's already accused us of trying to ruin the wedding," I explained. "Pearl showed up drunk and looking like hell."

The smile slowly eased off my brother's face. He shook his head and said, "I'll go on over there." He pulled his dirt-caked cap down over his clean hair.

The phone rang. Mason answered it. His face turned serious and flat. Then he nodded and hung up the phone. "Pearl left Blue sleeping in a booth at Riordan Chagall's bar last night. Riordan's wife just found him when she came in to clean."

I stared at him, shocked. "Pearl told me she left him at her friend's," I blurted out in protest.

Mason shook his head. "She must have forgot. She does that when she drinks," he added matter-of-factly. "Or she lied. She does that, too. Momma wants me to go get him. Wanna ride with me?"

I was already out the door. Mason had to jog to catch up with me in the driveway. He slung himself into the car as I started to pull out onto the road. "Slow down, sister," he said. "Riordan says he's fine."

I was fuming. "Why haven't you done anything about this? Why hasn't Momma? What are you waiting for? Blue to go missing?"

"Momma's tried," Mason answered seriously. "She's done everything she can short of calling the law. Hell, we've all tried to help Pearl out."

"How?" I sneered. "You been screwing her, too?"

Mason's face turned an angry red, but he said nothing.

I pushed the gas pedal to the floor.

≈

Riordan Chagall's bar was a squat structure made of cinder block. His gravel parking lot was half an acre at least, but come Friday night people would still have to park in the ditch along the highway. This morning the lot was empty and bleak. We drove right up by the door and climbed out.

Mason caught my arm as I reached for the door handle. We hadn't spoken the whole trip, but now it seemed he had something he wanted to tell me.

"You know," he said somberly, "you may think I'm a sonofabitch, Kat, but at least I've never done this. Never left my kids in a bar."

Mason released my arm and tested the door. It was unlocked. He held it open for me. Feeling oddly mollified, I stepped past him into the gloom of the bar.

≈

Riordan and Lew Chagall stood by the bar. Riordan was nearing sixty now, but still a big man. He wore a leather vest over his round belly. His bushy beard and long braided hair were white.

Lew only came up to his father's shoulder, but he was tough and lean. He had a seriously mean face, and his skin had the deep, leathery tan of a year-round outdoor laborer. He wore his hair short and slicked back.

Riordan and Lew squinted through the gloom at Mason and me. "Well, fuck me," Lew said in obvious surprise, when he saw me.

Riordan smiled. He gave me a sweaty hug as I came to the bar. It was like being wrapped in a piece of raw steak. He smelled of beer and smoke, and I couldn't tell if it was from last night or this morning. The fond look in his eye was undeniable.

I looked away.

This bar had been Tea's second home. She'd worked here as long as I could remember. Even when she wasn't working, she was here until late, talking with the regulars, playing pool, getting slowly but steadily drunk. More often than not, I tagged along. I was there the night Lew introduced Tea to his cousin, Billy Chagall.

Lew was still staring at me as if I'd just risen from my grave when Blue came running out from behind the bar. He hugged my legs and buried his face in my thigh. I scooped the boy up into my arms. He smiled, tired, and touched my face.

I looked anxiously into his eyes for some sign of deep hurt or lasting damage. He was damp and sleepy, but otherwise none the worse for wear. I felt the knot of tension I'd been carrying in my chest uncoil like a snake and slide out of me.

Clutching Blue, I let Mason make our apologies and started for the door. Lew followed me out, not speaking as he watched me settle Blue into the car. When I straightened, Lew handed me the boy's shoes. "I found these in the bathroom," he said awkwardly. "He's missing his socks, though. I don't know where they went."

"Thank you," I said.

I was surprised at how hard this meeting was for the man. I'd known Lew for a long time. He was even my date for Tea's wedding. I was just sixteen then. Now he hooked his thumbs nervously into his belt and said quietly, "This is the second time Pearl's left him here."

I frowned and glanced from Lew to my nephew in the backseat. Out in the light, his face was gray and drawn. He seemed to be ready to doze off. It'd been a long night for him.

"It's bad with your sister, Kat," he told me sadly. "She's worse than your old man."

My throat was tight. I nodded.

Mason emerged from the bar. He and Lew shook hands. We got in the car and drove away, leaving Lew alone in the dusty lot.

We were halfway back to his place when Mason said, "I haven't talked with Lew in years." He was silent for a moment, watching the corn slide by outside the car window.

"It's funny how things get away from you, isn't it?" Mason spoke again. "Lew was a pallbearer at Billy's funeral. After the ceremony, Tea, Lew, Riordan, and I went back to the bar. We closed the bar down and just sat and drank." Mason suddenly shuddered. "I don't think I've ever seen two people as bombed as Lew and Tea that night."

Surprised, I looked over at Mason. He watched the road, not looking at me as he spoke. "Billy's first wife died, too. Must be three years ago now. Their kids live with her parents."

He shook his head. "It's strange that they're all gone now. All those years of fighting and hurt. Can't think of three people who hurt each other more. And now they're all gone . . . " Mason trailed off sadly. "They're all just gone," he repeated.

≈

Back at Mason's, I scrambled from the car. I wanted to get away from my brother before something shattered the tenuous peace growing between us. He must have felt it, too, and barely waved as he drove off to Momma's.

I carried Blue into the house. Amazingly, Constance was still chopping vegetables. She smiled at me in relief when she saw Blue.

Jordan was still playing the ineffectual guardian of the living room. One of the boys now had a bloody nose. I plopped Blue down among his wrestling, squalling, laughing, TV-watching cousins and returned to the kitchen. Smiling, Constance handed me a knife. I suddenly felt the need to hack and slice.

≈

Constance and I worked mostly in companionable silence, smearing cream cheese onto tiny sandwiches, adding marshmallows to Jell-O, and making deviled eggs. Occasionally we spoke about the kids, Jordan, and Abra's wedding. Constance turned on an old radio over the sink. Randy Travis sang mournfully to us about love while we butchered celery. The morning heated up and turned into early afternoon. Taylor made a few trips back and forth, carrying food up to the house.

He reported that Pearl was sitting upright in a chair, calmly drinking coffee. Mason had taken over setting up the tables and things for the reception. Momma had wandered off and sat herself down under Tea's old apple tree. It was amazing how much food Constance and I generated in a short amount of time. We ran out of space on the counters, so we packed the food in coolers. Constance let me carry these out to Tea's car. I packed them into the backseat and trunk. The car gleamed today. It looked as if the kids had scrubbed it down from fender to bumper for the wedding.

When I got back to the kitchen, as if reading my mind, Constance said, "Jordan and the boys cleaned it for the wedding."

I stared out the screen door at the car. "Did you ever think of having it painted?" Cherry red didn't seem like Constance's color.

She looked surprised. "No, I like that red. It reminds me of Tea. I like to think that Tea and I were close, in a manner of speaking," she said softly.

Picking up my knife, I halved one of Constance's homemade pickles.

"I think Tea knew I was a friend," she continued. "I cared more than most, at any rate. I wasn't born into this family. I always thought that gave me a little distance, you know, to see things clearer. People just got used to thinking about Tea in a certain light. Sometimes she enjoyed it, but sometimes I could tell she felt real trapped by it."

Constance drained another jar of pickles. "No one in this town had an ounce of sympathy for Tea," she said sadly. "You take what happened with her and Billy Chagall. She was still in high school when she started up with him. And he was a grown man and a teacher. He knew better, but everyone acted like it was Tea's fault he did all that to his wife."

Constance stopped slicing pickles and gazed out the window at the car. Then she said at last, "Everybody, especially Billy, acted like he was some great thing for Tea. God's gift. But you know, he really just made it all worse. He never could decide where he wanted to be. And every time he left Tea, she drank from the misery of it. Then when she was on her last legs, suddenly he'd come back to save her. And when they were together, she drank for fear of losing him again."

I stared at Constance. Evidently, Mason's and my trip to Chagall's bar had stirred up memories for her as well. For a while we made casseroles in silence, mixing can after can of cream of mushroom soup with noodles and rice and hamburger. When this was done, Constance asked, "I never thanked you for giving me that car, did I?"

Feeling awkward, I said, "Mason did all the work on that car. He put a lot of time into it."

"No matter that," Constance said firmly, brushing the idea away as she scraped bits of wet vegetable from her cutting board. "It was Tea's car. She left it to you."

I wanted desperately for this conversation to end. "It's all right," I stammered, feeling my face get hot.

"The car's worth some money. It's in good shape." Constance rinsed her knife under the tap. "I've seen families get ugly over a lot less. Someone dies, it seems to shake people up and they start fighting over just about anything."

I felt so uncomfortable I could have run. The crazy urge to blurt out my secret rose in me again. I wedged myself between the refrigerator and the counter so that I wouldn't. I was out of things to chop. I reached for another jar of homemade pickles; it felt solid and cool in my hand. For some reason it calmed me. "Did you do all this canning yourself?" I asked, opening the jar.

Constance allowed me to change the subject. "This last year I did," she said. "Used to be that your momma, Tea, and I would get together and do it all in one day. Now it's just me." Constance grimaced. "But remember the last time we all did it together. Boy, that was a mess. There was so much to do. I'd never seen things grow like they did that summer."

My knife slipped. One moment I was fine, the next I was bleeding all over the pickle tray and feeling faint. Constance gasped and put her hand to her heart. We just stood there staring at each other for a moment. I'd never been good with blood, especially my own. When I started to wobble, Constance woke up and led me into the bathroom, where I settled gratefully on the edge of the tub.

Strangely, when Constance poured the iodine in the cut and it stung like hell, I started to feel better. It distracted me at least from thinking about Tea and Mason. I could finally look Constance in the eyes. I started to cry. Constance smiled apologetically as my blood and the iodine ran down the side of the tub and into the drain. "Iodine stings more than that other stuff. But I use iodine because of Jordan," she explained. "I can't imagine how she does it, but that girl never gets little scrapes or cuts. She always cuts herself deep and bad. Mason laughs and says it's part of being a kid. I think he's just tired of paying the emergency room bills, but I'm always terrified of infection."

Constance handed me some toilet paper to dry my eyes. "She's not like you, though," she smiled, misinterpreting my tears. "Once Jordan got thrown off a horse into a barbwire fence. She was maybe eight years old. She didn't so much as cry out."

I blushed. Constance took the toilet paper from me and dabbed gently at my eyes. "I know you don't like to talk about it," she said softly, "but I'm really glad you came home, Kat. Thank you for helping today. And thanks again for the car. It means all the freedom in the world to me."

The sting in my hand must have died down, because I was having trouble looking Constance in the eye again. I felt the redness of my checks deepen. Since it felt like I needed to say something, I said, "Mason put a lot of work into the car. With everything he's replaced, it's almost like he already owned it."

To my surprise, Constance laughed. "You know I used to tell him that when Tea was alive. Seemed like he built that car three times over."

I gave her a quick look. Constance fished some rolled-up gauze and tape out of the medicine cabinet. She sat down on the closed toilet and began wrapping my hand.

"It seems silly now that she's gone," she said apologetically, "but Mason and I used to fight over that car. It seemed like I was drowning in kids and housework, and where was he? Off at your mother's tinkering with that car. And for what? He never even so much as talked to Tea when she was around. And she never paid him a dime. But the minute some little thing was busted on that car, off he'd go. I was always sending Jordan off to look for him." Constance shook her head with regret. "It seems silly now with all the trouble that happened. I feel selfish."

Constance looked up at me and our eyes met for one long, painful moment. I felt my face working, trying to disguise my guilty expression, and looked away, unable to think of anything to say, so I watched my blood pool in the drain.

I never meant to tell her. Constance was holding my hand, bandaging my wound. Somehow the knowledge just leaked out, without my saying a word, moving from my body to hers by some process like osmosis. Or maybe it didn't happen all that suddenly. Maybe all along, since Mason first told me, I'd been looking like a woman with a secret and Constance had been wondering all that while, guessing. Soon it got silent, like the moment after a train rushes through and then drops out of hearing.

Constance knew. She kept bandaging my hand anyway. She kept on going and going, trying to stuff everything back into place, wrap it all up so tightly that it wouldn't move again.

I began to lose feeling in my hand from lack of circulation. "We should get going," I said hastily, trying to keep my voice calm. "It's not long until the wedding."

Constance nodded and taped off the bandage.

≈

I had my clothes for the wedding in a brown paper sack out in the trunk of my car. I retrieved the bag and dressed in Jordan's sparse room. Jordan herself had disappeared, abandoning her post as baby-sitter.

Since the clothes Blue was wearing smelled like beer and cigarettes, Constance found him a spare pair of pants and a shirt. They belonged to her youngest. They were too big for Blue, but he liked the cartoon character on the shirt. He plucked happily at it, while I scooped him up and carried him to the car.

Constance walked me out to the porch. We both kind of just stopped at the sight of Tea's car in the driveway. Constance didn't come any farther than that with me.

Still, when she spoke her voice was steady. "You go on to the church," she said as if nothing were the matter. I glanced quickly at her. She didn't exactly smile, but her face softened. For a moment I doubted what had just happened between us in the bathroom. From Constance I expected tears and weeping. "I have to wait for my sister," Constance explained easily. "She's going to watch the boys. When she gets here, I'll load up the rest of the vegetables and all the presents and bring them over to your mother's. I'll probably be a little late getting to the church." It all seemed logical, so I buckled Blue into the backseat and prepared to leave. Constance waved good-bye from the front porch as I started the ignition.

The car door on the passenger side opened and Jordan slipped in. "I'll ride with Aunt Katherine," she called out to her mother.

Constance nodded, waved good-bye again, and stepped inside her graying house.

≈

When we turned onto the road, Jordan fixed her luminous eyes on me. She was wearing the pale lavender dress my mother had sewn for her. Her hair was brushed and twisted into a loose bun at the nape of her neck. It made her neck look even longer and more graceful.

With a shock, I realized that she was wearing makeup, but not in the way kids do. Neither in the way I'd seen her mother and my sisters wear it, layering on blush and eye shadow, creating strange angles. Jordan had applied soft beiges and pale blushes to her cheeks. She had blended away her few freckles with powder. She wore a delicate pale pink on her lips, from a lipstick that I knew must bear a name involving the words *coral* or *kiss*.

I pictured her in the store alone, facing down the saleswoman, choosing her own colors with deliberation. She had not asked for any help on this. She had not come to me. To have asked any of her other aunts or mother would have been simply impossible for a child like Jordan. Alone, she had sat down in front of a mirror and made up the woman she wanted to be. Perhaps she had spent hours practicing at the vanity table near the foot of my bed, floating in the sweet scent of Tea's perfumes. It frightened me, the depths to which I did not understand this child.

Once we had pulled out of the driveway and out of her mother's sight, Jordan unbuckled her seat belt and turned so that she could watch all of me. Her scrutiny was unnerving. I couldn't imagine that she knew what had just happened between her mother and me. I wasn't even sure that I understood what had taken place. But I was nervous. Sometimes Jordan reminded me of myself as a child, which is to say that she was born with a sense for the truth. I had always known when my mother was the saddest, where my father hid his bottles all over our house, and when storms were brewing, like when Abra got pregnant.

So I searched desperately for a safe topic. I wanted to get Jordan talking, thinking, turning her intelligent eyes inward and not on me. "How come you never call me Kat, like everyone else? You make me feel old when you call me Aunt Katherine."

Jordan leaned back in the seat and put her feet up on the dash. I felt a definite drop in temperature the minute her eyes looked away. "I guess because you never looked like a cat to me."

"What do I look like?" I asked.

"Like a bird," she said. "Like one of those big old black crows, flying over the corn fields."

"Thanks," I said dryly.

"No, it's not a bad thing," she said, smoothing her skirt out across her lap. "People don't like crows, but I do. I watch them from my windows, out in the cornfield. They have the biggest wings and they're all one thing, you know. They're black all over, even their beaks and their eyes. Crows make up their minds to be the biggest, blackest birds around and never think twice about it. I like that."

# 21

The Evangelical Church of the Holy Redeemer was lost in backwater. I had never been there. For a while, I thought Jordan and I would never reach it. We seemed to make no progress on Old Comfort Road. The road merely dragged out to its natural conclusion, the edge of the flat world, and not the little church Abra had promised. Like everywhere, the road was walled in with corn. We were nearing the harvest, and the corn was at its tallest.

I kept glancing in the mirror behind me as I drove. I had this flash of insight that Abra had determined to get me lost. She had meant to distract her family in this maze of country roads and cornstalks, while her wedding progressed quietly elsewhere. I kept looking in the mirror, hoping to see a familiar car kicking up dust. None did.

Eventually, the church appeared as promised. It was after four o'clock by the time we arrived. The church wasn't much more than a pole barn at the end of a gravel driveway, barely scratched out of the fields itself. The building was narrow and windowless. The lot was filled with a dozen cars, but otherwise empty except for my family.

Pearl stood there, upright and apparently sober, her arms wrapped tightly around her chest. She was wearing one of Momma's church dresses, and seemed oddly diminished by the slightly fussy collar and bows. Taylor, Mason, and Momma stood nearby in a clump, casting uncertain glances at the church.

Pearl gave a dramatic cry of relief when I lifted Blue out of the car. I held the little boy close, trying to resist the urge to beat his mother down flat. But to my surprise, Blue reached out his thin arms for his mother, struggling a little in my grasp. Reluctantly I let him go to her. She hugged him, and he tucked his head comfortably under her chin.

Momma gave me a hard look. Evidently I hadn't been forgiven for this morning, even though I wasn't sure what I'd done.

I glanced quickly away at the church. The door was closed, and despite the many cars in the driveway, no voices could be heard from inside. The quiet in the yard was oppressive.

Whatever their quarrels elsewhere and in other times, right then some instinct made my family herd together. Mason stood protectively near my mother. Jordan bumped up against me as I walked, a soft, steady bumping like a boat tethered to a dock. Even Taylor and Pearl linked arms. Blue was now clinging to his mother, a worried crease on his brow.

"He's never been in a church," Pearl whispered to me, when Jordan and I approached. She added proudly, "I never even had him baptized."

Momma shot Pearl a steely look. Pearl avoided her eyes.

We all stood and stared at the closed church door, alert for some sound, some sign of welcome.

The wind picked up and the corn waggled its heavy stalks at us, like accusing fingers. Finally, Mason turned to me and asked, "Where's Constance?"

I knew that Jordan was watching me closely. My own saliva suddenly seemed a little hard to swallow. I tried to school my features into a blank, neutral expression. "She should be here any minute," I said, trying to sound calm and matter-of-fact.

Silently, they all turned, looking back down the road I'd come on, expecting Constance to be there. There was nothing.

"We should go in," I said as that hard little knot began to form in my stomach once again. I linked arms with Taylor and began to walk with him. Pearl followed so close behind us that she stepped on my heels. Mason looped his arm through Momma's. Jordan lagged behind, then suddenly loped up to Taylor's side and grabbed his other hand, swinging it wildly and smiling like a flirt.

The church was white—the door frame, the door, even the cement of the front steps had been painted white. The place had a new feel to it. The lumber hadn't mellowed yet and everything, the rough cross above the doorway included, seemed to still be on its first coat of paint.

At the door we halted once again. Taylor cast an unsure glance at me. Once again silence. We stared at each other. It seemed inappropriate to knock. None of us dared walk right in. Then Blue, perched on his mother's hip, lost a shoe. It fell to the front steps with a large bang that made us all jump.

The tension in us broke. Taylor grinned and we all broke out laughing, suddenly at ease. Even Momma giggled and squeezed Mason's arm. We laughed so hard we leaned even closer together, looking for physical support. I found myself hugging both my brothers, with Jordan somewhere behind me clinging to the skirt of my dress.

The door to the church flew open. The thinnest man I'd ever seen, in an ill-fitting gray suit, peered out of the shadows at us. His sternest expressions couldn't stop our laughing. We had snapped. Our nervousness had overtaken us, and no thin man could stand in the way of it.

It was Momma who finally wiped her eyes and, arranging herself neatly on Mason's arm, nodded at the man and managed a hello. She started to enter the church with as much dignity as she could muster. The thin man stood in her way.

Momma drew herself up. "We're the bride's family," she said crisply and plowed past him. Like a combine through the corn, Momma swept to the front of the church. We trailed in her wake.

Inside, the church was as white and silent as outside. The air seemed to carry the musty scent of unclean bodies and windowless spaces, where the oxygen could not circulate. Too many people breathed the same air. Too many people murmured the same prayer, too often. The Jesus nailed to the cross at the front of the church looked weary. I bet, that like us, he wouldn't have been there either, given a choice.

As we walked down the aisle, the small congregation of perhaps forty solemn men, women, and children turned in their seats to watch us wordlessly. We seemed to have interrupted something.

The minister was already at the front. My sister and Lovell sat in chairs on either side of him. A Bible was open in his hands. And I felt as if a faint word were frozen on the air, but couldn't grasp it. The mouths of the congregation were sealed shut, puckered faintly like old scars.

Abra's head was turned down in prayer. She didn't look up when we entered. Lovell shifted his weight from side to side in the chair. He knew we were there, but his eyes stayed elsewhere.

The church had kindly left us five rows of pews at the front. More than we needed. We filled the first one. Jordan sat in the pew behind us by herself. In our isolated little island, I could feel eyes fixed on the back of our heads. None of us squirmed, though, I noticed with satisfaction. We all stared straight ahead.

The minister nodded at us and closed his Bible. He bent and whispered something to Abra. She opened her eyes and looked up, though not at us. Lovell smiled at Momma. Momma chose to focus her attention on arranging the pleats of her dress.

Someone coughed. I had the feeling again that we had interrupted something grave, the sacrificing of a virgin or the burning of a martyr. Who the hell knew what those people did way out in the middle of nowhere, isolated by fifty miles of corn on every side?

The minister placed one hand on Abra's shoulder and the other on Lovell's. "Perhaps we should begin," he said. Turning towards us, he nodded. "You are welcome in our church."

Somewhere behind me, I heard the thin man close the door of the church with a solid whump. Nervously, I strained to hear any noise that sounded suspiciously like a bolt being drawn.

The ceremony was conducted without music. Near the middle of it all, Lovell's sisters emerged from some private recess of the church, with three men accompanying them. They formed a half-moon around my sister and Lovell. It was impossible to see through them. The minister droned on. Blue climbed onto my lap. He began to play with his shoelaces. Pearl rolled her eyes at me and giggled when Lovell's sisters emerged in their heavy white gowns with little pink rose bouquets clutched in their hands. I was still in no mood for Pearl. I ignored her.

Halfway through the ceremony, something strange flicked in and out of my vision. Over my left shoulder, I could see Jordan opening her purse. She drew out her compact, examined her face in its little mirror, and powdered her nose. A sparkle of light, reflected from the mirror, danced like a flame on the church's ceiling.

The minister's eyes flicked onto Jordan, then back to Lovell.

Jordan screwed her lipstick out to its full length. With a smooth and flowing gesture, she began to paint and repaint her lips. She admired her work in the mirror once more, twisting her head in all directions, scraping a little bit of lipstick off her front tooth. With her brilliant lips, she made a pouting kissing face at her own image. She coated her eyelashes with mascara. She applied eyeliner. And then, as the grand finale to her stellar performance, she reached up and, one by one, pulled the pins from her hair. Jordan shook her mane out around her shoulders, like a movie star. She pulled a brush from her bag and began to groom her thick hair. Down and down the brush went. Her hair was straight and thick like the mane of her horse.

Every eye in the congregation was riveted on the sight.

Momma didn't seem to notice. Taylor finally did with a quick start. But when he reached out his hand to give Jordan some signal, I neatly trapped it in my own, squeezed it, and smiled at him. By the end of the ceremony, she had done everything but shave her long, long legs in front of those people. Their mouths formed black, empty circles of disbelief.

We rose at the end of the ceremony. As Abra turned toward the congregation and took her first step down the aisle to lead the wedding party out of the church, Jordan clicked her compact closed, with a loud snap.

Abra's eyes widened and she froze, fixing on Jordan a stare that could have stopped a tornado on clear prairie. Oblivious, Jordan slid the compact into her purse. Then, without waiting for Abra to walk past, she slipped out of her pew and sashayed out of the church like a model on a runway. Her long, free hair swished from side to side, like a grown woman's full and heavenly hips. Hesitantly, Abra followed behind, her heavy, white dress hanging all around her like a defeated banner.

# 22

At the reception, Jordan sat on the rail of the porch, swinging her long legs freely over the side. Her heels kept banging into the wood of the porch, giving off a dull thud that she didn't seem to notice. She stared out at the reception with a look on her face that told me she was a greater distance away than anyone thought. I had to touch her shoulder to get her attention.

She grinned at me and slid off her perch. Like me, she'd traded her wedding clothes for jeans and a T-shirt. "Who are those two boys?" she asked. She pointed off somewhere. Turning around, I found Abednego and Samuel at the tip of her finger. "Those are Lovell's sons."

"Where's their mom?" she asked.

"She died."

"I bet they miss her." Jordan stared at the boys a little more, sizing them up. Finally she patted my arm. "I'll see you later, Aunt Katherine," she said, sauntering off in the direction of the two pale boys, who looked to me as if they were hiding from the sun in the shade of Momma's lilac bushes.

I had to squint into the sun to watch her maneuver. She seemed about to walk past her new cousins, then stopped as if she'd just noticed them. Her lips moved as she said hello. I glanced skyward. No angels raced down from heaven to save those boys, but a foursome of crows regally shook out their wings in the elm above Jordan. Lovell must not be in as good with God as he thought.

The reception didn't seem to suit Jordan, because she disappeared after that. So did Lovell's boys. The reception didn't suit me either, and for a long time I sat on the porch, simply watching. Abra's fellow churchgoers settled into the lawn chairs in our front yard as if they were still in their pews at church. They said little, their faces marked with silent disapproval.

Constance's boys and a dozen of their maternal cousins showed up. They poured out of their aunt's car like water from a jug. The boys cut warpaths between the rows of church members, running and screaming at the top of their lungs, playing or dying, I wasn't quite sure which. The church children did not play with our children, but sat serenely at the feet of their elders, looking pale and ill.

The neighbors filed in but didn't stay too long. The women from Momma's work came to eat and seemed determined to outlast the church people. I wasn't sure if this was a gesture of solidarity with Momma or just their love of potato salad. They lined up at the food table, their big hips bumping softly against one another as they moved. In their flowered and polka-dot dresses, the effect was slightly hypnotic, dizzying. Eventually I fled into the house, towards the shelter of my attic, taking the stairs two at a time.

≈

I wouldn't have been surprised to find any other member of my family in Tea's attic. I couldn't blame them for hiding when that was what I was after. But when I found Abra standing there, her skirts hiked up to avoid the dust, a certain dangerous stillness settled over me.

Abra flicked a brief scowl at me. She was standing by a stack of boxes, with Tea's open jewelry chest on top. I could hear its contents softly bumping into each other as her hand swirled among them, creating disorder in the order I had made. Occasionally she took something out and set it on the box beside her. A wave of hot heat spread through me that had nothing to do with the temperature outside.

When I moved closer, I saw that she had a little pile of earrings building up. They were pieces of jewelry that Tea had made from cut glass and vintage beads she collected. She sold them in the galleries downtown. The beads caught the sun and winked at me, red and green and blue tangled in silvery nets. "What are you doing?" There was a silence that buzzed around my ears. It whispered patience.

Abra glanced at me again. "I need some gifts for my bridesmaids. I thought these earrings Tea used to make would do."

I said nothing.

Abra clamped the box shut. "Why not?" she said absently, beginning to sort through the little pile she had made. "They're new. Tea never wore them. It's not like I'm giving them someone else's old jewelry. They were made to be sold. There's even little boxes to put them in. Just like at the store."

"This isn't the mall," I spat out. "Were you even going to ask me?"

Abra's head snapped up. She took a good long look at me for the first time.

Her eyes narrowed. "Oh, come on, Kat," she sneered. "They're just earrings. And besides, they're for my bridesmaids." She stressed the word bridesmaids as her voice rose to a whine.

"No," I said firmly.

"What?" her voice cut sharply.

"No. Thank you for asking, but no, you can't have them." I swept the little piles into my hand and closed a tight fist around them.

Abra held out her open hand and spoke as if she were dealing with a rather dense child. "I really don't have time for this. Just give them to me."

"They're not yours."

Abra clenched her hand. "They're not yours, either. This isn't up to you. This has nothing to do with you." Her voice rose another decibel. "Momma already said I could have them. Now give them to me."

My voice had a quality to it that I didn't recognize, some tone that could have been attributed to Tea once. "We're not kids anymore, Abra. If you want to take something of mine, you can't play favorites with Mom to get it. If you want to hurt me, if you want to steal from me, you have do it yourself."

The muscles in Abra's face tightened and then spasmed.

I still felt calm, but my rage was double Abra's and more. "I'll knock you flat if I ever find you up here again," I hissed. "If I ever catch you touching Tea's things, you'll regret it."

"It's my wedding day," Abra gasped, her voice ragged like a saw. "I can't believe how selfish you are."

"I can't believe how badly I'd like to knock you on your ass." I took a threatening step forward.

Abra's eyes widened in alarm. She took a step back. I took another step forward. "I hated her!" she screamed shrilly. "That bitch, I hated her!" She pushed past me, fleeing from the attic.

I settled the earrings back into their box. I was flushed with victory, but my hands were shaking. Clutching the earrings had made my injured hand bleed again. I stared at the blood, feeling vague and nauseated.

I stumbled to the steps and nearly tripped over a bottle. It made a hollow sound as my foot connected with it. I stared down at it, blinking. It was the vodka bottle I had retrieved from under my bed. It seemed like a long time ago, almost as distant in my memory as the night Tea left it there, ten years or more ago.

The bottle's label was peeling off, but the gold lettering hadn't faded any. There was still maybe a finger of vodka left in it.

I reached down to pick it up, then paused. A soft rustle, maybe a slight change of temperature in the still attic told me that I had another guest. When I straightened, Momma stood at the top of the stairs. She had seen the bottle in my hand. She shook her head in disgust and turned to go. "You know," I said, "Lovell wouldn't give Abra any money for gifts. She was embarrassed not to have anything."

"She should have asked."

"You think Tea wouldn't have given them to her?"

"What do you know about Tea, Momma?" I demanded.

"Quite a lot," she said. "Most of it things you've never had the courage to face."

Momma turned her back on me. I held up the bottle, toasting her exit, and downed the vodka. For a long while, I could hear her high-heeled shoes hitting the steps.

≈

Eventually even the shame of facing Momma couldn't keep me from needing another drink. I started down, only to find Pearl sitting at the head of the second flight of stairs, drinking gin. She shook her head when she saw me. "Abra came running out of there crying not too long ago. Momma followed. I figured you'd be next." She took a tentative sip from her glass, grimaced, and added sugar. "What'd you do this time?" she asked.

Pearl's feet were bare and crusted with mud. She had traded her borrowed dress for a pair of low-slung jeans and a T-shirt that was so small it couldn't be hers. Her eyes were a little cloudy.

After this morning, the last thing I wanted to do was sit and talk with Pearl. Still, I eyed her bottle and wavered.

"Where's Blue?" I asked, trying to keep my voice neutral.

"Asleep under your bed."

I said nothing.

Pearl sloshed some more gin in her glass. "I tried to put him down in Momma's bed, but he wouldn't have it. Figures you'd come home and make my son weird."

It seemed best not to say anything, so I stretched out on the steps beside her and took her bottle. The gin smelled reassuringly chemical, like pine-scented furniture polish. Even the smell of it cleared my head. I took a long drink. "Did the wedding shake him up any?" I asked.

"He'll have nightmares for weeks," Pearl replied flatly. She gave a mock shudder. "So will I. Those people are crazy. Jesus nuts."

We talked trash about Abra's church for a while and passed the bottle back and forth. My head started to feel floaty, and Pearl and I fell into a companionable silence.

"When do I get those boots you promised me?" Pearl said at last.

I drank, not answering.

"A deal's a deal, right?" she persisted. "I told you something about Tea, about Tea screwing Mason, so get the boots."

I tried the concoction in Pearl's glass, feeling the sugar slide down my throat like sandpaper. I shook my head and went back to drinking from the bottle.

"You know what I don't get, Pearl?" I said after awhile. "None of you could stand Tea when she was alive, but now that she's gone it seems like you all want something from her." I took another swallow of gin. "It's disgusting, that's what it is."

Pearl took her bottle back. It sloshed a little onto her front. She cast a bemused look at her wet shirt, but was too far gone to really care. "You never give up, do you, Kat?" She shook her head.

I eyed her suspiciously. "What'd you mean?"

Pearl shrugged and poured herself some more gin. Her unsteady hands dumped sugar on the stairs. "You're all pissed because I said something bad about Tea. But you know what? Keep the damn boots. I don't need them. Tea was trash and that's the truth. She was a cold, mean-hearted bitch and things have been nice and quiet around here since she offed herself."

"What about you?" I asked harshly. "Left your son in any bars lately?"

"Are you saying I'm trash?" Pearl demanded.

"You're a drunk."

To my surprise, Pearl almost smiled, her eyes growing cloudier. "Yeah, guess I am," she said comfortably.

"And a whore too," she added, stretching her legs out on the stairs. She took a long drink from her glass and wiped her chin with the back of her hand. "You know why I named my son Blue, Kat? Because that's all I remember about his daddy. I think he had blue eyes. I don't think I ever knew his name."

I stared at her, at the bottle she held so negligently in her hand, dangling between her legs. I had the uneasy feeling that some part of Pearl was laughing at me. I looked away. Silently, I rose to go.

"I'm serious," she called after me. "Keep the damn boots. I don't want anything that belonged to Tea. Why would I? We never meant a thing to her. Not even you, Kat."

"How would you know?"

Pearl laughed. "I know a lot. More than you, big sis. Where have you been all these years? You missed the best part of the show hiding out in California. Or was it Louisiana? Who the hell knows with you? Took Momma a whole week to find you after Tea died."

I stared at Pearl, not knowing what to say.

She took another drink. "Here's a memory for you, Kat. A real good story. Billy's wife drove up here once, with her kids all packed into the back of the hot car. She cried and begged Tea to let her know where Billy was. Just cried and cried. And Tea wouldn't. Never let out one word."

"So?" I said grimly.

Pearl shook her head. "She was sick, Kat, real sick with lupus. She needed Billy to watch the kids and to talk to them. She was in a lot of pain. Terrible pain."

"I didn't know that," I said softly.

"You don't know a lot."

"But you're the wise drunk, I suppose," I said acidly, turning to leave again. "No thanks, Pearl. I've had enough of that already for this life."

"You know, Kat," she said quietly, "sometimes the things you love about a person keep you from deciding if they're trash or not. That's the awfulest thing, to go on like that. To go on loving trash and not knowing it.

"You don't know it, but I do, so I'm gonna tell you once and for all. Tea was real garbage. She was a waste of whatever talent God gave her and she's a waste of your love, Kat. All those people that bought her paintings—if they knew what kind of person she really was . . . " Pearl shook her head. "They would have burned down McCreedy's gallery a long time ago."

"That's not true," I said hoarsely.

Pearl shook her head. "If it's not true, then where have you been all these years? Where were you when Tea killed herself?"

My eyes burned and my throat was too constricted to talk.

Pearl nodded, satisfied. She'd finally struck a blow that hit home. She smiled at me. "That got you, didn't it?"

Pearl hauled herself up, holding onto the railing. "Now, if you'll excuse me," she said stumbling past me, "I'm going to go pass out on the bed my son's sleeping under." She pressed the gin into my unwilling hand. "Have a drink, Kat. Drink the whole damn bottle. Maybe it'll help."

"Tea didn't kill herself," I called after her. "It was an accident."

Pearl barked out a short, hard laugh. It almost knocked her off her feet. She steadied herself against the wall and shot a pitying look back at me. "People don't die that way by accident, Kat."

# 23

My father ended up incontinent. Every morning we'd wake to the sight of him sleeping on the living room floor, wet with his own urine. Momma tried to make him drink out on the porch, but in winter she was afraid of him falling asleep and freezing to death. So she tried to make him quit drinking completely.

Despite Momma's best efforts, I'd say that until the day he died my father never had a bottle more than five inches away from him. He was so good at hiding bottles that more than eight years after his death, Momma and Abra still found bottles at the back of cupboards and closets. Me, I'd known all along where the old man laid in his stash, but never bothered to tell anyone. As a teenager, it had given me a lot of pleasure to be able to outsmart my father.

When I finished Pearl's bottle, I found myself needing another drink. Right away. And I knew where to find one. In an old roll of carpet in the basement there was a bottle. There was another in the basement closet, hidden among ragged tennis racquets and snowshoes. In the living room there was one in the piano and others in the heating vents. The entire house was like this, the outside as well, a minefield of forgotten booze. If we ever caught fire, we'd go off like a bomb.

Like a crazed squirrel, my father had even buried bottles along the fence posts in the far pasture. He'd tried to bury some out among the roots of Tea's apple tree, but she wouldn't let him. As I pulled out one dusty bottle after another, I got to thinking how close to insanity my father's whiskey love was.

≈

I made it through the bedrooms and the living room, collecting bottles and drinking as I went. On my way through the dining room, I heard the voices.

Maybe it was that they said my name, or maybe they said my cousin's, but either way, as I was standing in the dining room I heard the voices of Momma's coworkers drifting out from the kitchen. I paused and listened.

For a while all I heard were women's voices, scattered, broken up by the running of water in the kitchen sink and the rattle of dishes. Then the conversation began to float to me in whole strains, complete phrases, accompanied by the hum of the microwave.

"Kat took it real hard," said a voice.

"It's sad, but I could have told you from day one how Tea was gonna end up."

Murmurs.

"Still, it's strange how long it took them to find the body. You'd think someone would've gotten worried sooner. Or called the police, you know."

"Tea was always coming and going," someone said. "Who would notice?"

"Still, can't help thinking that if someone had gone out to check on her sooner, she would've been all right."

"A woman like her? She was never all right." There was a short laugh. "You know what she was like. It was just a matter of time."

Just inside the kitchen Momma had set up a folding table covered with white paper and gold ribbon. All of Abra's gifts were stacked up on it—a pile of sparkling gold and silver paper and vases of flowers. I bumped into it, stumbling a little as I entered the kitchen.

Most people probably would've thrown one of the vases. The glass would have made an impressive crash. Some people would've risked throwing a gift, hoping whatever was inside would shatter and make a point. But I heaved the entire table and sent it crashing to the kitchen floor.

The women stood frozen. I walked into the kitchen on their silence. I tramped right across their disbelief, as if I hadn't noticed it. The water from the flowers seeped through the soles of my sandals. I squished a little when I walked.

Opening the cupboard, I pulled out a glass and found myself holding one of the china teacups Momma and I had washed the other night. I cradled Tea's little cup against my chest. I was hot from drinking and my hands felt too large and unwieldy for something so delicate. I walked out of the kitchen, the silence behind me as solid as ice.

Taylor was standing in the doorway, his face tense, watching me. I faltered a little. Looking over my shoulder, I got a full view of the damage I had done. Momma's friends had backed right up against the walls. Abra's presents lay in a heap, the bent boxes and torn paper growing soggier by the minute. There were petals everywhere.

Funny, I couldn't seem to locate the unmistakable shape of the hibachi I had bought for Abra. I would have thought that it would have made an impressive crash. The complimentary bag of charcoal should have ripped open and been staining the floor black. "Where are the rest of the gifts?" I asked Taylor.

Taylor shook his head and seemed to wobble a little, the way calves do when the brand hits them.

I felt the need to giggle.

Taylor evidently decided to act at that moment, because he took a couple of quick steps toward me and tried to steer me away by my elbow. I wouldn't go.

"I would've thought there'd be more damage," I told him. "Where are the rest of the presents?"

Taylor tried to move me once again. "They're with Constance," he whispered real low. "She hasn't shown up yet."

The women had begun to shift and whisper in the kitchen. Evidently it made Taylor nervous, because he urged in a soft, pleading voice, "Please, Kat, let's go. Let me get you outside and cleaned up."

I patted his cheek. "I just came in for a cup," I explained. I began to gather up all of my father's bottles. I needed a bag, I decided, and weaved back into the kitchen, where Momma's coworkers had begun to show some signs of life, but when I entered the room they again pressed up against the walls, immobilized. It was almost as if the spinning room had pressed them flat, as if we were caught in some sort of powerful centrifugal force. The spinning sensation began to make me feel ill, so I ignored it, concentrating on my task.

Momma kept the grocery bags under the sink. I piled my bottles into one, along with Tea's lone little cup.

Taylor studied me. Then I was falling. It looked to me that he had been expecting that all along, because he was right there at exactly the right moment, holding me up.

"What d'you say we go out to Tea's apple tree and get drunker?" I asked his neck.

So it was agreed.

≈

Taylor kept his arm around me the whole way out there. We walked slowly and carefully, because the ground was so uneven. He kept talking soft and low, and I gladly wrapped my arms around his neck. I liked to hear his voice. He smiled down at me, and it seemed to me that he was glowing a little.

Out by the tree, Taylor hugged me tight one more time and then eased me to the ground. He flopped down beside me and peeked into the bag. Carefully he started sorting through the bottles, sniffing some, brushing dust off others. It looked to me like he was settling in for the duration, so I uncapped a bottle of scotch and lay back on the sun-scorched grass. "I suppose Abra hates us now," I said, looking up at the branches.

"Most likely," he answered, opening a bottle.

"Of course, she always did." I was so far into drinking my liquor straight that there was no longer a burn from it. Taylor still grimaced a little at each sip. "Where's Dinah?"

Taylor shook his head. "She's back up on the reservation. Another funeral."

I gave him a quizzical look.

He settled himself more comfortably in the grass. "You know how I told you before she was up there to bury a great-aunt?"

I nodded.

"Her husband got real sick all of a sudden. He didn't last more than a few weeks without her. It's sad, you know, but all of it is kind of reassuring too. Those two were real old. They lived their whole lives together. Look at Momma and Dad's marriage—all that time together just seemed to make them hate each other more. But Dinah's great-uncle, he loved his wife so much he couldn't live without her."

I uttered a drunken, romantic, exaggerated sigh.

Taylor shot me a suspicious glance. "Go ahead and laugh. But I can't help thinking I'd like to have that with someone. With Dinah."

I reached over and patted his shoulder. "I didn't mean that. I just meant, I couldn't imagine it for me."

"That's surprising."

"Why?"

"I guess because when Tea died we were all so scared of what you'd do. We half thought you'd try something. You know, maybe think about going to visit her."

"You think our cousin is up in some kind of heaven, waiting for me?"

Taylor plucked a handful of grass, then let it scatter. "I don't know what to think. I do know that you loved Tea more than you ever loved any of us. Why was that?"

"It wasn't like it was a choice."

"Then what was it?"

No matter how much I drank, my throat seemed to get drier. "Why do you love Dinah? Why does Mason love Constance?"

Taylor pulled a face. "I find it hard to believe that Mason loves Constance.

If he loved her so much, do you think she would've run off?"

I knew distinctly that if I had been sober, what Taylor just said would've hit me like an electric shock. Instead, the hurt just clicked, like a broken toy, somewhere off in a far corner of my mind. "You think she ran off?" I asked calmly.

"If you were married to Mason, wouldn't you?"

We drank in silence. Finally I said, "Well, if she's gone, she went in Tea's car. She's gone and I don't blame her."

"Mason's out looking for her now." Taylor rummaged for another bottle. Between the two of us, one bottle didn't seem to last very long. The sky started to get dusky.

Taylor squinted at the pink horizon. "Lindstrom's hopping tonight," he said with a grin. "Look at all those people."

It was an old joke of Tea's. She'd been born in Tennessee and had never gotten over the flatness of the prairie.

Sometimes she'd say that you couldn't help but feel a little crazy because of all that emptiness. The thought made me speed up my drinking. We drank with a steady determination for a long while, lounging back on the long grass.

"Where'd you find all this booze?" Taylor asked, his eyes half closed, sleepy.

"Daddy," I explained. "This was his stash." I swished some scotch around in the bottle. "We're finishing off what's left of our father." I toasted my brother silently and drank again, a little of it dribbling out the corner of my mouth and down my chin.

Taylor's eyes widened a little. His mouth turned down in distaste. "That's a strange way of putting it, sis. Pretty creepy actually." A shiver ran through him, like wind through the prairie grass.

I leaned close to him and drained the bottle, reached for another. "Some cultures eat the ashes of their dead. I learned that in college, Anthropology 101. You should take an anthropology class at the community college when you and Dinah get to Colorado."

Taylor stared at me, then at the bottles, then at me again. Resolutely he picked out a bottle and propped it up on a hump of grass beside him. "Let's set this one aside for Dad," he said.

"Suit yourself."

"I hate bourbon anyway."

"So did Dad."

Taylor grinned. "I know."

≈

Hours later, when Mason and Jordan arrived, the sky was definitely done for the day, its brilliant colors faded. Mason stood, quiet and solemn, his hands looped into his wide belt, watching us for a while. Jordan fidgeted beside him, like one of his colts.

Mason pulled off his hat and rolled the brim between his two powerful hands. He beat it against his thigh, absently. "I need you to help me look for Constance," he said, and it seemed to me he got smaller. His shoulders stooped a little.

We stared blearily up at him.

Mason's cap seemed to interest him a lot. He studied it in his hands, turning it over and over as he spoke, like he was looking for it to be something else, his wife maybe.

"Her sisters haven't seen her since this afternoon. No one's seen her since she dropped off the food," Mason continued, clearing his throat. "So I thought we could split up. You know, each of us take the back roads. I think she probably had car trouble," he added, though all of us knew this wasn't true.

Mason bobbed in my vision like a boat way out on the water. "Is she in Tea's car?" I blurted out.

He chewed on my words for a while, then slowly he nodded.

Taylor rolled over. He was looking a little pale in the coming darkness. "I can't drive, Mason," he moaned. "I'm one brick short of being in the shithouse."

Mason's jaw tightened. It was like the band of a slingshot being pulled back. Sensing danger, I was suddenly scrambling to my feet. I held back the nausea with clenched teeth and hoped I looked more sober than I felt.

"Kat, Jordan can drive you," Mason was saying from somewhere off in the distance. "She doesn't have her permit yet, but she knows how."

I leaned into Jordan and we limped back across the field, up to the house, and over to my car. All the way there she whispered gentle encouragement. "It's okay, Aunt Katherine. Okay, " she kept saying. The shame of needing her help made me feel even sicker.

I gave Jordan my car keys and fell into the passenger seat.

Mason was a little rougher on Taylor. Behind us, I could hear him yelp in pain as Mason hurled him into his truck.

It wasn't until Jordan had me belted into the car and closed the door that I realized I was clutching the bottle of bourbon Taylor had set aside for Daddy. I cradled it to my chest, while Jordan eased the car out of the driveway and onto the road.

# 24

In my dream I was lost in a cornfield. High above my head, the corn was ripe, the ears as distant and yellow as the sun. I reached for them until my arms ached, but kept falling down to the earth. I was so hungry I ate the dirt, and woke because I was choking on dirt.

I was amazed things could be so clear, considering my condition. I knew I was choking on my own vomit. I knew I was running out of air and consciousness. I struggled to breathe, collapsing across the front seat. Jordan's door was open. Outside the car the world was black and starless. Inside the car a dusty white moth clung to the overhead light, its wings fluttering. Jordan was gone. I was desperately alone.

My door flew open and I was being pulled out by my ankles. The car seat was slick with vomit. I slid out like a breech birth. My head hit the running board. I think the blow knocked my windpipe clear, but I was still too much in shock to communicate this to my rescuer.

Strong arms pulled me to my feet and shoved me across the hood of the car. Hands pounded on my back. The blows came down harder and harder, never pausing, not hesitating once, until the thought began to form that maybe being saved wasn't worth the suffering. I howled. The sound of it filled me up. I could feel that cry in my lungs like a separate thing, as if some animal had crawled inside me.

My rescuer, my attacker, retreated. I sank to the ground beside the wheel, still shielding my face. Silence. Silence all around me.

When I opened my eyes. Jordan loomed over me, struggling to keep her breath in her chest, her fists clenched and red like hard apples. She was damp with sweat and my vomit. My body ached. I shrank away from her.

Wordlessly, she walked around the front of the car. She pulled some grass from the side of the road and used it to wipe her seat as best as she could. She got behind the wheel and sat stock still, staring into the distance. She said nothing when I crawled meekly into the car beside her.

There was a frog, one of those gray, thumbnail-size frogs, on the window, its sticky toes splayed and its belly squashed flat against the glass. Jordan stepped out of the car and gently set the frog down at the side of the road.

Climbing back in, she leaned across me and closed the passenger side door. She turned the key in the ignition. "You were sleeping so peacefully," she said and then added, "I'm sorry." She talked at the windshield and not to me.

≈

All during the ride home, I was painfully awake. I suspected I would be for a long while. My body throbbed. It reeked. As we turned into Momma's driveway, I saw that there were no lights on in the house.

Neither of us had a watch, so there was no way to tell how long we'd been gone. The night was absolute; it gave us no clues. Nothing seemed disturbed, although I suspected we could have been gone a hundred years and this remote patch of prairie would never have missed us. The thought seemed to blow across an ember of anger in me. The little coal blazed into life. Suddenly I was too tired and filthy. I flung the car door open and clambered out. Jordan followed me to the house, at a pace that lagged a few cautious steps behind.

My hand was reaching for the door when the phone rang, breaking off a chunk of the night's silence. Jordan bolted, taking off like a spooked horse.

The phone rang again. It dawned on me that no one was home. Fortunately, the front door was unlocked. I surged into the house. I didn't think I'd make it, but the phone kept ringing, reflecting either the urgency or the patience of the person on the other end of the line. Maybe it was Constance. I knocked over Momma's chair in the process of getting to the phone. "Hello," I panted, fumbling for the light switch. "Hello," I said again, my voice sounding hollow and lost in the dark house.

≈

I was suddenly sober and didn't want to be. The night was closing in, shutting me down. I went outside to breathe and remembered my father's bottle of bourbon, nestled in the front seat of my car. I fetched it out and climbed onto the hood of the car. I took a big swig and hurled the bottle out onto the driveway, relishing the noise it made when it shattered. Then I lay back against the windshield, the way Tea and I used to do when we went to the drive-in.

Mason, Taylor, Pearl, and Blue came back together. Pearl was at the wheel of Mason's clunker. Mason was driving Taylor's new truck and rolled over the remains of the bottle. It crunched beneath the wheels.

Taylor climbed out of his truck murmuring, "Goddammit." He stooped to pick up the pieces. I could hear the hissing noise of one of his tires deflating.

"We didn't find Constance," Pearl said, carrying Blue.

I hadn't expected that they would. I reached out and hugged Pearl and Blue. She drew back in surprise, studying me carefully.

I said as calmly as possible, "Take Blue inside and make us something to eat. Momma's got all those leftovers. And make some coffee."

I fooled no one.

Mason stared at me, like a man preparing to get hit by a semi. Pearl didn't budge. She clung to Blue, shivering a little.

Mason's face was twisting slowly, like barbwire being strung around a fence post. He was getting angry, not sad. As if somehow he knew it was going to be bad and the rage was going to help him deal with whatever was coming.

I reached out and put my hand on his chest and he flinched like an animal, with that motion that sets a deer running, but he stood, his legs locked.

"Stay here with me," I said low, so just he could hear. "It's Taylor. I've got something I have to tell him." A bubble floated up from the lake of Mason's rage and confusion crossed his face. He relaxed a little, just one finger of one fist maybe.

So that's how they do it, I thought. That's how men control grief. They take it in their hands and they break it over their knees like kindling wood.

"Go on," I told Pearl. She shuffled off, still carrying Blue and casting a frightened look back at us. Once she got inside, she switched on the porch light and whiteness spread over us.

I turned to Taylor and tried to say it all in straight words, laying them down one after the other, solid like bricks. I wanted to use those words like a path he could follow through the pain to the other side. I told him everything Dinah's sister had said on the phone. I told him how Dinah had stopped at her sister's house on the way back from the funeral. How all her cousins and nephews had come over for a meal, how there were leftovers to take home in Tupperware dishes covered in tin foil. I told him how Dinah had felt good, so she didn't leave until after ten, after the news, when she should have been home by eight. She had carried a box of food and some clothes her sister wanted to send down. She had kissed everyone good-bye, even her youngest nephews, who were out playing basketball in the dark. That meant a lot to them, that she had kissed everyone good-bye. Kissed her mother and father.

Then she had started toward home and it was a long, long drive and somewhere, sometime before she finished, before the car was parked on the curb outside her apartment, before she had a chance to put the leftovers in the fridge or her clothes in the machine, before all the pieces were arranged and the tasks completed, she died.

Because you see, it was dark when she left her sister's house and she was in a hurry to get home. Dinah saw the eyes of the doe light up like two flames in the reflection of her headlights, and she didn't have time to stop before they went out.

The doe had a baby, maybe four months old, and it didn't know what to do. Dinah went through the windshield, her neck snapped, and she landed four feet from where the doe lay dying, too. That fawn wandered back and forth between the two, nuzzling one, then the other, until the sheriff arrived. The sheriff had to run it off. I finished. We all waited in a long silence that reached out and away from us, like the highway. I flicked a nervous glance behind me, and there were Pearl and Blue, folded into one another on the steps. Pearl held a coffee pot, but she seemed to have forgotten its existence. Mason scuffed his foot against the gravel and that brought us back to the present. Taylor shook as the words blew through him in a gust, disturbing every molecule of his being. Then a puzzled look crossed his face.

He looked down at his hands. We all watched, a sense of horror leaking out of us, as one by one he peeled his fingers open. Shards of glass from Daddy's bottle fell to the ground and glistened wetly in the porch light. Taylor held his ragged hands out to us.

In an instant, I could remember each time he had reached out for me. Taylor had always been my baby as much as anyone else's. He'd been a part of my hip since the day he was born, until he was just too plain heavy to carry.

"Jesus," Mason whispered. Pearl let out a ragged cry. I jumped forward to catch Taylor as Mason leapt for the door of his truck. We maneuvered Taylor into the cab. Mason started the engine as Taylor slumped down in the seat between Mason and me, his head resting on my shoulder. He stared at his hands.

"Jesus," Mason whispered again.

Neither Taylor nor I answered as we rocketed out of the driveway and down the road toward the hospital. I tried to get Taylor to elevate his hands, but each time I picked them up, he let them fall back on his lap. He wasn't hearing me. I held his hands up myself, my arms cramping with the effort. My hands first grew wet, then sticky with blood. I could feel it trickle down my forearms and over my elbows.

"Jesus," Mason kept whispering. "Jesus Christ." He kept shaking his head as if he'd just been punched and his ears were ringing.

A passing car flashed us with its brights. The driver slammed his fist down on the horn. Mason and I realized that we were driving without lights, careening blindly down the highway.

We sped along Highway 8, the hospital still more than three towns down the line. Taylor didn't stir. His head grew heavier and heavier on my shoulder. His breathing was my only reassurance; it was steady and sure. He didn't seem to be in any pain, but he kept flexing his hands open and closed, like a cat does when it sleeps in the sun. All the way to our elbows, there was no skin visible, just blood.

I rolled the window down and the wind poured in around us, tugging at my hair. Taylor stirred a little, shifting on the seat. He was probably still a little drunk. Maybe that was helping with the pain. It was also probably making him bleed more.

We passed through Comfort Lake, then Lindstrom. Just outside of Lindstrom, Riordan Chagall's bar lit up the prairie like a fire. You could see it coming from a long way off, glowing faintly green with neon.

Taylor lifted his head off my shoulder. "Let's stop," he said.

I shot a panicked look at Mason, who then hunched over the wheel. Our speed climbed. "No," he said firmly.

"Let's stop," Taylor repeated insistently. "I feel like a drink."

"We've got to get you to a hospital," I told him, my voice crackling with panic.

"How 'bout I hop out here then," Taylor said easily, freeing his hands from mine. "I need a drink." Wildly, I shook my head and tried to catch his hands. He shifted in the seat, leaning hard into me.

The round knob of the door handle pressed into my spine.

"Taylor, please, you're hurting me," I begged him, tears stinging my eyes.

"Just calm down," Mason said tightly.

"Just fuck off," Taylor's voice lashed out. Without warning, he pushed into me hard, trying to shove me out of the way. I gasped as the door handle once again dug into my back.

"Taylor, stop!" I screamed. He wrenched me away, trying to reach the handle. The door was unlocked, and I knew if he succeeded, we would both tumble out onto the highway and under the wheels. We struggled. Mason knuckled down and drove.

Taylor drew back and struck me straight in the face. His fist bounced off me. The cramped space hampered his movements. I knew the blow wasn't as hard as he'd intended it to be. Still, I was stunned. Once again he leaned into me, crushing me with the weight of his body.

Somehow, he got hold of the handle. I heard it unlatch.

"Mason, stop!" I screamed.

As we screeched to a halt, my forehead hit the dash. My head rebounded, and hit the window at the back of the cab. I heard the glass crack. Miraculously, we weren't thrown from the car.

Dazed, I sank back into Taylor's arms. He grinned at me, then calmly untangled himself and climbed out. The overhead light came on as the door opened. Suddenly everything in my vision seemed blurry around the edges and washed out, like an old photo. A crime scene photograph. I was covered in blood, my own from where my forehead had hit the dash and Taylor's. The door was smeared. The dashboard and vinyl seemed to bleed from deep wounds. My nose was bleeding—I could taste it in my mouth.

"Jesus," Mason whispered, shrinking away, repulsed by the blood and the sight of me. His hands gripped the steering wheel, growing white at the knuckle. "If he wants a drink that bad, let him go."

"Fuck that," I yelled and stumbled out of the truck, falling headlong into the ditch. Taylor was a few feet ahead of me, climbing up the ditch's other side, making his way through the tall Johnson grass towards the lights of the bar.

With the first step I took, I knew I had twisted my ankle falling out of the truck. I tried to go after Taylor, but I couldn't manage it with one lame foot.

"Taylor, you son of a bitch!" I screamed. "Get back here!"

He just kept walking, with a steadier stride than I would have thought possible.

"Get back here! I'll call the goddamn police!" I shrieked, pushed beyond all vestiges of control.

Taylor half turned, still walking. "I need a drink," he said. "That's not against the law. Go on, Kat, let me be."

I watched him go. His figure disappeared somewhere off in the distance between the dark and the lights.

It took me a long time to hobble back to the truck. Mason didn't say a thing as he climbed in. His door was half open, and he was turned a little, with one leg hanging out, almost as if he'd been coming to help. He stared straight ahead, a man caught on some unseen border.

I slammed my door closed. That moved him. He slowly turned his head in my direction, but he was somewhere else, far away. He seemed to be chewing on a thought, something more than his dazed sister or the trouble with Taylor. For the first time since the phone call about Dinah, Constance crossed my mind.

"Lord knows," Mason said hoarsely, "how many times I've been out on this same godforsaken highway, looking for Tea or Pearl or, hell, even Daddy." He paused. "But Constance . . . "

I wanted to comfort him. Somehow, it just didn't happen like that. I reached over to touch his shoulder and a drop of blood rolled off my fingertip, staining the white of his shirt, just above the elbow. It was a new shirt. My brother had so few good clothes. This one, I knew, Constance had bought special for Abra's wedding. "Mason," I sobbed. "Mason, I'm bleeding."

Mason looked down at the drop of blood, his face haunted by absolute defeat.

≈

The doctor who examined my head and decided I didn't need stitches had a familiar but tired face. It wasn't so much wrinkled as deeply grooved. She had seen most of everything. People died all the time. People hurt themselves in unimaginable ways every day. Last time I had seen her, I was trailing, half blind from crying, behind my father and Mason. Mason and Daddy carried Tea between them, Mason at the head, Daddy at the feet. Tea was somewhere between life and dreaming, hollering for her mother.

At the time, this doctor's face had made me feel calm. She'd seemed too collected to let people die on her shift, least of all my cousin, who meant the world and more to me.

Back then I'd been too shy to look the doctor in the face. Now, she made me feel old. While she bandaged my head and wrapped my sprained ankle, I wanted to ask her to compare notes. I thought she might be something of an expert on human pain.

All my life people I loved died long, slow deaths. Alcohol is like the tide. It wears you away, little by little, sucking out your strength. It was the worst way to die. I always thought nothing could hurt more than watching that. But now I wasn't sure.

Tonight Taylor had died in front of me, the life pouring out of him like blood from a wound. And I wasn't sure I could live with myself anymore. I told the doctor that my head hurt and asked her for something, codeine maybe, to dull the pain.

Something flickered in her calm eyes, recognition perhaps. I wondered if she suddenly remembered me. Remembered Tea.

"I don't usually like to prescribe pain killers, absent severe trauma," she said calmly, stripping off her gloves and dropping them into the trash. "When the body feels pain, its first instinct is to run, to change, to fight, to do something to stop the discomfort. That's a healthy human reaction. Drugs tend to numb that."

There was a rolling cart beside the examining table. She pulled open a drawer and pressed a sample package of Tylenol into my hand. "You might have a concussion," she said. "I can't give you anything stronger. But you need to keep awake and have someone check on you. You smell of alcohol," she added clinically, her face neutral. "I advise that you not drink anything else tonight."

With the flick of a curtain she was gone. I heard her moving on to the next patients, a family with a young child with a finger in a splint. I stared at the Tylenol in my hand, then tossed it into the trash.

# 25

Mason dropped me off at the end of the drive. He was anxious to be home, to learn firsthand that Constance hadn't called and probably never would. I slowly made my way up to the house on my lame foot. The whole house was dark. No one answered my knock. For the second time since I had arrived, I found myself locked out of my mother's house.

I got in my car and tried to keep awake. I never realized how far away dawn could be until that night. Maybe I slept some. Mainly I blinked myself awake and tried hard not to die in my sleep.

I was waiting for the sun when Momma walked up the driveway. She was all in pink, still wearing the dress she'd made for Abra's wedding. She looked worn out. Evidently I looked bad too, because she gasped a little when she saw me.

"What happened to you?" she asked. "When did you get in?"

Truthfully, I was wondering the same thing. My mouth was too dry to answer and my throat felt stuck closed. I ran my sandpapery tongue over my cracked lips and winced.

Momma's face creased with concern. "Why aren't you inside? You weren't thinking of driving somewhere like this?" she demanded sharply.

I shook my head. "Locked," I croaked, pointing at the door. Glad that my voice was working again, I added, "No one home. Couldn't get in."

"I went to Mason's," Momma explained. "I was afraid the boys would run wild. Sure enough, I found the pack of them out in the barn. The older two, who know better, were torturing the horses, shooting them with their pellet guns. Your grandmother has barricaded herself in her house. I can't get in. And Constance is still nowhere to be found.

"How's Taylor?" she asked quietly, coming to the subject that I knew must be hurting her.

"Didn't Mason tell you?" I asked in surprise.

"Mason was home for all of five minutes last night," Momma said with a touch of exasperation. "And what he said made no sense. He's still out looking for Constance. Pearl's the one who came over and told me about Dinah."

"I don't know how Taylor's doing," I told her honestly. "He's off medicating himself at Dr. Riordan Chagall's."

Momma's eyes flared.

"We tried to get him to the doctor, but he . . . " There was more that I wanted to say, but I felt my eyes stinging dangerously. I looked away from Momma, down at my hands. I still had blood under my fingernails. Slowly, I began to climb out of the car. My body was difficult to move, stiff from its injuries and the long hours of immobility. I sank back into the seat.

Momma was studying me. "You look like hell, Kat."

"Thanks." I made one more effort to get out of the car and almost made it, but wobbled at the last moment. Momma caught me easily. The moment she touched me, my throat tightened. I couldn't place the feeling, until I realized that this was the closest Momma and I had been in years. I couldn't remember the last time she had touched me, but now there she was, with her arms around me, supporting me. It was almost like an embrace.

It seemed to take us years to inch up the sidewalk, up the four steps, and into the house. By the end, we were both sweating with the exertion of being so close to one another. Momma lowered me into a kitchen chair and stepped away. I could feel in the air how grateful she was to let go.

"I'll make you breakfast," she said gruffly. Touching Momma left a strange ache inside me. I could tell she was aware of it too, but preferred to describe the feeling as hunger. From the table, I watched Momma in silence as she moved around the kitchen. She took out a skillet and some eggs, then lit the gas burner with a match.

"I called Abra to tell her the news," she said, glancing up at me quickly, then back at the stove. "I know it's her honeymoon and all, but I wanted to let her know about Dinah." Momma faltered a little when she had to say Dinah's name.

"What'd she say?"

Momma cracked an egg against the edge of the skillet. She didn't answer. I figured I'd give her a little time. I reached over and flipped on the radio that Momma always kept on the kitchen table. Then I turned it off. Momma pulled a carton of milk from the refrigerator. She put some bread in the toaster.

In my memories of her she is often cooking. Sorrow always seemed to find her in the kitchen.

"What'd Abra say?" I asked again.

Momma turned the eggs. She pursed her lips, as if she'd broken the yolks, and set the spatula down. "Abra said she had her own family now. She said she'd pray for Dinah, but she wants us to leave her in peace."

When they fell, Momma's tears sizzled on the hot skillet. A noise like a sob escaped her. She pressed her hand to her mouth. I stared at her, a hot wail of misery rising within me. I had never seen Momma cry. Not like this.

The eggs began to smoke. Momma blinked at the pan. "Goddammit!" she screamed and threw the whole mess into the sink. Several dishes in the basin shattered explosively and egg went flying everywhere.

"Momma . . . " I began, but she had already turned to flee to the far part of the house. The bathroom door slammed, and shortly after that I heard water running in the bathtub.

I sat stonelike in my chair. My body hurt all over. Above the range gray smoke hung, as wispy as a veil.

Sound carries well in an emptied house. Momma's tears broke over me like a great wave of sorrow. The weight of it pushed me down into my chair and held me under until my own lungs ached. Then slowly, I began to move against the pressure. I put away the eggs and butter before heading for higher ground, away from the onslaught. I climbed clumsily to the attic, wincing every time I put weight on my ankle.

It was only when I got up there in that long space, like an ark, with the morning light emptying into the windows, illuminating snug beams and my half-finished work, that I could breathe. There was a peaceful calm in the attic, sudden and complete, polished with wear and time. I could turn it over in my hand like a stone from the ocean's depths. A branch of the old elm tree tapped gently on the window as it swayed in the soft wind. Opened boxes yawned. Half full. Half empty.

Then the wind picked up and the tapping grew louder until I realized that it must be someone downstairs at the front door. Momma wasn't answering. I turned back to the steps, then hesitated. The knocking ceased. The tree began. I was caught, not knowing which to answer. I was contemplating the stairs when a sense of vertigo came over me. I felt myself turn in it, like a whirli-gig, held on to the railing and eased myself to the floor. My ankle throbbed. I closed my eyes. The spinning stopped and I opened my eyes. The tree was tapping. Down below, I heard voices. Momma had gone to let the person in. From the sounds, I knew it must be Mason and Jordan or Pearl, and tried to sneak a glance at the stairs. Sure enough, the moment I looked at them, I began to spin. When I looked away, the spinning slowed and I hugged myself. Still sitting, I scooted to the center of the attic. The spinning ended completely.

I was all right, I decided, if I didn't look at the stairs, and made my way over to Tea's great iron bed and lay down.

Once again, the attic's gray calm spread over me, until I felt that my interiors had the same color and quality as the shadows. I felt as bare as the curtainless windows and as thick as the settled dust, and realized that I should stay here forever.

# 26

$M$y work progressed steadily. I was not lonely. I was not idle. I could hear my family, moving and living beneath me, though not their words. The pine boards transformed all emotions—laughter, anger, wrath—and all conversations, whatever the subject or concern, into murmurs of the same tone and quality that made the floorboards vibrate, a calming music. Sometimes I would lie flat, press my ear against the floor, and listen to the steady hum of their voices without words. Maybe Tea had done the same thing.

I packed her old magazines into boxes and wrote the names on the side. I subdivided the magazines—housekeeping in one box, art and trade in another, and so on. I sealed the cartons with silver crosses of duct tape, dusted again, and took a broom to the cobwebs in the corners. Then I moved on to Tea's clothes, folding everything neatly into trunks.

That first day, I worked without stop, only pausing when night fell and I could no longer find my way around. I banged my toes on a desk and swore. I had forgotten to replace the attic's single light bulb. It was too late now.

By the fourth day, the darkness was a blessing. Each time my purpose threatened to wear me down to exhaustion, night would come and I would be forced to sleep. I got up when the sun woke me, found a comforting rhythm that grew more solid, more reassuring to me each day. Dark. Sleep. Light. Wake and clean.

Sometimes I took a peek at the stairs, to see if I could make it down, and I would get so crazy dizzy that I would have to lie for hours, flat like the prairie, on Tea's bed. When I had to go near the stairs, I walked backward.

Momma and Mason came up to visit me and once even Pearl. But it was easy to ignore them, to concentrate on my work. If I listened hard enough, their voices were just mumbles through the floorboards. If I concentrated long enough, they just went away, leaving bottles of juice and stacks of sandwiches behind.

≈

Momma must have called him. I suppose that's what she did, but I wasn't expecting it. When he appeared, it unsettled me. The plate I was wrapping slipped from my hand and broke into three jagged pieces. "How about you and I take a ride?" Shepherd asked with a grin.

"Where?" I asked, kneeling to pick up the broken plate.

Shepherd knelt beside me so that we were eye to eye. He took my hand. "I don't know. How about Memphis? I've always been partial to it. Or we could roll out to Bakersfield, take a good long look at California." He squeezed my hand.

"Why don't you go without me?" I said. "I'm not very good company."

He kissed the palm of my hand. "But I want to do you good."

I pulled away from him. "You can't help me with this, Shepherd," I said.

"Why not?"

I just stared at the sunlight from my window. It gathered in a perfect rectangle on the floor, glowing from within.

Strong arms entwined around me. "I could carry you out. I could put you in my car and drive off with you," he whispered. He was so close, so dangerous that his lips brushed my ear. I shivered. His arms squeezed me a little tighter. "Would that work?" he asked.

I turned my face away, shaking my head.

"Maybe I'll try it anyway," he said roughly. "Maybe you just don't know what's good for you. Maybe I'm good for you."

It was so hard to look into his sad, familiar eyes. I reached over and touched his face, first his cheek, then the strong sweep of his forehead. "Can I ask you something, Shepherd?"

He nodded, his face cautious.

"How long have you loved me?"

He smiled. "Since I first saw you in a painting."

I kissed his forehead, then kissed it again in the same spot. "I'm not her, Shepherd. I'm not the woman in those paintings. She's not real."

"You're more real than you know," he said, his voice as jagged as a wound. "You need to leave here, Kat," he pleaded. "We'll go wherever you want. Anywhere. I promise."

"Anywhere?" I smiled sadly at him. "Then take me to Tea. I miss her."

"She's gone, honey," he said. "She's dirt in a field. You don't want to go there."

I said nothing.

Shepherd gingerly touched a piece of the plate I had broken. "You know,

Tea's mother read her horoscope in the paper every single morning of her life. She wouldn't leave the house until Tea or I went and got the paper for her so that she could see what was in her stars. We always used to make fun of that." He smiled. "But now I'm starting to think that people do have fates, don't they, Kat? And no matter how much you love them or how many obstacles you try to throw in their paths, they're still going to reach their destiny. No matter what." He looked at me one more time, his eyes stark with pain.

I tried to look away, but he caught my face in his hands. He kissed me, pulling me so tightly to him that I could feel his heart in his chest, pressed right to mine. "If you decide to join the living, Kat," he said, "call me. Let me know where I can reach you."

Then he rose and turned to go. I tried to smile for him before he left, but never managed it. At least I didn't cry.

Long after he left, while I was lying on Tea's heavy iron bed, I could picture myself curled up in Shepherd's car with my cheek against the seat, listening to the road move beneath us. I could almost hear it when I closed my eyes, that clean sound. The world passed effortlessly under us and the horizon parted, like clean halves, never touching.

≈

Pearl appeared in the attic later that afternoon, looking pale and anxious. "Go away, Pearl," I groaned, rolling over. I had almost been asleep. I let my eyes droop closed again but, a moment later, peered back at her. She was still there. She was dressed for the heat in cutoffs and a T-shirt. Her belly poked out between the two; her navel eyed me sternly. "You have to come down now, Kat," she said directly. "Momma's going to send Mason up next to carry you down. She would have already, but he's out looking for his damned horses again. She says you turned that McCreedy man away today." Wearily, I pulled myself out of bed. Since I wasn't going to get any rest, I resumed work. Before Shepherd's arrival, I had been wrapping decorative plates and figurines. Tea had bought them by the boxful at auctions. I was packing them according to theme. Evidently Tea had a fondness for ceramic rabbits. I had a whole box of rabbits already. I picked up a statuette of a peasant girl and her sheep. Grimly, I began wrapping it in newspaper.

"Kat, are you listening to me?" Pearl persisted. "You're worrying Momma. She's down there crying right now."

I could feel the ink of the newsprint rubbing off on my hands. My hands were turning black with ink. Momma crying for me was an odd thought.

I took up another sheet of newsprint and seized a lamb figurine a little too violently. It hit the corner of the dresser and a little paint chipped off one foot. I swore.

"Look," Pearl said, "you've got to come down and help me with Taylor. He's in bad shape."

I paused and grew very still. The image of my brother walking across that field in the dark, the bar in the distance, rose up in my mind, like a crow startled from the corn. When I got to thinking about him, the light in my attic seemed less gray. The air around me heated up a few degrees. I looked over at Pearl, expecting her to ripple, like a mirage. I felt an odd flutter of panic in my stomach.

"Taylor?" I said slowly, almost reluctantly.

"Yes, Taylor," Pearl bit out. "If you hadn't been hiding in the attic like a total nut case you might know what's going on." She lit a cigarette. "He's smashed up his new truck. The whole front end is ruined. And he hasn't been working since Dinah's accident." Pearl flicked ash onto my floor. "He even asked me to buy him some groceries." Pearl misinterpreted my silence as interest and continued. "I drove him over to the supermarket and pretty soon there was sixty dollars' worth of stuff that I had to pay for. I told him he should come home for a while, but he just laughed and said he had enough problems already. Then," she fumed, "he told me the groceries aren't really for him. They're for Maddie Loux, and she's got three kids. Are you listening, Kat?"

I was thinking of Taylor, with his bloody hands. Distracted, I nodded.

"I'm telling you, this is bad. He's staying with Maddie. She's got a trailer on some land in Scandia. An old farm. They don't own the land, but it doesn't look like anyone's making them move. Her Daddy lives out there, too."

"He told you all this?"

Pearl shook her head. She cleared the smoke from her lungs. "Most of it. I know Maddie from high school. She's a year younger than me. She dropped out with that first kid."

"What's she like?"

"She's a real pig," Pearl said flatly. "She only lives way out in the sticks like that so she can do her drugs in peace. Everybody knows that."

"Did you tell Momma?"

"Yeah."

I shrugged, as if to say, Well, that's all then.

Apparently Pearl didn't think so, because she practically howled at me. "Are you hearing me, Kat? I'm telling you that Taylor is seriously fucked up. His life. Everything. He didn't even go to Dinah's funeral."

She waved wildly as she spoke. I was afraid that the ash flying from her cigarette might start a fire in the highly combustible attic. "And now he's pissed her family off," Pearl continued. "Dinah's sister Fern called Momma yesterday wondering why he didn't come to the funeral. Momma didn't know what to say, so she gave her the phone number Taylor gave me."

Pearl stomped her cigarette out on the floor. "And I don't know what he said, but after Fern talked to him she and her brothers came down real quick to collect Dinah's things. Taylor ran them off. He just ran them off. Fern called Momma. She says that if she can't get her sister's stuff from Taylor, she'll call the police."

"What does Fern want?" I asked. I was holding a rabbit figurine in my hand. I didn't remember picking it up. Numbly, I reached for another sheet of newsprint.

"I don't know. Looks like Taylor went by and cleared out Dinah's apartment. All her stuff is gone. Fern gave Momma a list. She's pretty upset. If Fern got a look at that pig Taylor's living with, I don't blame her."

The newsprint slipped from my hand. I looked down at the rabbit again. It was silly, painted with pink flowers. It had swirling blue hearts for eyes. I knew Fern. She and Tea had been friends for years, and cousins in a vague and distant way. Fern was not the type of woman that my brother should have run off. In fact, she was not the type of woman you talked to in a voice above a whisper.

I closed my eyes.

"Momma wants us to go over there today. You, me, and her. You can talk sense into Taylor better than any of us." Pearl spoke from behind the curtain of my closed eyes. I felt myself frown. It seemed to me for some reason that if I couldn't see her, Pearl should simply not be there. What a relief it would have been to have her not be there. To maybe have Taylor standing in front of me instead, grinning as he had a few weeks ago, making plans to run away to Colorado with Dinah. It was still a brilliant plan. They should try to do that, I thought.

"I'm real tired now, Pearl," I said with my eyes closed. "I can't come down and help you now. Not today."

"When then?" she demanded. "Tomorrow? Kat, you've been up here for more than a week!"

I shrugged.

"How long are you going to stay up here?" Pearl demanded.

I shrugged again. "You hear from Abra?"

"No."

"When you hear from Abra, I'll come down."

I could sense my sister's frustration. It had the taste of paint. Her voice was painted red with it. "You know Abra is never going to call."

I opened my eyes. "And I'm not coming down."

We stared at one another.

"Look," Pearl blurted out, "I'm sorry about what I said at the wedding. We all just had a bad day. Then Dinah died and Constance ran off. But I didn't mean to shoot my mouth off about Tea. Does that make you feel better?"

I shook my head, almost disbelieving.

"I didn't mean half of that stuff about Tea," she continued. "And if I'd known you were going to go nuts, I wouldn't have said any of it."

"Go away, Pearl," I said.

"Look—"

"This isn't about you, Pearl."

"Then what is it about?"

"Me," I yelled. "Me. My life. My ceramic rabbit." I waved it at her. "So get the hell out. Go take care of your son if you've got so much goddamn time on your hands!"

Pearl fled.

# 27

"What goes to and fro over the threshold, but never enters?" Tea would ask as she brushed my hair and dressed me for school. Thinking about riddles usually kept me still for a while.

"A door," I would answer.

Perhaps the same door that Jordan entered through and closed a little too loudly. The whole house shook as she thundered up the stairs.

"Today was the last day of summer school," she announced, appearing in a cloud of dust. I set aside the picture frames I'd been packing.

"I will never see Engel again," she continued dramatically. "His mother is sending him to Catholic school."

Somehow I knew she was lying to me. Knowing that didn't make me angry. I felt no need to reproach her. I simply did not expect Jordan to tell me the truth. Of course she wouldn't give him up. She didn't know how.

Tea had once written me that Jordan had broken her arm and two ribs because she had fallen off her horse and it had dragged her clear across the field. She wouldn't have been hurt half so bad, Tea had explained, if she had just let go of the reins. Tea had been so proud of Jordan, and I, reading her words a thousand miles away, had at least understood.

Jordan wandered in circles, touching everything, stirring up dust. I tried to interest her in sitting, in stillness, anything.

Sometimes I thought the only reason Tea had wanted to paint me so much was because it kept me still. When she first came to us, she tried to paint landscapes, but I was always in the way. Seeing Jordan pace in the confined area made me bone-weary. I wondered if Tea had ever felt the same way.

At last, Jordan sat down for a moment to talk. "I've never been up here before," she said. "What's in those?" She pointed toward a group of trunks lined up against the walls.

"Clothes."

"Can I look?" I would have told her no, but already her hands were plunged into layers of cloth and color. She seized a purple T-shirt and held it against her chest. "I like this. Can I have it?" she asked bluntly.

"It probably won't fit."

She slid the T-shirt over her shoulders. It fit perfectly. She put a sweater on next. The clothes seemed to have been made for her. She reached down through a few more layers, pulling out blue jeans and cutoffs. She quickly put those aside when she came across a knee-length spaghetti-strap dress of a certain soft red that I remembered well. She held it up against her and twirled. She smelled the dress. Her nose wrinkled. "It smells like cigarettes."

"Well," I said with a little difficulty, "Tea smoked Old Golds."

Jordan shrugged. "Dad smokes them, too. They always smoked the same brand." I felt myself flush a little as she let the dress fall to the floor. "I'll have to wash it, I guess."

Jordan pulled on a gauzy skirt right over her blue jeans. She turned and turned, flaring out the skirt. I carried Tea's old mirror over to her. She looked at herself briefly, then impatiently shucked the skirt. She tried on clothes for almost half an hour. I couldn't remember Tea being that thin. Jordan was tall for her age, but she was too slim, too slight. Tea had always seemed like a lot more in my eyes. Maybe too much sometimes. Already, I realized, my mind was beginning to play tricks on me. My cousin was becoming more and more of a memory than a person to me.

Jordan found another dress, this one carefully wrapped and sealed with tape in green tissue. She threw the wrapper to one side and shook out the dress. It was slightly pink, slightly cream, sleeveless, with a low bodice. Tea had married Billy in this dress. My heart contracted when I saw it.

Jordan held the dress close to her chest. I could tell she didn't recognize or trust the expression on my face. "Can I have it?" she asked.

"It's not really a casual dress," I told her gently. "It's not for everyday."

She shrugged and tossed it aside. She dove into the trunk, fishing out a beaded shirt. I reached over and folded the dress. The silk and satin felt cool to the touch. "Can I have this?" she chirped, holding up the shirt.

"Of course," I said, setting the dress aside. "There's more in here." I dragged out another trunk. "All of Tea's things. Tea loved clothes."

Jordan stripped down to her bra and tried on her new shirt. "Aren't you going to ask me for a story?" she demanded. "Like Uncle Taylor, when he asked you for the bed?"

I rummaged in the trunk, taking out some scarves. Maybe I was hoping to distract her, because I didn't feel like talking about Tea or Taylor just then.

"I have a story," she insisted.

"That's okay. You can just have the things."

But Jordan was frowning. "Do you think I haven't got one?"

She spoke so fiercely that I found myself staring at her in surprise.

"Tea was my cousin, too." Her voice rose steadily. "I went to the funeral even though Momma told the boys they couldn't go."

I tossed the scarves back into the trunk and rocked back on my heels. "Okay, shoot," I said, resigned. "What did Tea do to you?"

Jordan rose and shook her head. "It's not a story like that." She settled comfortably on the edge of Tea's great bed.

Cautiously, I settled into a nearby chair. "It's about Dad, too," she said almost apologetically, "and Roche Healy."

"Who's Roche Healy?"

"He's dead," Jordan said with blithe unconcern. "He died awhile before Tea. In the spring. He had the farm behind ours. Dad owns it now," Jordan explained. "If you walk through the corn beyond the far pasture toward the river, you'll run across Roche Healy's place. He was an old man.

"Dad knew him," she continued, "so when Mr. Healy died, his son asked Dad to keep an eye on the place until he sold it. Mr. Healy's son wasn't a farmer, so at the end of the season, Dad took in the corn. It kept growing after he died. No reason it wouldn't, but Dad couldn't stand the idea of that corn rotting out in the fields.

"Ma never liked Mr. Healy. She liked him less after he died, because one day Dad showed up with this big basket of tomatoes. He'd found them growing among the weeds in Mr. Healy's garden. Ma said it was like grave robbing to pick stuff from a dead man's garden.

"But the next day Dad brought back some carrots and beans. A few days later he walked in with two grocery bags full of little green peppers. That made Ma even more angry, because the peppers sat in the refrigerator for a week and she didn't know what to do with them.

"Then Grandma had the idea that we could can them. Tea found a recipe somewhere and they both came over to help Ma and me out.

"It took us awhile to get the peppers cleaned and cut right. We must have been halfway through the batch when Tea's hands started to burn and Ma's started to swell. Pretty soon Grandma got to feeling just as bad as Ma and Tea. I guess it was the juice in the peppers.

"Ma started to cry and wave her hands in the air. Tea and Grandma tried to help her rinse her hands off under the tap, but pretty soon they were all jostling to rinse their hands off. Kinda like the horses when you first fill their trough up.

"Their hands swelled until it looked like they were all wearing red mittens. Not me, though," Jordan added proudly, "not me. I didn't have any problems." She gave me a hard look to see if I doubted her. "I was just fine. So I took care of all of them. I turned off the stove and brought them all big bowls of ice water to soak their hands in. When the burning finally stopped, I made them all sit around the kitchen table and I salved their hands with udder balm.

"Even then they all looked pretty miserable. Grandma's fingers swelled as big as state fair pickles. Every time Ma's nose itched she'd get balm all over her face and I'd have to wipe it off and rub new balm on her hands.

"Then all of a sudden Tea started to laugh and everybody stared at her like she'd gone crazy. She kept laughing until she started wobbling in her chair. And then she looked at Ma and Grandma and me too, and she said, 'You know, we deserve this. Here we are, grown women, and yet we let Mason bully us into this.'

"Grandma and Ma just stared at her and Tea said, 'I hate canned peppers. I don't know anyone who likes them.'

"Then she turned to me and asked me to go out to the car and fetch her thermos. I poured her a glass and she drank and said, 'I feel better already.' Then Tea smiled at Grandma, and Grandma smiled back at her. Then Grandma said, 'Jordan, I believe I'd like a sip of that, too.'"

Jordan paused and smoothed the beaded shirt she wore. "Can I really have this?" she asked doubtfully.

"Finish your story first," I told her. "What happened next?"

"Not much," Jordan said. She rose from the bed and started digging through the trunks again. "Whatever it was in Tea's thermos, they got really drunk. I would have, too, if I hadn't just got sleepy." Jordan glanced at me shyly. "I don't drink much. But every time I woke up, they'd be sitting there, smiling, drinking, laughing. I don't think I ever saw them like that before. Seemed kinda nice, you know, especially Tea and Grandma, because usually they were just always fighting.

"At the end of the night Tea and Grandma sorta staggered home together, their arms wrapped real tight around each other's waist, like they were on a horse or something and they were each afraid the other would fall off. I could hear them laughing all the way home."

Jordan shook her head in bemused wonder. "I'd never heard them laugh like that before. I can remember it so clearly because it was about a month before Tea died. It was such a clear night and the corn had just been taken in so you could see for miles and miles."

Jordan pulled a pair of cowboy boots out of the trunk. "Can I have these, too?" she asked.

"No."

"Why not?"

"Your aunt Pearl's already asked me for Tea's boots."

"Oh," she said, seeming to go back to her inspection of the trunk, but she kept glancing at the boots, then at me. "I have another story," she offered with an air of studied nonchalance. "It's a secret."

I sighed. "I can't give you the boots, Jordan. But you can have whatever you want from the trunks."

"The boots were in the trunks."

"Everything in the trunks but the boots," I clarified.

She seemed to think it over, then she nodded. "Okay, I'll tell you my story then." She came back over and sat down on the bed. She kept her head down, but her face was hard and set. She examined her hands, both sides, than she said to me quietly, "It's about the horses getting out."

"Yeah?"

"You know how they get out?" She shot me a nervous glance. "Me," she said in a rush. "I let them out. Dad thinks there's a hole in the fence or that the boys keep forgetting to close the gate when they play, but it's not that. It's me."

Once again, I was overwhelmed by the feeling that whole stretches of prairie separated Jordan's understanding of the world and mine. "Why do you do that?" I asked carefully.

Jordan hugged herself and let out a nervous little laugh when she squeezed. She started to speak, then stopped several times. Then she turned and looked me in the eye when she spoke, straightening her shoulders a little. "At first it was because Dad would always tear into Ma. Just ragging on her. And they would fight and Ma would cry. They always fight."

Jordan shrugged. "I guess I just wanted some quiet. One night, in the middle of a real battle, the idea just hit me and I went out and let the horses out, and the cows, too. Then I ran back up to the house, as if I had just noticed they were gone. And the fighting stopped. Everyone went looking for the stock. After we finally got them all in again, Dad was just too tired to keep on fighting with Ma. He went straight to bed."

Jordan was watching me closely to see how I would react. She sat tense, on the edge of the bed, ready to fly away, if necessary. When I said nothing, she continued. "At first I let them out when there was a fight. After awhile, I started letting them out before the fights started. It's real easy to tell when a fight's coming on," she explained. "Ma's eyes get pink and Dad sits at the kitchen table and smokes one cigarette after another without saying a word. Things have been quiet at our house lately. Ma and Dad actually seemed to be getting along pretty well. A couple of times Dad got angry and smacked one of the boys, but that's never anything serious."

Jordan suddenly touched my arm. I jumped. Her hand rested there. "I didn't mean for Grandma's little white calf to die," she said softly. "If I had known that would happen, I would've just let the horses out and not the cows."

Downstairs, Momma turned on the television. The television man spoke to us in a language we couldn't understand. Something Pearl had said during her visit fluttered across my mind on moth's wings. "Jordan, why did you let the horses out yesterday?"

Jordan's hand tightened painfully around my forearm. Her eyes seemed to get a little pink, but she didn't cry. I had the feeling that she rarely, maybe never, cried. She pressed her lips down to a tight line. Her voice was flat and hard when she said, "I did that to remind him, you know, about Ma."

She came to me like the horse erupting from the corn, surprising me with the stampede of her grief. Jordan threw herself at me, wrapping her arms around my waist and burying her face in my lap. She began to sob. As her cries grew louder, her hold on me tightened, until it was painful to breathe, as if Jordan thought that by the sheer force of her grip she could wring sympathy from me.

I felt at that moment what a terrible thing it would be to love this child. It would be something akin to grabbing hold of an electric fence and feeling your hand tighten against your will around the shock. Sorrow for this broken girl planted itself like a seed in the waiting furrow of my heart, at the same time that I felt fear of her strength. Jordan was a child, but somehow stronger than any child should be, sinewy and muscled with desperation. She had a strength that seemed to shake and vibrate in the bone.

Only when her grief had run its course, and not a minute before, did Jordan release me. The air rushed back into my lungs. She knotted her hand into mine. Together we made a double fist. She squeezed my hand and said, "You can't tell anyone, Aunt Katherine. Promise me you won't tell."

# 28

Jordan and I walked down the stairs and out to Mason's pickup. The sun was too bright for my eyes, but I helped her load armfuls of clothes into the back. We made several trips. My ankle throbbed, but dully. My body was healing, at least.

When Jordan was nearby, it was possible to move up and down the stairs. Her presence seemed to hold the dizziness at bay. I only stumbled once, and Jordan caught me.

As she headed off, I followed the truck to the end of the driveway, waving her on. Along the road, some distance ahead of her, an impossible number of crows wheeled in the sky, cawing insistently. I tried to locate the source of their disturbance. They were in a frenzy.

Two great combines rolled through the corn. They were harvesting our neighbor's fields. Near the road I could see a few patches of earth that were already shaved. The labyrinth of corn was falling. My own breathing sounded suddenly harsh and loud in my ears. I was so dizzy that I could barely walk back up the driveway, and when I got to the house, I needed to cling to the porch rail.

≈

I ran the tap in the kitchen until the water was cool, and then filled myself a glass. Looking for ice, I opened the freezer door and an avalanche crashed over me. Some of the containers ruptured upon impact. The remains of Abra's wedding cake splattered across the refrigerator door, the floor, and me. The disorder was as absolute as it was sudden. Scattered among patches of smooshed cake were plastic bowls, ice cubes, several mysterious foil-wrapped packages, leftovers from the wedding, and many of Tea's tiny plastic containers.

I picked Tea's things out of the mess, trying to scrape the frosting off them with my fingers. I didn't bother with the rest. I would come back to it later. For now, Tea's jars had my attention. I carried them to the kitchen table and pried open every one of them.

They were filled with dirt. Not remarkable dirt. Just dirt—all three dozen of them were packed to the rim with crumbling earth. I sat and stared at the little pots. They didn't stir.

"I can't explain it," my mother said from nearby, and I jumped. She was standing a few inches behind me but hadn't registered her presence until she spoke. "Right after her funeral, when everyone had gone home, I opened them all up. For the life of me, I don't know what they mean. Do you?"

I shook my head.

Momma seemed genuinely disappointed. "For a while there after she died, I kept thinking I'd come to understand it." She shook her head sadly. "I don't just mean her death—that was only a part of it. I mean that I wanted to understand all of it, the real reason why she was the way she was. I keep thinking I should understand it. For her whole life I was there. Most of it anyway."

It was hard for me to muster pity for Momma where Tea was concerned. "Maybe if you could've loved her, it might have helped," I suggested baldly.

She didn't flinch. "Sometimes I think that too. I don't know why, but right from the start Tea could make me so mad, it was like I'd go blind. From the very first day she could do that to me. It got so I was frightened that a child could make me that angry." Momma settled into the chair beside me. "Whenever Tea pushed me too far, I used to count to ten and tell myself that it wasn't her fault, that something really terrible must have happened to that child for her to be that mean. Something terrible," she repeated sadly, thoughtfully. "Then sometimes I would think, maybe it wasn't like that at all. Maybe it was just a lot of little things that built up over time, like grime on windows. Maybe Tea just grew steadily into being crazy, the way a tree grows toward the moon."

We were quiet. Momma poked her finger into a pot. "You want to know what I finally decided?"

"Sure."

"I decided it didn't matter much," she said evenly, stirring the dirt. "However it happened, by the time Tea was thirteen, every door to her heart was nailed closed. The only way in was through the window, and that was so tiny that only a child was able to squeeze through."

I looked away, feeling uncomfortable.

"And," Momma continued, "I decided that the man her mother ran off with, that man Moses, was probably messing with Tea when she was a little girl, though I never could prove it one way or the other."

I poured the dirt from one of the containers into my hand. It was still cool from the freezer. Frozen earth, like winter in my hand. I closed my fist around it, feeling it calm me.

"You can't live like this," Momma said softly, wrapping her hands around my fist. "Katherine, you've got to let it go."

I smiled painfully at her and opened my fist. The dirt streamed through my fingers. "You know already that I can't. Maybe it's exactly like you say, Momma. When I was six years old, I crawled into the window of my cousin's heart, and once I was in, she reached over and closed it behind me."

I brushed the spilled dirt back into its container and put the lid on. "I know that you blame me and you blame Tea for having a love that was too narrow," I said. "It hurts that I never loved anyone the way I loved her." I looked into my mother's drawn face. "But I don't know how to change that now."

I began replacing all the lids. They made a soft and final snap as they popped back into place. Momma's face was so sad I had to look away. "I didn't make that choice. Tea made it for me," I told her softly, "but even now I don't regret it."

"It must be cold, a dead woman's love."

"Probably as cold as a mother's love is warm," I said, staring at the containers, trying hard not to look at Momma. "But I wouldn't know."

Momma drew a ragged breath and rose abruptly. She stood over me for a moment like the shadow of a cloud, then moved away just as silently. I could hear her sloshing water around in the sink. I could hear things shifting and being rearranged. When I looked around, she was kneeling by the refrigerator, sponging up the mess I had made.

"Momma," I called to her. She paused. "I'll go with you tomorrow to see Taylor, if you still want me to."

Grimly, my mother nodded.

# 29

Early the next morning Momma was waiting in the kitchen with her white purse in her hand. She wore brown slacks and one of Daddy's old shirts.

Pearl sat silently at the kitchen table watching me, watching Momma. She had on Tea's old boots. She gave me an encouraging smile as we filed silently out to my car. As I turned the key in the ignition, a riddle of Tea's came to mind.

Which dark sister goes to see her fair brother and he flees from her? Tea's voice was so clear in my head, it was as if she were sitting beside me, her elbows jostling me and Pearl.

Night and day, I answered her silently.

Maddie Loux's place was truly in the middle of nowhere. She was about forty minutes north of us, squatting on the remnants of a farm. Her father lived at the top of the hill in a tumbling-down farmhouse. Maddie lived at the bottom in a trailer. Between them there was a collapsed barn.

As far as I could tell, the fields hadn't been plowed in years. Still, the corn grew, though only in occasional scraggly patches. Odd stalks poked up here and there, pointing shakily at the sky with heretical grace.

We rolled past the farmhouse, where an old man sat on the steps watching us. At the end of his arm, like a dog on a leash, was a girl of about eight or nine. She tried to pull free and follow us down the hill. She tugged at the old man's arm, but he wouldn't shift.

"She looks big enough to be Maddie's oldest girl," Pearl observed from the passenger seat. "Maddie started young."

Down by the trailer all the grass had long since been trampled to death. The trailer sat on bare dirt, listing to one side on crumbling cinder blocks. The front door was open and screenless. Two shirtless kids played out by the steps, enjoying a game that I noticed involved eating great quantities of dirt. They were three and five maybe, but I couldn't tell if they were boys or girls.

A skinny dog hovered nearby, sniffing and licking them by turns. They made a filthy trio. Both children had swollen bellies peeking out over their shorts.

When I cut the engine, a woman came to the door. This is her, I thought, the instant I laid eyes on her. My stomach tightened.

Maddie Loux was thin but lumpy. Her round face was pale and her hair utterly colorless. Her uneven breasts sagged, braless under her low-cut shirt. She watched us petulantly with dull blue eyes as Pearl and I got out of the car. Maddie gingerly climbed down from the trailer, and I realized that she was pregnant.

Momma did not move. I glanced back at her, surprised, but she stayed anchored in the backseat.

Maddie did not approach us and offered no greeting, though she seemed to recognize Pearl.

"Taylor's asleep," she told Pearl directly. "Who's that?" she asked pointing at me with her chin.

"I'm Taylor's sister, Kat."

"And that's my mother, in the car," Taylor said, appearing in the doorway, "but she doesn't want to talk to you."

Maddie whirled on him. "You told me to tell them you were asleep," she hissed angrily.

Taylor shrugged and scratched his bare chest. "I changed my mind." He waved at Momma. "Maybe you should try and make yourself look nice," he told Maddie without looking at her. "Then maybe Momma will talk to you. She's very particular about which trash she'll talk to, and whether it's clean or not."

Pearl and I gaped at him while Maddie's face turned an impressive red. Grabbing her two kids roughly by the arms, she hauled them into the trailer, pushing Taylor out of her path. The kids howled. The door slammed behind them. Seconds later, the sound of the TV climbed several decibels.

My brother grimaced and wobbled a little bit on his feet coming down the short steps. He kept on wobbling over to a lawn chair. He grinned and waved at Momma again. Momma made no move to respond.

"Come sit with me," Taylor urged, pointing at a pair of empty lawn chairs. "I'd offer Momma a chair too, but she seems comfortable already."

Neither Pearl nor I budged. The dog whined. Taylor kicked dirt at it.

"Dinah's family came out here?" I asked, looking around at the hopeless yard. There was a tub filled with dishes off to the back of the trailer and a half-full plastic tank of water. It looked like the trailer wasn't hooked up to running water. "Did you see Fern?"

Taylor appeared not to have heard me. "How have you been, sister Kat?" he asked. "Look here, I got my hands bandaged up after all." He held out his hands, which were wrapped in filthy, graying bandages.

"I met Maddie," he nodded toward the trailer, "at the bar that night. Hadn't seen her in years, but the moment I saw her, I knew she'd fix me up right. She wrapped my hands up for me and took me home with her, too." He laughed loudly. "I wish you could have seen yourself in that ditch. You were madder than a wet cat."

"Fern says you ran her off."

The smile faded from Taylor's face. "I see you didn't come out here to celebrate with me," he said.

"Celebrate what?"

Once more he nodded at the trailer. "My new life," he answered. "I quit my job yesterday. Told them to stick it good."

Pearl groaned.

Taylor seemed not to notice, but from the clouded look on his face I got the feeling that lately he hadn't been noticing a lot of things. His pupils were in about the same condition that I guessed his heart was in, contracted almost to the point of invisibility.

"Fern told Momma she'll call the police if you won't turn over Dinah's things."

"Yeah," he said, sounding unconcerned. "That's what Fern said when she was out here. Did she talk Momma's ear off too? The problem with that woman is that she won't shut up." Taylor stumbled to his feet, almost knocking over his lawn chair. "I would've given it all to her that day she was out, if she would've just closed her mouth for a minute." He sighed with long suffering. "Fern never liked me."

In silence, Pearl and I watched him fumble for his keys then pop open the trunk of what must have been Maddie's car. The car was so battered and rusted I couldn't even determine the make. Taylor waved us over. Inside were six neatly packed cardboard boxes. "It's all here," he said softly, gently brushing his fingertips across the top of one.

"This is what Fern really wants," he explained, opening up a box filled with a number of ordinary spiral-bound notebooks. "It's all Dinah's notebooks, her writing and stuff. Dinah wrote just about every day the whole time I knew her."

"It's not like a diary or anything," he said, gingerly touching the notebooks. His eyes reddened and his voice dropped so low I almost couldn't hear him. "It's all stories. Poems. Fern wants to make a little book, you know, for the family, with this stuff. Maybe she'll try and get it published."

"Yeah, right," Maddie snorted. She leaned against the trailer wall with a beer in one hand and a thick joint in the other. "You know, that's all you talk about. I get sick of hearing about those stupid stories. I read some of them. No big deal. Who wants to hear what some Indian has to say anyway?"

Taylor took maybe two, three steps, his face impassive.

I never expected what came next. Coolly, Taylor punched Maddie hard in the face. Her head slammed into the aluminum wall of the trailer with a solid whump. At first, she didn't go down. She just stared at him. Then slowly she slid down onto her backside. Taylor shook his hand like he'd hurt it.

It took a few stunned moments for Maddie to realize she should react. When she finally took it in, she howled. The children in the trailer came to the door. They started crying. Maddie curled up on the ground wailing, her arms wrapped around her swollen belly. Pearl and I stared at one another, speechless. The little girl we'd seen up at the farmhouse came streaking down the hill, shrieking as she threw herself between her mother and Taylor. She nearly pushed Taylor off his feet. Grabbing hold of Maddie, by sheer force of will the girl hauled her mother into the trailer and locked the door behind her. A terrible silence fell over the yard.

Behind me I heard the car door open. Momma got out. She and Taylor seemed to take each other in during one long, lingering look. Then slowly Momma turned from Taylor to me and said firmly, "We're through here, Kat. Gather up those things and take us home."

Once again Momma sealed herself in the car. Pearl started weeping. Numbly, I turned and began loading Dinah's things into the trunk of the car. Pearl tried to help, but she was sobbing so hard she wasn't much use.

Taylor never moved. He just stood, swaying, and staring at the trailer. It wasn't until I turned the key in the ignition that he stirred and sort of sleep-walked over to our car. He paused, resting his hand on the hood. He smiled as if he were surprised by its warmth. Then he shook his head, seeming to regain himself for a moment as he walked over to the driver's side.

He put his face through the window and kissed my cheek. I flinched.

"You know, Kat," he said, leaning into the car, "just yesterday I was thinking about that story I told you. I suddenly had this longing to sit under that apple tree and just watch the sunset, give it my full attention, you know?" Taylor shook his head regretfully. "I sure wish Tea were here now. I'd tell her that I found my reason to drink."

"Take us home," Momma said again from the backseat.

Taylor straightened. He nodded at Momma. "Tell Fern not to bother me no more," he said. "Don't anyone bother me no more."

"What do you want me to do with Tea's furniture?" I asked him.

He scratched his elbow. "It can burn in hell with her for all I care." He turned and walked unsteadily away.

# 30

No one was given to much conversation on the way home. Momma silently wept. Pearl smoked. I dropped her off at Mason's, where Blue sat on the front porch coloring with Jordan. At home, I helped Momma into the house and then to bed. I brought her a glass of water and for a while I settled on the edge of the bed, studying her.

She never said a word, and pretty soon it got so I couldn't stand her silence anymore. In the kitchen, I dialed Shepherd's number. I let the phone ring until the voice mail answered. I didn't leave a message. Instead, I climbed the two flights of stairs to the attic.

From my window there, I could look down on the cornfields as they died. The combines worked steadily. It was almost all cut down. The newly exposed earth looked tired and raw.

I don't know how long I sat there, but eventually it got dark. Down below, my mother stirred. I could hear her pacing, and several times I knew she paused at the foot of the stairs, wondering if she should come up.

≈

The last time I ever saw Tea was the summer after I graduated from high school, and that was years and years ago. I hadn't wanted to go to college. No one else in my family had ever gone, and I didn't see why I should either.

Tea had said I should. In fact, she insisted and I guess that hurt me, because it meant that for the first time since I was little, I would be away from her. That was a hard summer, because we both knew that it was time for me to decide about my life. I had a few acceptance letters, some of them from faraway places. Neither of us had a clue what that would mean. College was one thing, California was another. That summer, I sat for Tea for hours on end. I sat until my muscles cramped and I felt like fainting in the heat, but even then we didn't talk much.

Then one night, Tea crawled through my bedroom window. She crashed drunkenly to the floor, the vodka bottle she held in her hand banging impressively in the night. Pulling a chair up to my bed, she propped up her feet, resting her cowboy boots on my chest. She had me pinned. She smelled of cigarettes, lilac, paint, and drink.

When I resisted, she held me there firmly, and when I cried, she gathered me up in her arms and kissed me like a small child. Then she pulled me up out of my bed and began tugging off my nightgown and easing me into my jeans, dressing me the way she had when it had been her job to get me to school on time.

"I've got an idea, Kitten," she whispered as she tugged me into a T-shirt. "We've got to get going."

"Where are we going?" I asked apprehensively. Usually, when Tea was this drunk, it meant that her husband Billy had disappeared somewhere. Tea was never good company in these instances.

Tea kissed me full on the lips. "You have to promise me not to be scared." She was holding tight onto me, so when she stumbled, so did I. My bare toes hit the bottle Tea had dropped. I yelped in pain as it skittered under the bed. Its ornate letters glinted there in the dark, like a fire in the night. "Put some shoes on, Kitten," she ordered.

"Where are we going?" I asked again while I pulled on my boots.

Tea shrugged and pulled my jacket out of the closet. She handed it to me. "What's the first thing you gotta do when you set out on a journey?"

I waited patiently.

"You pick a direction," she said happily. "You find a direction and you stick to it. And you keep going until there's nothing left of you behind."

Tea lost her balance again and I sprang forward to catch her. We stood there in our strange embrace for a while. I was half holding her up and half falling. She buttoned my jacket and tenderly straightened the collar.

"You see, when you were a kid," she explained, "I thought I was just waiting for you to grow up. Then one day I come to find out you're going to college. You got all smart, and I'm still here. I never thought that would happen.

"I hate it here," she continued. "But hating it has gotten into me. It's made me heavy. I can't stay. I'm too drunk to leave. I love Billy too much." Tea glanced down at my feet. "Did you tie your laces? You always forget to tie your laces."

"I'm wearing boots, Tea," I told her gently.

She nodded almost absently. I let her lead me by the hand. She talked as we maneuvered through the house, out the front door, and across the yard, where the fields stretched out through the night, as black as the deep of an ocean.

"I have this idea about direction," she told me. "The only true way to find a direction is to do it blindly. Like you, Kat," she smiled. "You did it once before and you found me. But now we've got to do it together. We've got to let our feet show us our direction."

I had a sudden inkling of what she meant, and froze right there. I had no intention of going into the corn in the dark.

Tea talked me into it, of course. In fact, it didn't take her very long. It never did. We stumbled into the corn and away from the light of the house. Now it was my turn to cling to Tea, afraid not so much of being alone, but of losing her in the dark field.

Tea wrapped her arm around me. Then we began to run. The leaves slapped our faces. We cut across several rows, then seemed to zigzag back and forth for a while. Maybe we wandered in circles. When panic hit me and my feet began to drag, Tea would stop and kiss my cheeks, my forehead, my wrists.

≈

Suddenly, from the maze of corn, we poured out into a space the size of my mother's kitchen. Not a thing grew out of the floor of thick mud. The area was circular, defined by the dense corn all around. My feet were cold and numb. We were sinking into the earth. The mud was already up to the tops of my feet.

"Where are we, Tea?" I whispered.

"Dunno." We turned a slow circle.

Despite the warmth of Tea's body, I shivered. "It's strange. Why doesn't the corn grow here? It's like a fairy ring."

"It's the perfect place to get lost then." Releasing me, Tea held her arms out wide, like a crow spreading its wings. Slowly at first because of the thick mud, then with rising momentum, she began to spin. "Come on, Kat!" she cried out.

It was a game I hadn't played since I was a child. Pin the tail on the donkey, at the playground, when falling down and being dizzy had seemed fun. Tea and I spun.

We spun until our feet caught in the mud. We fell on our butts and got back to our feet and began again. The air was cool and good, the way it feels when you're running. We kept falling. The mud stained our clothes. My arms were covered up to the elbow.

We fell and fell and fell until we were too tired to dare stand again. Finally, out of breath, I found myself lying flat on my back. I lay in my tracks, feeling the mud slowly draw me down. My heart beat wildly in my chest, like a great bird trapped in a cage.

I looked down at my feet. They pointed off a good distance away from me. I had found my direction. Just like Tea had said, I knew which way I had to go. All I needed was for the world to stop spinning.

Despite my dizziness, I eased my head to one side. Tea lay next to me. She wasn't moving just then, but our feet pointed in the same direction.

"Tea," I called to her softly. Slowly she turned her head and smiled. Her lips were almost lost in the muck that covered her face, but her teeth stood out, white in the moonlight.

"I can't move, Kat," she whispered faintly, her eyelids fluttering. "I can't feel anything anymore. I'm too drunk. I'm too stoned."

And then I think she lost consciousness. I crawled over to her and shook her and shook her. She said nothing. I tried to lift her, but we sank back down just as soon as we rose. Not only could I not get Tea to her feet, I had lost all sense of direction. I had no idea how to get us home.

It was cold. Tea felt frigid. Once again, I tried collecting her in my arms and rose to go. I made it a few steps before the mud tripped me up. That's when I noticed that she was chuckling softly while I fought for breath. Her eyes drifted open. She considered me thoughtfully. "It's a beautiful night, Kat. Why don't you just lie back with me and watch the stars."

"I have to get you home," I gasped, feeling a bright thread of panic unwind within me. I clutched at the thread, trying to keep it with me, but felt it sail steadily away and out into the night. I had never been so scared in my life, not even when I was lost in the corn alone, as a child. Tea didn't seem to notice, though. She rolled her head to one side, looking up at the sky.

"Our home is the stars and the stars are at home in us," she said dreamily. "We're all made of the same thing."

It seemed to me that we were having two separate conversations. In my frustration, I could have swallowed my own tongue along with the dirt I felt grinding around in my mouth. "I need to get you to a hospital," I said, my voice cracking with fright, "but I can't find the way."

Tea smiled softly. "Poor, Kat," she whispered, "how tiring I must be to you."

Weakly, she pointed up at the sky. "There's the North Star, Kat. We need to go straight that way." She pointed off again. "The house is south." She let her hand fall back. It rested on her heart. "You won't be lost, you can't ever be lost. The stars are always there to remind you."

My relief was so powerful that it was too much for me. I started to cry. "I need to get you home."

"I know," she said. Then she sighed so long and sorrowfully that for a moment, I was afraid she'd take one last dramatic breath and die right there in my arms. But Tea didn't. She kept living. She let me hoist her to her feet. She didn't struggle, though she didn't really help. Some parts of the journey I had to carry her. Other parts I dragged her. We walked forever until even the forever of it didn't seem to matter anymore.

≈

Later on, in the early morning that followed that night, the gray-eyed emergency room doctor told me that it was probably all that walking that saved Tea's life. They pumped her stomach. She'd ingested so much alcohol mixed with pills, the doctor said it seemed like a deliberate attempt at suicide. Tea couldn't tell us, though, because at that point she was somewhere beyond drunk and stoned, over the line screaming at her mom, while Daddy, Mason, and I sat slumped in the waiting room drinking too-sweet hot chocolate from the vending machine. I had never seen my father look so sober.

Daddy had been asleep in his chair when I finally managed to carry Tea into the house. I made so much noise trying to be quiet, trying to hold her up, trying not to cry and to keep her talking, that Daddy woke up.

He flipped the light on and stood there staring at the two of us. He went pale and stared until he needed to rub his face, hoping maybe to erase the sight of us covered in mud and half dead. I was so startled at the sudden presence of the light and my father that I let Tea fall to the floor.

"She can't walk," I explained stupidly.

Daddy stood so quiet for so long, his face filled with such knowing dread that I would remember that moment years later. When the news reached me about Daddy, all I could think about was that night. I believe it was at that moment that my father seemed to know his own death. After that time in Momma's kitchen, with Tea dying before us, he knew that finding his own death at the bottom of his bottle was just a simple matter of days, months, years. I'd never seen a man look so scared, but so resigned.

Daddy ran his hand through his hair and seemed to go taut, like he was a rope being pulled at both ends. He picked Tea up and headed for the door. "Stop crying," he said harshly. "You'll wake your mother."

≈

That was the first time they put Tea into a recovery center for addicts. She was there two months. By the time she got out I was gone, away at school in California. I never came home again, not once, not even to my own father's hospital bed, where moments before he died, he absently patted my mother's hand, turned his head to the wall, and said, "Naomi, just let me be."

After college, I got a job in Colorado, but that didn't last long. Then I went to Texas, and after that I went other places. No matter how far away, though, I could always sense that Tea was there, on the prairie, staring off across that great blank expanse, watching for me. Even after she died, for years after her funeral, I could still feel her there waiting for me.

Until late one night, more towards morning really, the phone woke me. When I picked it up, no one answered, and strangely, I found myself heading toward home.

# 31

In my dream there was a powerful wind that seemed to come from the north. It blew me to the south. Then the south wind rallied and I was caught between them. I was almost pulled apart. I was pulled heavenward, flung like a limp rag doll. My body sailed over the cornfields. My desperate hands fought to find a hold and caught one of the stalks. In my dream, the corn grew tall, with roots as strong as oak and as deep as the lake. I clung to their green arms until my hands bled while the winds raged over me. Then Momma was there, shaking me. I knew then that I was awake because I could feel the warmth of her hands on me. She stood over me in the dark attic in an old V-neck undershirt of Daddy's.

Her hair was loose and fell long and dark around her elbows. She was barefoot, looking like a woman startled from an uneasy sleep. Her face was red and streaked, and I could tell she'd been crying again. Crying for Abra, for me, and Taylor, weeping as if he'd died.

Something about Momma standing there touched my heart like the sound of a child crying. I reached up and wrapped my arms around her and pulled her down onto my lap. For a long time, I just held her, rocking us both a little.

Momma buried her head in my shoulder. "Kat," she whispered, "I want you to do something for me."

I stroked her hair. It was as rough as prairie grass. "What is it, Momma?"

"I want you to come downstairs with me now. I want you to walk with me to your car and kiss me good-bye before you leave, and then don't ever come back."

I tried to push her away. "You know I can't do that," I said wearily.

She wrapped her arms around my neck, holding me to her. "You have to come down, Kat," she whispered, her voice almost too soft to hear. "Tea was a sad drunk. She was selfish. She twisted you all up inside, just to ease her own loneliness, but she wouldn't have wanted this for you." She hesitated, then added, "I don't want this for you."

"Don't, Momma," I said, rising abruptly and pushing her to her feet. "Don't talk about Tea like that."

She shook her head helplessly. She tried to pull me into her arms, to hold me. I shrugged her off.

"You won't come down, Kat?" she asked, almost pleading.

"No."

"You won't come down for me, Kat?" she begged.

"No."

She was crying again. It startled me to think she would cry for me. She drew a long jagged breath. Wearily she pushed away from me. She touched my cheek longingly, her fingers fluttering softly. Her voice was low but clear when she said, "Kat, I've set the house on fire."

I felt my body go numb.

"Right now, beneath us, it's smoldering," Momma continued. "I came up here to tell you that. We still have time to get out. But nothing," she said firmly, "nothing in this world or the next, can save this house."

"Momma—" I gasped.

She shook her head and turned away, taking a step towards the stairs. Behind her, I saw the moon outside my window. It seemed to glow a little bit brighter. I thought I could smell smoke.

"I didn't come up here to save you, Kat, because I know I can't," Momma said, her voice breaking. "I just came up here to tell you that the road you're on leads one way and that it's time to choose. It's time for you to save yourself." The smoke was beginning to rise thick and black into the room. It crept up the stairs and through the floorboards. "I'm tired of wasting my life, waiting for the inevitable," Momma explained. "If you want to die, be kind to us all and have the guts to die now. Don't hang around for the next twenty years just thinking on it over a bottle of beer. I'm too old a woman for that now." And that was that. Momma turned and disappeared down the stairs.

# 32

I sat in my chair until the smoke was too thick to see through. Until the heat got to my lungs. I thought about Tea. And then I stood up. A part of me went on, stood up and walked out of that house, and a part of me remained there and burned to ashes.

But it wasn't quite as clean as that, not really. The fire almost killed me first. I stumbled down the stairs and practically fell into the kitchen. The smoke from the fire in the back rooms was so intense that I was disoriented for a moment. I flattened out on the linoleum, trying to see through the smoke. My eyes began to burn.

And then I heard a soft, strange sound, not like anything I had ever heard before. It was chilling, almost like a wail, a heartrending wail, but so muted by smoke that it was barely a whisper. I whirled around.

Huddled under the kitchen table was Blue. The ceiling was on fire above him. I slid over to him on my belly.

He was so scared that I don't believe he even saw me. But when I pulled him from under the table, he clung to me with such strength that I thought we both might break. Like someone drowning, I struggled to heave us both upright. It was painful work. My lungs felt ready to explode, and everything swam black before me. I hugged Blue to me and ran, ran blindly through the house, through the blackness, pushing against the front door. I pushed so hard that I felt the bone of my arm crack against the wood. It went numb, but I pushed until the door popped open and Blue and I tumbled out together into the clean night air.

We rolled on the grass and it was some minutes before I realized that we were both all right. Blue's hair was singed and my eyes felt as if they were on fire. But we were all right.

Then Momma was there, looking as pale as white, hot fire. She seized Blue with a strangled cry and wept into his hair, rocking him back and forth on the lawn. "I didn't know," she sobbed hysterically. "I didn't know he was in the house."

The heat was fierce, so I pulled them both towards the garage. I rummaged around in the dark and found a piece of old canvas to wrap around them.

Momma clutched my arm. "I didn't know," she repeated. "Pearl must have left him and I didn't know."

He was probably sleeping under my bed, I thought grimly. I wanted to tell Momma this, but I was too tired to talk just then. The flames had reached the porch and smoke billowed out, climbing high into the sky, like a black scratch on the night. My legs were weak. I sank down on the ground next to Momma.

≈

Eventually the roof of the house caught fire. Through the window, I could see the flames begin to snake their way through the attic. Once that caught fire, the flames roared to new heights.

I looked over at Momma and Blue, huddled together in the filthy canvas. Blue had his face pressed tight to his grandmother's breast. He shivered as he clung to her. He would fear fire for the rest of his life. Like me and the corn.

My throat was burned. It was almost too hard to speak. "You almost killed me, Momma," I managed at last. "You might not have known about Blue, but you almost killed me. On purpose."

"But you got out all right," Momma said.

"Did you think I wouldn't?"

Momma said nothing. I stared at her. Something in the house exploded, and I jumped.

I had never seen anything so bright as our lives going up in flames. I could picture the photos of our family for five generations burning under Momma's bed. I could picture Momma's china blackening, and Daddy's old easy chair being swiftly reduced to ash.

"Kat," Momma called. Numbly, I turned from the flames to look at her. "I just wanted you to know something about the way Tea died. Maybe you're right," she said softly. "Maybe it was an accident. But if she died by accident, she stayed alive all those years by accident, too. Every day God worked a miracle just to get her home in one piece."

I looked away, tears stinging my eyes.

Momma touched me and I started. "She wanted to die, Kat," she said quietly. "Nothing could change her. Her whole life was a slow suicide. You're the only one who won't believe that. But you've got to. You've got to let her go."

The tears that had been pooling in the corners of my eyes began to flow freely. They drew long tracks down my sooty face and fell dark with ash onto my clothes. For a long while the three of us sat in silence. Another series of small explosions echoed from the house.

At last I said, "Tea would've liked this, huh, Momma?"

Momma looked surprised, then almost smiled. "I guess she wasn't the only one in this family with a flair for drama."

It took me awhile to register that my mother was making a joke. I never had a chance to laugh, though, because just then we heard the distant wail of the fire engines. Blue let out a cry when he heard them.

Momma rose abruptly. "It's time to go, Kat," she told me. She led me to my car and opened the door. I sank into the driver's seat. "I've packed some things for you in the trunk," she said. "And there's money in the glove compartment."

She opened the back door. She kissed Blue and slid him inside. "You be real good," she told him, as she buckled his seat belt. "Your Aunt Kat will take care of you now."

"Momma," I said, shaking my head, "I don't think—"

Momma held up her hand. I fell silent. "I'll take care of Pearl," she said grimly. "Don't worry about that."

I stared at her, then looked back at Blue. He was only wearing a T-shirt and his cartoon underwear. His face was smudged with smoke and tears. His dark curly hair was almost invisible in the night. He had Daddy's eyes. He didn't look quite like a child sitting in the backseat. He didn't look quite grown either. He simply looked like a little boy who'd been through too much.

I turned and nodded at Momma, in that quiet of agreement that can never be cast aside, and the windows of our house exploded. A wave of heat billowed towards us as Momma smiled at me. She reached into the car and wrapped her arms around me. "Good girl, Kat," she said. It was the first time in my life that I experienced the warmth of my mother's love. It crackled, like the fire. I could still feel her heat long after she pulled away. I started the engine.

"Do you need a ride anywhere, Momma?" I asked. She shook her head and waved me on.

Looking back from the end of the long driveway, just as I pulled out onto the road, I saw Momma's calm, beautiful face. It stood out in the darkness, bright with fire. She was hugging herself and swaying slightly.

I told myself that I wouldn't look back again. And I didn't, except once, and that was for a glance so brief I could say to myself later that I didn't look back at all. That I didn't see the dark form of Jordan, clinging to the back of her horse, riding it like anger, running circles around the burning house, enraging the flames.

# Biography

Rachel Coyne is a novelist and poet who resides in Lindstrom, Minnesota. As a girl she went ice fishing on Lake Comfort with her father and grandfather. Coyne is a graduate of the Perpich Center for Arts Education, a public arts high school in Golden Valley, and Macalester College in St. Paul. She is a devotee of Pablo Neruda, a lover of Don Williams' songs and a collector of vintage editions of *Jane Eyre*. Her previously published works include a children's book titled *Daughter, Have I Told You?*